TANGLED TRAILS

TANGLED TRAILS

William MacLeod Raine

CHIVERS

British Library Cataloguing in Publication Data available

This Large Print edition published by BBC Audiobooks Ltd, Bath, 2008.
Published by arrangement with Golden West Literary Agency.

U.K. Hardcover ISBN 978 1 405 64364 1
U.K. Softcover ISBN 978 1 405 64365 8

Printed and bound in Great Britain by
Antony Rowe Ltd., Chippenham, Wiltshire

CHAPTER ONE

NO ALTRUIST

Esther McLean brought the afternoon mail in to Cunningham. She put it on the desk before him and stood waiting, timidly, afraid to voice her demand for justice, yet too desperately anxious to leave with it unspoken.

He leaned back in his swivel chair, his cold eyes challenging her. 'Well,' he barked harshly.

She was a young, soft creature, very pretty in a kittenish fashion, both sensuous and helpless. It was an easy guess that unless fortune stood her friend she was a predestined victim to the world's selfish love of pleasure. And fortune, with a cynical smile, had stood aside and let her go her way.

'I . . I . . .' A wave of color flooded her face. She twisted a rag of a handkerchief into a hard wadded knot.

'Spit it out,' he ordered curtly.

'I've got to do something . . . soon. Won't you—won't you—?' There was a wail of despair in the unfinished sentence.

James Cunningham was a grim, gray pirate, as malleable as cast iron and as soft. He was a large, big-boned man, aggressive, dominant, the kind that takes the world by the throat and shakes success from it. The contour of his

1

hook-nosed face had something rapacious written on it.

'No. Not till I get good and ready. I've told you I'd look out for you if you'd keep still. Don't come whining at me. I won't have it.'

'But—'

Already he was ripping letters open and glancing over them. Tears brimmed the brown eyes of the girl. She bit her lower lip, choked back a sob, and turned hopelessly away. Her misfortune lay at her own door. She knew that. But—The woe in her heart was that the man she had loved was leaving her to face alone a night as bleak as death.

Cunningham had always led a life of intelligent selfishness. He had usually got what he wanted because he was strong enough to take it. No scrupulous nicety of means had ever deterred him. Nor ever would. He played his own hand with a cynical disregard of the rights of others. It was this that had made him what he was, a man who bulked large in the sight of the city and state. Long ago he had made up his mind that altruism was weakness.

He went through his mail with a swift, trained eye. One of the letters he laid aside and glanced at a second time. It brought a grim, hard smile to his lips. A paragraph read:

There's no water in your ditch and our crops are burning up. Your whole irrigation system in Dry Valley is a fake.

You knew it. but we didn't. You've skinned us out of all we had, you damned bloodsucker. If you ever come up here we'll dry-gulch you, sure.

The letter was signed, 'One You Have Robbed.' Attached to it was a clipping from a small-town paper telling of a meeting of farmers to ask the United States District Attorney for an investigation of the Dry Valley irrigation project promoted by James Cunningham.

The promoter smiled. He was not afraid of the Government. He had kept strictly within the law. It was not his fault there was not enough rainfall in the watershed to irrigate the valley. But the threat to dry-gulch him was another matter. He had no fancy for being shot in the back. Some crazy fool of a settler might do just that. He decided to let an agent attend to his Dry Valley affairs hereafter.

He dictated some letters, closed his desk, and went down the street toward the City Club. At a florist's he stopped and ordered a box of American Beauties to be sent to Miss Phyllis Harriman. With these he enclosed his card, a line of greeting scrawled on it.

A poker game was on at the club and Cunningham sat in. He interrupted it to dine, holding his seat by leaving a pile of chips at the place. When he cashed in his winnings and went downstairs it was still early. As a cardplayer he was not popular. He was too keen on the main chance and he nearly always won. In spite of his loud and frequent laugh, of the effect of bluff geniality, there was no genuine humor in the man, none of the milk of human kindness.

A lawyer in the reading-room rose at sight of Cunningham. 'Want to see you a minute,' he said. 'Let's go into the Red Room.'

He led the way to a small room furnished with a desk, writing supplies, and a telephone. It was for the use of members who wanted to be private. The lawyer shut the door.

'Afraid I've bad news for you, Cunningham,' he said.

The other man's steady eyes did not waver. He waited silently.

'I was at Golden today on business connected with a divorce case. By chance I ran across a record that astonished me. It may be only a coincidence of names, but—'

'Now you've wrapped up the blackjack so that it won't hurt, suppose you go ahead and hit me over the head with it,' suggested Cunningham dryly.

The lawyer told what he knew. The promoter took it with no evidence of feeling other than that which showed in narrowed eyes hard as diamonds and a clenched jaw in which the muscles stood out like ropes.

'Much obliged, Foster,' he said, and the lawyer knew he was dismissed.

Cunningham paced the room for a few moments, then rang for a messenger. He wrote a note and gave it to the boy to be delivered. Then he left the club.

From Seventeenth Street he walked across to the Paradox Apartments where he lived. He found a note propped up against a book on the table of his living-room. It had been written by the Japanese servant he shared with two other bachelors who lived in the same building.

Mr. Hull he come see you. He sorry you not here. He say maybe perhaps make honorable call some other time.

It was signed, 'S. Horikawa.'

Cunningham tossed the note aside. He had no wish to see Hull. The fellow was becoming a nuisance. If he had any complaint he could go to the courts with it. That was what they were for.

The doorbell rang. The promoter opened to a big, barrel-bodied man who pushed past him into the room,

'What you want, Hull?' demanded Cunningham curtly.

The man thrust his bull neck forward. A heavy roll of fat swelled over the collar. 'You know damn well what I want. I want what's comin' to me. My share of the Dry Valley clean-up. An' I'm gonna have it. See?'

'You've had every cent you'll get. I told you

that before.'

Tiny red capillaries seamed the beefy face of the fat man. 'An' I told you I was gonna have a divvy. An' I am. You can't throw down Cass Hull an' get away with it. Not none.' The shallow protuberant eyes glittered threateningly.

'Thought you knew me better,' Cunningham retorted contemptuously. 'When I say I won't, I won't. Go to a lawyer if you think you've got a case. Don't come belly-aching to me.'

The face of the fat man was apoplectic. 'Like sin I'll go to a lawyer. You'd like that fine, you double-crossin' side-winder. I'll come with a six-gun. That's how I'll come. An' soon, I'll give you two days to come through. Two days. If you don't—hell sure enough will cough.'

Whatever else could be said about Cunningham he was no coward. He met the raving man eye to eye.

'I don't scare worth a cent, Hull. Get out. *Pronto.* And don't come back unless you want me to turn you over to the police for a blackmailing crook.'

Cunningham was past fifty-five and his hair was streaked with gray. But he stood straight as an Indian, six feet in his socks. The sap of strength still rang strong in him. In the days when he had ridden the range he had been famous for his stamina and he was even yet a formidable two-fisted fighter.

But Hull was beyond prudence. 'I'll go when I get ready, an' I'll come back when I get ready,' he boasted.

There came a soft thud of a hard fist on fat flesh, the crash of a heavy bulk against the door. After that things moved fast. Hull's body reacted to the pain of smashing blows falling swift and sure. Before he knew what had taken place he was on the landing outside on his way to the stairs. He hit the treads hard and rolled on down.

A man coming upstairs helped him to his feet.

'What's up?' the man asked.

Hull glared at him, for the moment speechless. His eyes were venomous, his mouth a thin, cruel slit. He pushed the newcomer aside, opened the door of the apartment opposite, went in, and slammed it after him.

The man who had assisted him to rise was dark and immaculately dressed.

'I judge Uncle James has been exercising,' he murmured before he took the next flight of stairs.

On the door of apartment 12 was a legend in Old English engraved on a calling card. It said:

James Cunningham

The visitor pushed the electric bell.

7

Cunningham opened to him.

'Good-evening, Uncle.' the younger man said. 'Your elevator is not running, so I walked up. On the way I met a man going down. He seemed rather in a hurry.'

'A cheap blackmailer trying to hold me up. I threw him out.'

'Thought he looked put out,' answered the younger man, smiling politely. 'I see you still believe in applying direct energy to difficulties.'

'I do. That's why I sent for you.' The promoter's cold eyes were inscrutable 'Come in and shut the door.'

The young man sauntered in. He glanced at his uncle curiously from his sparkling black eyes. What the devil did James, Senior, mean by what he had said? Was there any particular significance in it?

He stroked his small black moustache. 'Glad to oblige you any way I can, sir.'

'Sit down.'

The young Beau Brummel hung up his hat and cane, sank into the easiest chair in the room, and selected a cigarette from a gold-initialed case.

'At your service, sir,' he said languidly.

CHAPTER TWO

WILD ROSE TAKES THE DUST

'Wild Rose on Wild Fire,' shouted the announcer through a megaphone trained on the grand stand.

Kirby Lane, who was leaning against the fence chatting with a friend, turned round and took notice. Most people did when Wild Rose held the center of the stage.

Through the gateway of the enclosure came a girl hardly out of her teens. She was bareheaded, a cowboy hat in her hand. The sun, already slanting from the west, kissed her crisp, ruddy gold hair and set it sparkling. Her skin was shell pink, amber clear. She walked as might a young Greek goddess in the dawn of the world, with the free movement of one who loves the open sky and the wind-swept plain.

A storm of hand-clapping swept the grand stand. Wild Rose acknowledged it with a happy little laugh. These dear people loved her. She knew it. And not only because she was a champion. They made over her because of her slimness, her beauty, the aura of daintiness that surrounded her, the little touches of shy youth that still clung to her manner. Other riders of her sex might be rough, hoydenish, or masculine. Wild Rose

9

had the charm of her name. Yet the muscles that rippled beneath her velvet skin were hard as nails. No bronco alive could unseat her without the fight of its life.

Meanwhile the outlaw horse Wild Fire was claiming its share of attention. The bronco was a noted bucker. Every year it made the circuit of the rodeos and only twice had a rider stuck to the saddle suit horn pulling leather. Now it had been roped and cornered. Half a dozen wranglers in chaps were trying to get it ready for the saddle. From the red-hot eyes of the brute a devil of fury glared at the men trying to thrust a gunny sack over its head. The four legs were wide apart, the ears cocked, teeth bared. The animal flung itself skyward and came down on the boot of a puncher savagely. The man gave an involuntary howl of pain, but he clung to the rope snubbed round the wicked head.

The gunny sack was pushed and pulled over the eyes. Wild Fire subsided, trembling, while bridle was adjusted and saddle slipped on. The girl attended to the cinching herself. If the saddle turned it might cost her life, and she preferred to take no unnecessary chances.

She was dressed in green satin riding clothes. A beaded bolero jacket fitted over a white silk blouse. Her boots were of buckskin, silver-spurred. With her hat on, at a distance, one might have taken her for a slim, beautiful boy.

Wild Rose swung to the saddle and adjusted her feet in the stirrups. The gunny sack was whipped from the horse's head. There was a wild scuffle of escaping wranglers.

For a moment Wild Fire stood quivering. The girl's hat swept through the air in front of its eyes. The horse woke to galvanized action. The back humped. It shot into the air with a writhing twist of the body. All four feet struck the ground together, straight and stiff as fence posts.

The girl's head jerked forward as though it were on a hinge. The outlaw went sunfishing, its forefeet almost straight up. She was still in the saddle when it came to all fours again. A series of jarring bucks, each ending with the force of a pile-driver as Wild Fire's hoofs struck earth, varied the programme. The rider came down limp, half in the saddle, half out, righting herself as the horse settled for the next leap. But not once did her hands reach for the pommel of the saddle to steady her.

Pitching and bucking, the animal humped forward to the fence.

'Look out!' a judge yelled.

It was too late. The rider could not deflect her mount. Into the fence went Wild Fire blindly and furiously. The girl threw up her leg to keep it from being jammed. Up went the bronco again before Wild Rose could find the stirrup. She knew she was gone, felt herself shooting forward. She struck the ground close

11

to the horse's hoofs. Wild Fire lunged at her. A bolt of pain like a red-hot iron seared through her.

Through the air a rope whined. It settled over the head of the outlaw and instantly was jerked tight. Wild Fire, coming down hard for a second lunge at the green crumpled heap underfoot, was dragged sharply sideways. Another lariat snaked forward and fell true.

'Here, Cole!' The first roper thrust the taut line into the hands of a puncher who had run forward. He himself dived for the still girl beneath the hoofs of the rearing horse. Catching her by the arms, he dragged her out of danger. She was unconscious.

The cowboy picked her up and carried her to the waiting ambulance. The closed eyes flickered open. A puzzled little frown rested in them.

'What's up, Kirby?' asked Wild Rose.

'You had a spill.'

'Took the dust, did I?' He sensed the disappointment in her voice.

'You rode fine. He jammed you into the fence,' explained the young man.

The doctor examined her. The right arm hung limp.

'Broken. I'm afraid,' he said.

'Ever see such luck?' the girl complained to Lane. 'Probably they won't let me ride in the wild-horse race now.'

'No chance, young lady,' the doctor said

promptly. 'I'm going to take you right to the hospital.'

'I might get back in time,' she said hopefully.

'You might, but you won't.'

'Oh, well,' she sighed. 'If you're going to act like that.'

The cowboy helped her into the ambulance and found himself a seat.

'Where do you think you're going?' she asked with a smile a bit twisted by pain.

'I reckon I'll go far as the hospital with you.'

'I reckon you won't. What do you think I am—a nice little parlor girl who has to be petted when she gets hurt? You're on to ride inside of fifteen minutes—and you know it.'

'Oh, well! I'm lookin' for an alibi so as not to be beaten. That Cole Sanborn is sure a straight-up rider.'

'So's that Kirby Lane. You needn't think I'm going to let you beat yourself out of the championship. Not so any one could notice it. Hop out, sir.'

He rose, smiling ruefully. 'You certainly are one bossy kid.'

'I'd say you need bossing when you start to act so foolish,' she retorted, flushing.

'See you later,' he called to her by way of good-bye.

As the ambulance drove away she waved cheerfully at him a gauntleted hand.

The cowpuncher turned back to the arena.

13

The megaphone man was announcing that the contest for the world's rough-riding championship would now be resumed.

CHAPTER THREE

FOR THE CHAMPIONSHIP OF THE WORLD

The less expert riders had been weeded out in the past two days. Only the champions of their respective sections were still in the running. One after another these lean, brown men, chap-clad and bowlegged, came forward dragging their saddles and clamped themselves to the backs of the hurricane outlaws which pitched, bucked, crashed into fences, and toppled over backward in their frenzied efforts to dislodge the human clothes-pins fastened to them.

The bronco busters endured the usual luck of the day. Two were thrown and picked themselves out of the dust, chagrined and damaged, but still grinning. One drew a tame horse not to be driven into resistance either by fanning or scratching. Most of the riders emerged from the ordeal victorious. Meanwhile the spectators in the big grand stand, packed close as small apples in a box, watched every rider and snatched at its thrills

14

just as such crowds have done from the time of Caligula.

Kirby Lane, from his seat on the fence among a group of cowpunchers, watched each rider no less closely. It chanced that he came last on the programme for the day. When Cole Sanborn was in the saddle he made an audible comment.

'I'm lookin' at the next champion of the world,' he announced.

'Not unless you've got a lookin'-glass with you, old alkali,' a small berry-brown youth in yellow-wool chaps retorted.

Sanborn was astride a noted outlaw known as Jazz. The horse was a sorrel, and it knew all the tricks of its kind. It went sunfishing, tried weaving and fence-rowing, at last toppled over backward after a frantic leap upward. The rider, long-bodied and lithe, rode like a centaur. Except for the moment when he stepped out of the saddle as the outlaw fell on its back, he stuck to his seat as though he were glued to it.

'He's a right limber young fellow, an' he sure can ride. I'll say that,' admitted one old cattleman.

'They don't grow no better busters,' another man spoke up. He was a neighbor of Sanborn and had his local pride. 'From where I come from we'll put our last nickel on Cole, you betcha. He's top hand with a rope too.'

'Hmp! Kirby here can make him look like

15

thirty cents, top of a bronc or with a lariat either one,' the yellow-chapped vaquero flung out bluntly.

Lane looked at his champion, a trifle annoyed. 'What's the use o' talkin' foolishness, Kent? I never saw the day I had anything on Cole.'

'Beat him at Pendleton, didn't you?'

'Luck. I drew the best horses.' To Sanborn, who had finished his job and was straddling wide-legged toward the group, Kirby threw up a hand of greeting. 'Good work, old-timer. You're sure hell-amile on a bronc.'

'Kirby Lane on Wild Fire,' shouted the announcer.

Lane slid from the fence and reached for his saddle.

As he lounged forward, moving with indolent grace, one might have guessed him a Southerner. He was lean-loined and broad-shouldered. The long, flowing muscles rippled under his skin when he moved like those of a panther. From beneath the band of his pinched-in hat crisp, reddish hair escaped.

Wild Fire was off the instant his feet found the stirrups. Again the outlaw went through its bag of tricks and its straight bucking. The man in the saddle gave to its every motion lightly and easily. He rode with such grace that he seemed almost a part of the horse. His reactions appeared to anticipate the impulses of the screaming fiend which he was astride.

16

When Wild Fire jolted him with humpbacked jarring bucks his spine took the shock limply to neutralize the effect. When it leaped heavenward he waved his hat joyously and rode the stirrups. From first to last he was master of the situation, and the outlaw, though still fighting savagely, knew the battle was lost.

The bronco had one trump card left, a trick that had unseated many a stubborn rider. It plunged sideways at the fence of the enclosure and crashed through it. Kirby's nerves shrieked with pain, and for a moment everything went black before him. His leg had been jammed hard against the upper plank. But when the haze cleared he was still in the saddle.

The outlaw gave up. It trotted tamely back to the grand stand through the shredded fragments of pine in the splintered fence, and the grand stand rose to its feet with a shout of applause for the rider.

Kirby slipped from the saddle and limped back to his fellows on the fence. Already the crowd was pouring out from every exit of the stand. A thousand cars of fifty different makes were snorting impatiently to get out of the jam as soon as possible. For Cheyenne was full, full to overflowing. The town roared with a high tide of jocund life. From all over Colorado, Wyoming, Montana, and New Mexico hard-bitten, sunburned youths in high-heeled boots and gaudy attire had gathered for the Frontier Day celebration. Hundreds of cars had poured up from Denver. Trains had disgorged thousands of tourists come to see the festival. Many people would sleep out in automobiles and on the prairie. The late comers at restaurants and hotels would wait long and take second best.

A big cattleman beckoned to Lane. 'Place in my car, son. Run you back to town.'

One of the judges sat in the tonneau beside the rough rider.

'How's the leg? Hurt much?'

'Not much. I'm noticin' it some,' Kirby answered with a smile.

'You'll have to ride tomorrow. It's you and Sanborn for the finals. We haven't quite made up our minds.'

The cattleman was an expert driver. He wound in and out among the other cars speeding over the prairie, struck the road before the great majority of the automobiles had reached there, and was in town with the vanguard.

After dinner the rough rider asked the clerk at her hotel if there was any mail for Miss Rose McLean. Three letters were handed him. He put them in his pocket and set out for the hospital.

He found Miss Rose reclining in a hospital chair, in a frame of mind highly indignant. 'That doctor talks as though he's going to keep me here a week. Well, he's got another guess coming. I'll not stay,' she exploded to her

18

visitor.

'Now, looky here, you better do as the doc says. He knows best. What's a week in your young life?' Kirby suggested.

'A week's a week, and I don't intend to stay. Why did you limp when you came in? Get hurt?'

'Not really hurt. Jammed my leg against a fence. I drew Wild Fire.'

'Did you win the championship?' the girl asked eagerly.

'No. Finals tomorrow. Sanborn an' me. How's the arm? Bone broken?'

'Yes. Oh, it aches some. Be all right soon.'

He drew her letters from his pocket. 'Stopped to get your mail at the hotel. Thought you'd like to see it.'

Wild Rose looked the envelopes over and tore one open.

'From my little sister Esther,' she explained. 'Mind if I read it? I'm some worried about her. She's been writing kinda funny lately.'

As she read, the color ebbed from her face. When she had finished reading the letter Kirby spoke gently.

'Bad news, pardner?'

She nodded, choking. Her eyes, frank and direct, met those of her friend without evasion. It was a heritage of her life in the open that in her relations with men she showed a boylike unconcern of sex.

'Esther's in trouble. She—she—' Rose

19

caught her breath in a stress of emotion.

'If there's anything I can do—'

The girl flung aside the rug that covered her and rose from the chair. She began to pace up and down the room. Presently her thoughts overflowed in words.

'She doesn't say what it is, but—I know her. She's crazy with fear—or heartache—or something.' Wild Rose was always quick-tempered, a passionate defender of children and all weak creatures. Now Lane knew that the hot blood was rushing stormily to her heart. Her little sister was in danger, the only near relative she had. She would fight for her as a cougar would for its young. 'By God, if it's a man—if he's done her wrong—I'll shoot him down like a gray wolf. I'll show him how safe it is to—to—'

She broke down again, clamping tight her small strong teeth to bite back a sob.

He spoke very gently. 'Does she say—?'

His sentence hung suspended in air, but the young woman understood its significance.

'No. The letter's just a—a wail of despair. She—talks of suicide. Kirby. I've got to get to Denver on the next train. Find out when it leaves. And I'll send a telegram to her tonight telling her I'll fix it. I will too.'

'Sure. That's the way to talk. Be reasonable an' everything'll work out fine. Write your wire an' I'll take it right to the office. Soon as I've got the train schedule I'll come back.'

20

'You're a good pal, Kirby. I always knew you were.'

For a moment her left hand fell in his. He looked down at the small, firm, sunbrowned fist. That hand was, as Browning has written, a woman in itself, but it was a woman competent, unafraid, trained hard as nails. She would go through with whatever she set out to do.

As his eyes rested on the fingers there came to him a swift, unreasoning prescience of impending tragedy. To what dark destiny was she moving?

CHAPTER FOUR

NOT ALWAYS TWO TO MAKE A QUARREL

Kirby put Wild Rose on the morning train for Denver. She had escaped from the doctor by sheer force of will. The night had been a wretched one, almost sleepless, and she knew that her fever would rise in the afternoon. But that could not be helped. She had more important business than her health to attend to just now.

Ordinarily Rose bloomed with vitality, but this morning she looked tired and worn. In her eyes there was a hard brilliancy Kirby did not like to see. He knew from of old the fire that could blaze in her heart, the insurgent impulses that could sweep her into recklessness. What would she do if the worst she feared turned out to be true?

'Good luck,' she called through the open window as the train pulled out. 'Beat Cole, Kirby.'

'Good luck to you,' he answered. 'Write me soon as you find out how things are.'

But as he walked from the station his heart misgave him. Why had he let her go alone, knowing as he did how swift she blazed to passion when wrong was done those she loved? It was easy enough to say that she had refused to let him go with her, though he had several times offered. The fact remained that she might need a friend at hand, might need him the worst way.

All through breakfast he was ridden by the fear of trouble on her horizon. Comrades stopped to slap him on the back and wish him good luck in the finals, and though he made the proper answers it was with the surface of a mind almost wholly preoccupied with another matter.

While he was rising from the table he made a decision in the flash of an eye. He would join Rose in Denver at once. Already dozens of cars were taking the road. There would be a vacant place in some one of them.

He found a party just setting out for Denver

22

and easily made arrangements to take the unfilled seat in the tonneau.

By the middle of the afternoon he was at a boarding-house on Cherokee Street inquiring for Miss Rose McLean. She was out, and the landlady did not know when she would be back. Probably after her sister got home from work.

Lane wandered down to Curtis Street, sat through a part of a movie, then restlessly took his way up Seventeenth. He had an uncle and two cousins living in Denver. With the uncle he was on bad terms, and with his cousins on no terms at all. It had been ten years since he had seen either James Cunningham, Jr., or his brother Jack. Why not call on them and renew acquaintance?

He went into a drug-store and looked the name up in a telephone book. His cousin James had an office in the Equitable Building. He hung the book up on the hook and turned to go. As he did so he came face to face with Rose McLean.

'You—here!' she cried.

'Yes, I—I had business in Denver,' he explained.

'Like fun you had! You came because—' She stopped abruptly, struck by another phase of the situation. 'Did you leave Cheyenne without riding today?'

'I didn't want to ride. I'm fed up on ridin'?'

'You threw away the championship and a

thousand-dollar prize to—to—'

'You're forgettin' Cole Sanborn,' he laughed. 'No, honest, I came on business. But since I'm here—say, Rose, where can we have a talk? Let's go up to the mezzanine gallery at the Albany. It's right next door.'

He took her into the Albany Hotel. They stepped out of the elevator at the second floor and he found a settee in a corner where they might be alone. It struck him that the shadows in her eyes had deepened. She was, he could see plainly, laboring under a tension of repressed excitement. The misery of her soul leaped out at him when she looked his way.

'Have you anything to tell me?' he asked, and his low, gentle voice was a comfort to her raw nerves.

'It's a man, just as I thought—the man she works for.'

'Is he married?'

'No. Going to be soon, the papers say. He's a wealthy promoter. His name's Cunningham.'

'What Cunningham?' In his astonishment the words seemed to leap from him of their own volition.

'James Cunningham, a big land and mining man. You must have heard of him.'

'Yes, I've heard of him. Are you sure?'

She nodded. 'Esther won't tell me a thing. She's shielding him. But I went through her letters and found a note from him. It's signed 'J. C.' I accused him point-blank to her and she

24

just put her head down on her arms and sobbed. I know he's the man.'

'What do you mean to do?'

'I mean to have a talk with him first off. I'll make him do what's right.'

'How?'

'I don't know how, but I will,' she cried wildly. 'If he don't I'll settle with him. Nothing's too bad for a man like that.'

He shook his head. 'Not the best way, Rose. Let's be sure of every move we make. Let's check up on this man before we lay down the law to him.'

Some arresting quality in him held her eye. He had sloughed the gay devil-may-care boyishness of the range and taken on a look of strong patience new in her experience of him. But she was worn out and nervous. The pain in her arm throbbed feverishly. Her emotions had held her on a rack for many hours. There was in her no reserve power of endurance.

'No, I'm going to see him and have it out,' she flung back.

'Then let me go with you when you see him. You're sick. You ought to be in bed right now. You're in no condition to face it alone.'

'Oh, don't baby me, Kirby!' she burst out. 'I'm all right. What's it matter if I am fagged. Don't you see? I'm crazy about Esther. I've got to get it settled. I can rest afterward.'

'Will it do any harm to take a friend along when you go to see this man?'

25

'Yes. I don't want him to think I'm afraid of him. You're not in this, Kirby. Esther is my little sister, not yours.'

'True enough.' A sardonic, mirthless smile touched his face. 'But James Cunningham is my uncle, not yours.'

'Your uncle?' She rose, staring at him with big, dilated eyes. 'He's your uncle, the man who—who—'

'Yes, an' I know him better than you do. We've got to use finesse—'

'I see.' Her eyes attacked him scornfully. 'You think we'd better not face him with what he's done. You think we'd better go easy on him. Uncle's rich, and he might not like plain words. Oh, I understand now.'

Wild Rose flung out a gesture that brushed him from her friendship. She moved past him blazing with anger.

He was at the elevator cage almost as soon as she.

'Listen, Rose. You know better than that. I told you he was my uncle because you'd find it out if I'm goin' to help you. He's no friend of mine, but I know him. He's strong. You can't drive him by threats.'

The elevator slid down and stopped. The door of it opened.

'Will you stand aside, sir?' Rose demanded. 'I won't have anything to do with any of that villain's family. Don't ever speak to me again.'

She stepped into the car. The door clanged

26

shut. Kirby was left standing alone.

CHAPTER FIVE

COUSINS MEET

With the aid of a tiny looking-glass a young woman was powdering her nose. Lane interrupted her to ask if he might see Mr. Cunningham.

'Name, please?' she parroted pertly, and pressed a button in the switchboard before her.

Presently she reached for the powder-puff again. 'Says to come right in. Door 't end o' the hall.'

Kirby entered. A man sat at a desk telephoning. He was smooth-shaven and rather heavy-set, a year or two beyond thirty, with thinning hair on the top of his head. His eyes in repose were hard and chill. From the conversation his visitor gathered that he was a captain in the Red Cross drive that was on.

As he hung up the receiver the man rose, brisk and smiling, hand outstretched. 'Glad to meet you, Cousin Kirby. When did you reach town? And how long are you going to stay?'

'Got in hour an' a half ago. How are you. James?'

'Busy, but not too busy to meet old friends.

Let me see. I haven't seen you since you were ten years old, have I?'

'I was about twelve. It was when my father moved to Wyoming.'

'Well, I'm glad to see you. Where you staying? Eat lunch with me tomorrow, can't you? I'll try to get Jack too.'

'Suits me fine,' agreed Kirby.

'Anything I can do for you in the meantime?'

'Yes. I want to see Uncle James.'

There was a film of wariness in the eyes of the oil broker as he looked at the straight, clean-built young cattleman. He knew that the strong face, brown as Wyoming, expressed a pungent personality back of which was dynamic force. What did Lane want with his uncle? They had quarreled. His cousin knew that. Did young Lane expect him to back his side of the quarrel? Or did he want to win back favor with James Cunningham, Senior, millionaire?

Kirby smiled. He guessed what the other was thinking. 'I don't want to interfere in your friendship with him. All I need is his address and a little information. I've come to have another row with him, I reckon.'

The interest in Cunningham's eyes quickened. He laughed. 'Aren't you in bad enough already with Uncle? Why another quarrel?'

28

'This isn't on my own account. There's a girl in his office—'

A rap on the door interrupted Kirby. A young man walked into the room. He was a good-looking young exquisite, dark-eyed and black-haired. His clothes had been made by one of the best tailors in New York. Moreover, he knew how to wear them.

James Cunningham, Junior, introduced him to Kirby as his cousin Jack. After a few moments of talk the broker reverted to the subject of their previous talk.

'Kirby was just telling me that he has come to Denver to meet Uncle James.' he explained to his brother. 'Some difficulty with him. I understand.'

Jack Cunningham's black eyes fastened on his cousin. He waited for further information. It was plain he was interested.

'I'm not quite sure of my facts,' Lane said. 'But there's evidence to show that he has ruined a young girl in his office. She practically admits that he's the man. I happen to be a friend of her family, an' I'm goin' to call him to account. He can't get away with it.'

Kirby chanced to be looking at his cousin Jack. What he saw in that young man's eyes surprised him. There were astonishment, incredulity, and finally a cunning narrowing of the black pupils.

It was James who spoke. His face was grave. 'That's a serious charge, Kirby,' he said. 'What

29

is the name of the young woman?'

'I'd rather not give it—except to Uncle James himself.'

'Better write it,' suggested Jack with a reminiscent laugh. 'He's a bit impetuous. I saw him throw a man down the stairs yesterday. Picked the fellow up at the foot of the flight. He certainly looked as though he'd like to murder our dear uncle.'

'What I'd like to know is this,' said Lane. 'What sort of a reputation has Uncle James in this way? Have you ever heard of his bein' in anything of this sort before?'

'No, I haven't,' James said promptly.

Jack shrugged. 'I wouldn't pick nunky for exactly a moral man,' he said flippantly. 'His idea of living is to grab all the easy things he can.'

'Where can I see him most easily? At his office?' asked Kirby.

'He drove down to Colorado Springs today on business. At least he told me he was going. Don't know whether he expects to get back tonight or not. He lives at the Paradox Apartments,' Jack said.

'Probl'y I'd better see him there rather than at his office.'

'Hope you have a pleasant time with the old boy,' Jack murmured. 'Don't think I'd care to be a champion of dames where he's concerned. He's a damned cantankerous old brute. I'll say that for him.'

James arranged a place of meeting for luncheon next day. The young cattleman left. He knew from the fidgety manner of Jack that he had some important business he was anxious to talk over with his brother.

CHAPTER SIX

LIGHTS OUT

It was five minutes to ten by his watch when Kirby entered the Paradox Apartments. The bulletin board told him that his uncle's apartment was 12. He did not take the self-serve elevator, but the stairs. The hall on the second floor was dark. Since he did not know whether the rooms he wanted were on this floor or the next he knocked at a door.

Kirby thought he heard the whisper of voices and he knocked again. He had to rap a third time before the door was opened.

'What is it? What do you want?'

If ever Lane had seen stark, naked fear in a human face, it stared at him out of that of the woman in front of him. She was a tall, angular woman of a harsh, forbidding countenance, flat-breasted and middle-aged. Behind her, farther back in the room, the rough rider caught a glimpse of a fat, gross, ashen-faced man fleeing toward the inner door of a bedroom to escape being seen. He was thrusting into his coat pocket what looked to the man in the hall like a revolver.

'Can you tell me where James Cunningham's apartment is?' asked Kirby.

The woman gasped. The hand on the doorknob was trembling violently. Something clicked in her throat when the dry lips tried to frame an answer.

'Head o' the stairs—right hand,' she managed to get out, then shut the door swiftly in the face of the man whose simple question had so shocked her.

Kirby heard the latch released from its catch. The key in the lock below also turned.

'She's takin' no chances,' he murmured. 'Now I wonder why both her an' my fat friend are so darned worried. Who were they lookin' for when they opened the door an' saw me? An' why did it get her goat when I asked where Uncle James lived?'

As he took the treads that brought him to the next landing the cattleman had an impression of a light being flashed off somewhere. He turned to the right as the woman below had directed.

The first door had on the panel a card with his uncle's name. He knocked. and at the same instant noticed that the door was ajar. No answer came. His finger found the electric push button. He could hear it buzzing inside. Twice he pushed it.

32

'Nobody at home, looks like,' he said to himself. 'Well, I reckon I'll step in an' leave a note. Or maybe I'll wait. If the door's open he's liable to he right back.'

He stepped into the room. It was dark. His fingers groped along the wall for the button to throw on the light. Before he found it a sound startled him.

It was the soft faint panting of some one breathing.

He was a man whose nerves were under the best of control, but the cold feet of mice pattered up and down his spine. Something was wrong. The sixth sense of danger that comes to some men who live constantly in peril was warning him.

'Who's there?' he asked sharply.

No voice replied, but there was a faint rustle of some one or some thing stirring.

He waited, crouched in the darkness.

There came another vague rustle of movement. And presently another, this time closer. Every sense in him was alert, keyed up to closest attention. He knew that some one, for some sinister purpose, had come into this apartment and been trapped here by him.

The moments flew. He thought he could hear his hammering heart. A stifled gasp, a dozen feet from him, was just audible.

He leaped for the sound. His outflung hand struck an arm and slid down it, caught at a small wrist, and fastened there. In the fraction of a second left him he realized, beyond question, that it was a woman he had assaulted.

The hand was wrenched from him. There came a zigzag flash of lightning searing his brain, a crash that filled the world for him— and he floated into unconsciousness.

CHAPTER SEVEN

FOUL PLAY

Lane came back painfully to a world of darkness. His head throbbed distressingly. Querulously he wondered where he was and what had taken place.

He drew the fingers of his outstretched hand along the nap of a rug and he knew he was on the floor. Then his mind cleared and he remembered that a woman's hand had been imprisoned in his just before his brain stopped functioning.

Who was she? What was she doing here? And what under heaven had hit him hard enough to put the lights out so instantly?

He sat up and held his throbbing head. He had been struck on the point of the chin and gone down like an axed bullock. The woman must have lashed out at him with some weapon.

In his pocket he found a match. It flared up and lit a small space in the pit of blackness. Unsteadily he got to his feet and moved toward the door, His mind was quite clear now and his senses abnormally sensitive. For instance, he was aware of a faint perfume of violet in the room, so faint that he had not noticed it before.

There grew on him a horror, an eagerness to be gone from the rooms. It was based on no reasoning, but on some obscure feeling that there had taken place something evil, something that chilled his blood.

Yet he did not go. He had come for a purpose, and it was characteristic of him that he stayed in spite of the dread that grew on him till it filled his breast. Again he groped along the wall for the light switch. A second match flared in his fingers and showed it to him. Light flooded the room.

His first sensation was of relief. This handsome apartment with its Persian rugs, its padded easychairs, its harmonious wall tints, had a note of repose quite alien to tragedy. It was the home of a man who had given a good deal of attention to making himself comfortable. Indefinably, it was a man's room. The presiding genius of it was masculine and not feminine. It lacked the touches of adornment that only a woman can give to make a place homelike.

Yet one adornment caught Kirby's eye at

once. It was a large photograph in a handsome frame on the table. The picture showed the head and bust of a beautiful woman in evening dress. She was a brunette, young and very attractive. The line of head, throat, and shoulder was perfect. The delicate, disdainful poise and the gay provocation in the dark, slanting eyes were enough to tell that she was no novice in the game of sex. He judged her an expensive orchid produced in the civilization of our twentieth-century hothouse. Across the bottom of the picture was scrawled an inscription in a fashionably angular hand. Lane moved closer to read it. The words were, 'Always, Phyllis.' Probably this was the young woman to whom, if rumor were true, James Cunningham. Senior, was engaged.

On the floor, near where Kirby had been lying, lay a heavy piece of agate evidently used for a paperweight. He picked up the smooth stone and guessed instantly that this was the weapon which had established contact with his chin. Very likely the woman's hand had closed on it when she heard him coming. She had switched off the light and waited for him. That the blow had found a vulnerable mark and knocked him out had been sheer luck.

Kirby passed into a luxurious bedroom beyond which was a tiled bathroom, He glanced these over and returned to the outer apartment. There was still another door. It was closed. As the man from Wyoming moved toward it he felt once more a strange sensation of dread. It was strong enough to stop him in his stride. What was he going to find behind that door? When he laid his hand on the knob pinpricks played over his scalp and galloped down his spine.

He opened the door. A sweet sickish odor, pungent but not heavy, greeted his nostrils. It was a familiar smell, one he had met only recently. Where? His memory jumped to a corridor of the Cheyenne hospital. He had been passing the operating-room on his way to see Wild Rose. The door had opened and there had been wafted to him faintly the penetrating whiff of chloroform. It was the same drug he sniffed now.

He stood on the threshold, groped for the switch, and flashed on the lights. Sound though Kirby Lane's nerves were, he could not repress a gasp at what he saw.

Leaning back in an armchair, looking up at him with a horrible sardonic grin, was his uncle James Cunningham. His wrists were tied with ropes to the arms of the chair. A towel, passed round his throat, fastened the body to the back of the chair and propped up the head. A bloody clot of hair hung tangled just above the temple. The man was dead beyond any possibility of doubt. There was a small hole in the center of the forehead through which a bullet had crashed. Beneath this was a thin trickle of blood that had run into the heavy eyebrows.

The dead man was wearing a plaid smoking-jacket and oxblood slippers. On the tabouret close to his hand lay a half-smoked cigar. There was a grewsome suggestion in the tilt of the head and the gargoyle grin that this was a hideous and shocking jest he was playing on the world.

Kirby snatched his eyes from the grim spectacle and looked round the room, it was evidently a private den to which the owner of the apartment retired. There were facilities for smoking and for drinking, a lounge which showed marks of wear, and a writing-desk in one corner.

This desk held the young man's gaze. It was open. Papers lay scattered everywhere and its contents had been rifled and flung on the floor. Some one, in a desperate hurry, had searched every pigeon-hole.

The window of the room was open. Perhaps it had been thrown up to let out the fumes of the chloroform. Kirby stepped to it and looked down. The fire escape ran past it to the stories above and below.

The young cattleman had seen more than once the tragedies of the range. He had heard the bark of guns and had looked down on quiet dead men but a minute before full of lusty life. But these had been victims of warfare in the open, usually of sudden passions that had flared and struck. This was

38

different. It was murder, deliberate, cold-blooded, atrocious. The man had been tied up, made helpless, and done to death without mercy. There was a note of the abnormal, of the unhuman, about the affair. Whoever had killed James Cunningham deserved the extreme penalty of the law.

He was a man who no doubt had made many enemies. Always he had demanded his pound of flesh and got it. Some one had waited patiently for his hour and exacted a fearful vengeance for whatever wrong he had suffered.

Kirby decided that he must call the police at once. No time ought to be lost in starting to run down the murderer. He stepped into the living-room to the telephone, lifted the receiver from the hook, and stood staring down at a glove lying on the table.

As he looked at it the blood washed out of his face. He had a sensation as though his heart had been plunged into cracked ice. For he recognized the glove on the table, knew who its owner was.

It was a small riding-gauntlet with a device of a rose embroidered on the wrist. He would have known that glove among a thousand.

He had seen it, a few hours since, on the hand of Wild Rose.

CHAPTER EIGHT

BY MEANS OF THE FIRE ESCAPE

Kirby Lane stood with fascinated eyes looking down at the glove, muscles and brain alike paralyzed. The receiver was in his hand, close to his ear.

A voice from the other end of the wire drifted to him. 'Number, please.'

Automatically he hung the receiver on the hook. Dazed though he was, the rough rider knew that the police were the last people in the world he wanted to see just now.

All his life he had lived the adventure of the outdoors. For twelve months he had served at the front, part of the time with the forces in the Argonne. He had ridden stampedes and fought through blizzards, He had tamed the worst outlaw horses the West could produce. But he had never been so shock-shaken as he was now. A fact impossibly but dreadfully true confronted him. Wild Rose had been alone with his uncle in these rooms, had listened with breathless horror while Kirby climbed the stairs, had been trapped by his arrival, and had fought like a wolf to make her escape. He remembered the wild cry of her outraged heart, 'Nothing's too bad for a man like that.'

Lane was sick with fear. It ran through him

40

and sapped his supple strength like an illness. It was not possible that Rose could have done this in her right mind. But he had heard a doctor say once that under stress of great emotion people sometimes went momentarily insane. His friend had been greatly wrought up from anxiety, pain, fever, and lack of sleep.

In replacing the telephone he had accidentally pushed aside a book. Beneath it was a slip of paper on which had been penciled a note. He read it, without any interest.

Mr. Hull he come see you. He sorry you not here. He say maybe perhaps make honorable call some other time.

S. HORIKAWA

An electric bell buzzed through the apartment. The sound of it startled Kirby as though it had been the warning of a rattlesnake close to his head. Some one was at the outer door ringing for admission. It would never do for him to be caught here.

He had been trained to swift thought reactions. Quickly but noiselessly he stepped to the door and released the catch of the Yale lock so that it would not open from the out-side without a key. He switched off the light and passed through the living-room into the bedchamber. His whole desire now was to be gone from the building as soon as possible. The bedroom also he darkened before he

41

stepped to the window and crept through it to the platform of the fire escape.

The glove was still in his hand. He thrust it into his pocket as he began the descent. The iron ladder ran down the building to the alley. It ended ten feet above the ground. Kirby lowered himself and dropped. He turned to the right down the alley toward Glenarm Street.

A man was standing at the corner of the alley trying to light a cigar. He was a reporter on the *Times*, just returning from the Press Club where he had been playing in a pool tournament.

He stopped Lane. 'Can you lend me a match, friend?'

The cattleman handed him three or four and started to go.

'Just a mo',' the newspaper-man said, striking a light. 'Do you always'—puff, puff—'leave your rooms'—puff, puff, puff—'by the fire escape?'

Kirby looked at him in silence, thinking furiously. He had gone up to his uncle's rooms. Here was another to testify he had left by the fire escape. The best he could say was that he was very unlucky.

'Never mind, friend,' the newspaper-man went on. 'You don't look like a second-story worker to yours truly.' He broke into a little amused chuckle. 'I reckon friend husband who never comes home till Saturday night, happened around unexpectedly and the fire escape looked good to you. Am I right?'

The Wyoming man managed a grin. It was not a mirthful one, but it served.

'You're a wizard,' he said admiringly.

The reporter had met a bootlegger earlier in the evening and had two or three drinks. He was mellow. 'Oh, I'm wise,' be said with a wink. 'Chuck Ellis isn't anybody's fool. Beat it, Lothario, while the beating's good.' The last sentence and the gesture that accompanied the words were humorous exaggerations of old-time melodrama, Lane took his advice without delay.

CHAPTER NINE

THE STORY IN THE *NEWS*

From a booth in a drug-store on Sixteenth Street Kirby telephoned the police that James Cunningham had been murdered at his home in the Paradox Apartments. He stayed to answer no questions, but hung up at once. From a side door of the store he stepped out to Welton Street and walked to his hotel.

He passed a wretched night. The distress that flooded his mind was due less to his own danger than to his anxiety for Rose. His course of action was not at all clear to him in case he should be identified as the man who had been seen going to and coming from the apartment of the murdered man. He could not explain why he was there without implicating Rose and her sister. He would not betray them. That of course. But he had told his cousins why he was going. Would their story not start a hunt for the woman in the case?

Man is an illogical biped. Before Kirby had seen the glove on the table and associated it with the crime, his feeling had been that the gallows was the proper end of so cruel a murderer. Now he not only intended to protect Rose, but his heart was filled with pity for her. He understood her better than he did any other woman, her loyalty and love and swift, upblazing anger. Even if her hand had fired the shot, he told himself, it was not Wild Rose who had done it—not the little friend he had come to know and like so well, but a tortured woman beside herself with grief for the sister to whom she had always been a mother too.

He slept little, and that brokenly. With the dawn he was out on the street to buy a copy of the 'News.' The story of the murder had the two columns on the right-hand side of the front page and broke over to the third. He hurried back to his room to read it behind a locked door.

The story was of a kind in which newspapers revel. Cunningham was a well-known

44

character, several times a millionaire, His death even by illness would have been worth a column. But the horrible and grewsome way of his taking off, the mystery surrounding it, the absence of any apparent motive unless it were revenge, all whetted the appetite of the editors. It was a big 'story,' one that would run for many days, and the *News* played it strong.

As Kirby had expected, he was selected as the probable assassin. A reporter had interviewed Mr. and Mrs. Cass Hull, who occupied the apartment just below that of the murdered man. They had told him that a young man, a stranger to them, powerfully built and dressed like a prosperous ranchman, had knocked on their door about 9:20 to ask the way to the apartment of Cunningham. Hull explained that he remembered the time particularly because he happened to be winding the clock at the moment.

A description of Lane was given in a two-column 'box.' He read it with no amusement. It was too deadly accurate for comfort.

The supposed assassin of James Cunningham is described by Mrs. Cass Hull as dressed in a pepper-and-salt suit and a white, pinched-in cattleman's hat. He is about six feet tall, between 25 and 30 years old, weighing about 200 or perhaps 210 pounds. His hair is a light brown and his face tanned from the sun.

His age and his weight were overstated, and his clothes were almost a khaki brown. Otherwise Mrs. Hull had given a very close description of him, considering her state of mind at the moment when she had seen him.

There was one sentence of the story he read over two or three times. Hull and his wife agreed that it was about 9:20 when he had knocked on their door, unless it was a printer's error or the reporter had made a mistake. Kirby knew this was wrong. He had looked at his watch just before he had entered the Paradox Apartment. He had stopped directly under a street globe, and the time was 9:55.

Had the Hulls deliberately shifted the time back thirty-five minutes? If so, why? He remembered how stark terror had stared out of both their faces. Did they know more about the murder than they pretended? When he had mentioned his uncle's name the woman had been close to collapse, though, of course, he could not be sure that had been the reason. To his mind there flashed the memory of the note he had seen on the table. The man had called on Cunningham and left word he might call again. Was it possible the Hulls had just come down from the apartment above when he had knocked on their door? If so, how did the presence of Rose fit into the schedule?

Lane pounced on the fear and the evasion of the Hulls as an out for Wild Rose. It was only a morsel of hope, but he made the most

46

of it.

The newspaper was inclined to bring up stage the mysterious man who had called up the police at 10:25 to tell them that Cunningham had been murdered in his rooms. Who was this man? Could he be the murderer? If so, why should he telephone the police and start immediately the hunt after him? If not the killer, how did he know that a crime had been committed less than an hour before?

As soon as he had eaten breakfast, Kirby walked round to the boarding-house on Cherokee Street where Wild Rose was staying with her sister. Rose was out, he learned from the landlady. He asked if he might see her sister. His anxiety was so great he could not leave without a word of her.

Presently Esther came down to the parlor where the young man waited for her. Lane introduced himself as a friend of Rose. He was worried about her, he said. She seemed to him in a highly wrought-up, nervous state, He wondered if it would not be well to get her out of Denver.

Esther swallowed a lump in her throat. She had never seen Rose so jumpy, she agreed. Last night she had gone out for an hour alone. The look in her eyes when she had come back had frightened Esther. She had gone at once to her bedroom and locked the door, but her sister had heard her moving about for hours.

Then, suddenly, Esther's throat swelled and she began to sob. She knew well enough that she was at the bottom of Wild Rose's worries.

'Where is she now?' asked Kirby gently.

'I don't know. She didn't tell me where she was going. There's—there's something queer about her. I—I'm afraid.'

'What are you afraid of?'

'She's so—so kinda fierce,' Esther wailed.

It was impossible to explain, even to this big brown friend of Rose who looked as though his quiet strength could move mountains. He was a man. Besides, every instinct in her drove to keep hidden the secret that some day would tell itself.

Her eyes fell. They rested on the *News* some boarder had tossed on the table beside which she stood. Her thoughts were of herself and the plight in which she had become involved She looked at the big headlines of the paper and for the moment did not see them. What she did see was disgrace, the shipwreck of the young life she loved so much.

Her pupils dilated. The words of the headline penetrated to the brain. A hand clutched at her heart. She read again hazily—

JAMES CUNNINGHAM MURDERED

—then collapsed fainting into a chair.

CHAPTER TEN

KIRBY ASKS A DIRECT QUESTION

The story of the Cunningham mystery, as it was already being called, filled the early editions of the afternoon papers. The *Times* had the scoop of the day. It was a story signed by Chuck Ellis, who had seen the alleged murderer climb down by a fire escape from the window, of Cunningham's bedroom and had actually talked with the man as he emerged from the alley. His description of the suspect tallied fairly closely with that of Mrs. Hull, but it corrected errors in regard to weight, age, and color of clothes.

As Kirby walked to the Equitable Building to keep his appointment with his cousins, it would not have surprised him if at any moment an officer had touched him on the shoulder and told him he was under arrest.

Entering the office of the oil broker, where the two brothers were waiting for him, Kirby had a sense of an interrupted conversation. They had been talking about him, he guessed. The atmosphere was electric.

James spoke quickly, to bridge any embarrassment. 'This is a dreadful thing about Uncle James. I've never been so shocked before in my life. The crime was absolutely

49

fiendish.'

Kirby nodded. 'Or else the deed of some insane person. Men in their right senses don't do such things.'

'No,' agreed James. 'Murder's one thing. Such cold-blooded deviltry is quite another. There may be insanity connected with it. But one thing is sure. I'll not rest till the villain's run to earth and punished.'

His eyes met those of his cousin. They were cold and bleak.

'Do you think I did it?' asked Kirby quietly.

The directness of the question took James aback. After the fraction of a second's hesitation he spoke. 'If I did I wouldn't be going to lunch with you.'

Jack cut in. Excitement had banished his usual almost insolent indolence. His dark eyes burned with a consuming fire. 'Let's put our cards on the table. We think you're the man the police are looking for—the one described in the papers.'

'What makes you think that?'

'You told us you were going to see him as soon as he got back from the Springs. The description fits you to a T. You can't get away with an alibi so far as I'm concerned.'

'All right,' said the rough rider, his low, even voice unruffled by excitement. 'If I can't, I can't. We'll say I'm the man who came down the fire escape. What then?'

James was watching his cousin steadily. The

pupils of his eyes narrowed. He took the answer out of his brother's mouth. 'Then we think you probably know something about this mystery that you'll want to tell us. You must have been on the spot very soon after the murderer escaped. Perhaps you saw him.'

Kirby told the story of his night's adventure, omitting any reference whatever to Wild Rose or to anybody else in the apartment when he entered.

After he had finished, James made his comment. 'You've been very frank, Kirby. I accept your story. A guilty man would have denied being in the apartment, or he would have left town and disappeared.'

The range rider smiled sardonically. 'I'm not so sure of that. You've got the goods on me. I can't deny I'm the man the police are lookin' for. Mrs. Hull would identify me. So would this reporter Ellis. All you would have to do would be to hand my name to the nearest officer. An' I can't run away without confessin' guilt. Even if I had killed Uncle James, I couldn't do much else except tell some story like the one I've told you.'

'It wouldn't go far in a court-room,' Jack said.

'Not far,' admitted Kirby. 'By the way, you haven't expressed an opinion, Jack. Do you think I shot Uncle James?'

Jack looked at him, almost sullenly, and looked away. He poked at the corner of the

51

desk with the ferrule of his cane. 'I don't know who shot him. You had quarreled with him, and you went to have another row with him. A cop told me that some one who knew how to tie ropes fastened the knots around his arms and throat. You beat it from the room by the fire escape. A jury would hang you high as Haman on that evidence. Damn it, there's a bad bruise on your chin wasn't there when we saw you yesterday. For all I know he may have done it before you put him out.'

'I struck against a corner in the darkness,' Kirby said.

'That's what *you* say. You've got to explain it somehow. I think your story's fishy, if you ask me.'

'Then you'd better call up the police,' suggested Lane.

'I didn't say I was going to call the cops,' retorted Jack sulkily.

James looked at his cousin. Kirby Lane was strong. You could not deny his strength, audacious yet patient. He was a forty-horsepower man with the smile of a boy. Moreover, his face was a certificate of manhood. It was a recommendation more effective than words.

'I think you're wrong, Jack,' the older brother said. 'Kirby had no more to do with this than I had.'

'Thanks,' Kirby nodded.

'Let's investigate this man Hull. What Kirby

52

says fits in with what you saw a couple of evenings ago, Jack. I'm assuming he's the same man Uncle flung downstairs. Uncle told you he was a blackmailer. *There's* one lead. Let's follow it.'

Reluctantly Kirby broached one angle of the subject that must be faced. 'What about this girl in Uncle's office—the one in trouble? Are we goin' to bring her into this?'

There was a moment's silence. Jack's black eyes slid from Lane to his brother. It struck Kirby that he was waiting tensely for the decision of James, though the reason for his anxiety was not apparent.

James gave the matter consideration, then spoke judicially. 'Better leave her out of it. No need to smirch Uncle's reputation unless it's absolutely necessary. We don't want the newspapers gloating over any more scandals than they need.'

The cattleman breathed freer. He had an odd feeling that Jack, too, was relieved. Had the young man, after all, a warmer feeling for his dead uncle's reputation than he had given him credit for?

As the three cousins stepped out of the Equitable Building to Stout Street a newsboy was calling an extra.

'A-l-l 'bout Cunn'n'ham myst'ry. Huxtry! Huxtry!'

Kirby bought a paper. A streamer headline in red flashed at him.

53

HORIKAWA, VALET OF CUNNINGHAM, DISAPPEARS

The lead of the story below was to the effect that Cunningham had drawn two thousand dollars in large bills from the bank the day of his death. Horikawa could not be found, and the police had a theory that he had killed and robbed his master for this money.

CHAPTER ELEVEN

TIIE CORONER'S INQUEST

If Kirby had been playing his own hand only he would have gone to the police and told them he was the man who had been seen leaving the Paradox Apartments by the fire escape. But he could not do this without running the risk of implicating Wild Rose. Awkward questions would be fired at him that he could not answer. He decided not to run away from arrest, but not to surrender himself. If the police rounded him up, he could not help it; if they did not, so much the better.

He made two more attempts to see Wild Rose during the day, but he could not find her at home. When he at last did see her it was at the inquest, where he had gone to learn all that he could of the circumstances surrounding the murder.

There was a risk in attending. He recognized that. But he was moved by an imperative urge to find out all that was possible of the affair. The force that drove him was the need in his heart to exonerate his friend. Though he recognized the weight of evidence against her, he could not believe her guilty. Under tremendous provocation it might be in character for her to have shot his uncle in self-defense or while in extreme anger. But all his knowledge of her cried out that she could never have chloroformed him, tied him up, then taken his life while he was helpless. She was too fine and loyal to her code, too good a sportsman, far too tender-hearted, for such a thing.

Yet the evidence assaulted this conviction of his soul. If the Wild Rose in the dingy court-room had been his friend of the outdoor spaces, he would have rejected as absurd the possibility that she had killed his uncle. But his heart sank when he looked at this wan-faced woman who came late and slipped inconspicuously into a back seat, whose eyes avoided his, who was so plainly keyed up to a tremendously high pitch. She was dressed in a dark-blue tailored serge and a black sailor hat, beneath the rim of which the shadows on her face were dark.

The room was jammed with people. Every

aisle was packed and hundreds were turned away. In the audience was a scattering of fashionably dressed women, for it was possible the inquest might develop a sensation.

The coroner was a short, fat, little man with a highly developed sense of his importance. It was his hour, and he made the most of it. His methods were his own. The young assistant district attorney lounging by the table played second fiddle.

The first witnesses developed the movements of Cunningham during the evening of the twenty-third. He had dined at the City Club, and had left there after dinner to go to his apartment. To a club member dining with him he had mentioned an appointment at his rooms with a lady.

A rustling wave of excitement swept the benches. Those who had come to seek sensations had found their first thrill. Kirby drew in his breath sharply. He leaned forward, not to miss a word.

'Did he mention the name of the lady, Mr. Blanton?' asked the coroner, washing the backs of his hands with the palms.

'No.'

'Or his business with her?'

'No. But he seemed to be annoyed.' Mr. Blanton also seemed to be annoyed. He had considered not mentioning this appointment, but his conscience would not let him hide it. None the less he resented the need of giving the public more scandal about a fellow club member who was dead. He added an explanation. 'My feeling was that it was some business matter being forced on him. He had been at Colorado Springs during the day and probably had been unable to see the lady earlier.'

'Did he say so?'

'No-o, not exactly.'

'What did he say to give you that impression?'

'I don't recall his words.'

'Or the substance of them?'

'No. I had the impression, very strongly.'

The coroner reproved him tartly. 'Please confine your testimony to facts and not to impressions, Mr. Blanton. Do you know at what time Mr. Cunningham left the City Club?'

'At 8:45.'

'Precisely?'

'Precisely.'

'That will do.'

Exit Mr. Blanton from the chair and from the room, very promptly and very eagerly.

He was followed by a teller at the Rocky Mountain National Bank. He testified to only two facts—that he knew Cunningham and that the promoter had drawn two thousand dollars in bills on the day of his death.

A tenant at the Paradox Apartments was next called to the stand. The assistant district

57

attorney examined him. He brought out only one fact of importance—that he had seen Cunningham enter the building at a few minutes before nine o'clock.

The medical witnesses were introduced next. The police surgeon had reached the apartment at 10:30. The deceased had come to his death, in his judgment, from the effect of a bullet out of a .38 caliber revolver fired into his brain. He had been struck a blow on the head by some heavy instrument, but this in itself would probably not have proved fatal.

'How long do you think he had been dead when you first saw him?'

'Less than an hour.' Answering questions, the police surgeon gave the technical medical reasons upon which he based this opinion. He described the wound.

The coroner washed the backs of his hands with his palms. Observing reporters noticed that he did this whenever he intended taking the examination into his own hands.

'Did anything peculiar about the wound impress you?' he asked.

'Yes. The forehead of the deceased was powder-marked.'

'Showing that the weapon had been fired close to him?'

'Yes.'

'Anything else?'

'One thing. The bullet slanted into the head toward the right.'

'Where was the chair in which the deceased was seated? I mean in what part of the room.'

'Pushed close to the left-hand wall and parallel to it.'

'Very close?'

'Touching it.'

'Under the circumstances could the revolver have been fired so that the bullet could have taken the course it did if held in the right hand?'

'Hardly. Not unless it was held with extreme awkwardness.'

'In your judgment, then, the revolver was fired by a left-handed person?'

'That is my opinion.'

The coroner swelled like a turkey cock as he waved the attorney to take charge again.

Lane's heart drummed fast. He did not look across the room toward the girl in the blue tailored suit. But he saw her, just as clearly as though his eyes had been fastened on her. The detail that stood out in his imagination was the right arm set in splints and resting in a linen sling suspended from the neck.

Temporarily Rose McLean was left-handed.

'Was it possible that the deceased could have shot himself?'

'Do you mean, is it possible that somebody could have tied him to the chair after he was dead?'

'Yes.'

The surgeon, taken by surprise, hesitated.

'That's *possible*, certainly.'

James Cunningham took the witness chair after the police officers who had arrived at the scene of the tragedy with the surgeon had finished their testimony. One point brought out by the officers was that in the search of the rooms the two thousand dollars was not found. The oil broker gave information as to his uncle's affairs.

'You knew your uncle well?' the lawyer asked presently.

'Intimately.'

'And were on good terms with him?'

'The best.'

'Had he ever suggested to you that he might commit suicide?'

'Never,' answered the oil broker with emphasis. 'He was the last man in the world one would have associated with such a thought.'

'Did he own a revolver?'

'No, not to my knowledge. He had an automatic.'

'What caliber was it?'

'I'm not quite sure—about a .38, I think.'

'When did you see it last?'

'I don't recollect.'

The prosecuting attorney glanced at his notes.

'You are his next of kin?'

'My brother and I are his nephews. He had no nearer relatives.'

'You are his only nephews—his only near relatives?'

Cunningham hesitated, for just the blinking of an eye. He did not want to bring Kirby into his testimony if he could help it. That might ultimately lead to his arrest.

'He had one other nephew.'

'Living in Denver?'

'No.'

'Where?'

'Somewhere in Wyoming, I think. We do not correspond.'

'Do you know if he is there now?'

The witness dodged. 'He lives, there, I think.'

'Do you happen to know where he is at the present moment?'

'Yes.' The monosyllable fell reluctantly.

'Where?'

'In Denver.'

'Not in this court-room?'

'Yes.'

'What is the gentleman's name, Mr. Cunningham?'

'Kirby Lane.'

'Will you point him out?'

James did so.

The lawyer faced the crowded benches. 'I'll ask Mr. Lane to step forward and take a seat near the front. I may want to ask him a few questions later.'

Kirby rose and came forward.

'To your knowledge, Mr. Cunningham, had your uncle any enemies?' asked the attorney, continuing his examination.

'He was a man of positive opinions. Necessarily there were people who did not like him.'

'Active enemies?'

'In a business sense, yes.'

'But not in a personal sense?'

'I do not know of any. He may have had them. In going through his desk at the office I found a letter. Here it is.'

The fat little coroner bustled forward, took the letter, and read it. He handed it to one of the jury. It was read and passed around. The letter was the one the promoter had received from the Dry Valley rancher threatening his life if he ever appeared again in that part of the country.

'I notice that the letter is postmarked Denver,' Cunningham suggested. 'Whoever mailed it must have been in the city at the time.'

'That's very important,' the prosecuting attorney said. 'Have you communicated the information to the police?'

'Yes.'

'You do not know who wrote the letter?'

'I do not.'

The coroner put the tips of his fingers and thumbs together and balanced on the balls of his feet. 'Do you happen to know the name of the lady with whom your uncle had an appointment on the night of his death at his rooms?'

'No,' answered the witness curtly.

'When was the last time you saw the deceased alive?'

'About three o'clock on the day before that of his death.'

'Anything occur at that time throwing any light on what subsequently occurred?'

'Nothing whatever.'

'Very good, Mr. Cunningham. You may be excused, if Mr. Johns is through with you, unless some member of the jury has a question he would like to ask.'

One of the jury had. He was a dried-out wisp of a man wrinkled like a winter pippin. 'Was your uncle engaged to be married at the time of his death?' he piped.

There was a mild sensation in the room. Curious eyes swept toward the graceful, slender form of a veiled woman sitting at the extreme left of the room.

Cunningham flushed. The question seemed to him a gratuitous probe into the private affairs of the family. 'I do not care to discuss that,' he answered quietly.

'The witness may refuse to answer questions if he wishes,' the coroner ruled.

Jack Cunningham was called to the stand. James had made an excellent witness. He was quiet, dignified, and yet forceful. Jack, on the

63

other hand, was nervous and irritable. The first new point he developed was that on his last visit to the rooms of his uncle he had seen him throw downstairs a fat man with whom he had been scuffling. Shown Hull, he identified him as the man.

'Had you ever had any trouble with your uncle?' Johns asked him.

'You may decline to answer if you wish,' the coroner told the witness.

Young Cunningham hesitated. 'No-o. What do you mean by trouble?'

'Had he ever threatened to cut you out of his will?'

'Yes,' came the answer, a bit sulkily.

'Why—if you care to tell?'

'He thought I was extravagant and wild—wanted me to buckle down to business more.'

'What is your business?'

'I'm with a bond house—McCabe, Foster & Clinton.'

'During the past few months have you had any difference of opinion with your uncle?'

'That's my business,' flared the witness. Then, just as swiftly as his irritation had come it vanished. He remembered that his uncle's passionate voice had risen high. No doubt people in the next apartments had heard him. It would be better to make a frank admission. 'But I don't mind answering. I have.'

'When?'

'The last time I went to his rooms—two

days before his death.'

Significant looks passed from one to another of the spectators.

'What was the subject of the quarrel?'

'I didn't say we had quarreled,' was the sullen answer.

'Differed, then. My question was, what about?'

'I decline to say.'

'I think that is all, Mr. Cunningham.'

The wrinkled little juryman leaned forward and piped his question again. 'Was your uncle engaged to be married at the time of his death?'

The startled eyes of Jack Cunningham leaped to the little man. There was in them dismay, almost panic. Then, swiftly, he recovered and drawled insolently, 'I try to mind my own business. Do you?'

The coroner asserted himself. 'Here, here, none of that! Order in this court, *if* you please, gentlemen.' He bustled in his manner, turning to the attorney. 'Through with Mr. Cunningham, Johns? If so, we'll push on.'

'Quite.' The prosecuting attorney consulted a list in front of him. 'Cass Hull next.'

Hull came puffing to the stand. He was a porpoise of a man. His eyes dodged about the room in dread. It was as though he were looking for a way of escape.

CHAPTER TWELVE

'THAT'S THE MAN'

'Your name?'

'Cass Hull.'

'Business?'

'Real estate, mostly farm lands.'

'Did you know James Cunningham, the deceased?' asked Johns.

'Yes. Worked with him on the Dry Valley proposition, an irrigation project.'

'Ever have any trouble with him?'

'No, sir—not to say trouble.' Hull was already perspiring profusely. He dragged a red bandanna from his pocket and mopped the roll of fat that swelled over his collar. 'I—we had a—an argument about a settlement—nothin' serious.'

'Did he throw you out of his room and down the stairs?'

'No, sir, nothin' like that a-tall. We might 'a' scuffled some, kinda in fun like. Prob'ly it looked like we was fightin', but we wasn't. My heel caught on a tread o' the stairs an' I fell down.' Hull made his explanation eagerly and anxiously, dabbing at his beefy face with the handkerchief.

'When did you last see Mr. Cunningham alive?'

'Well, sir, that was the last time, though I reckon we heard him pass our door.'

In answer to questions the witness explained that Cunningham had owed him, in his opinion, four thousand dollars more than he had paid. It was about this sum they had differed.

'Were you at home on the evening of the twenty-third—that is, last night?'

The witness flung out more signals of distress. 'Yes, sir,' he said at last in a voice dry as a whisper.

'Will you tell what, if anything, occurred?'

'Well, sir, a man knocked at our door. The woman she opened it, an' he asked which flat was Cunningham's. She told him, an' the man he started up the stairs.'

'Have you seen the man since?'

'No, sir.'

'Didn't hear him come downstairs later?'

'No, sir.'

'At what time did this man knock?' asked the lawyer from the district attorney's office.

Kirby Lane did not move a muscle of his body, but excitement grew in him, as he waited, eyes narrowed, for the answer.

'At 9.20.'

'How do you know the time so exactly?'

'Well, sir, I was windin' the clock for the night.'

'Sure your clock was right?'

'Yes, sir. I happened to check up on it when

67

the court-house clock struck nine. Mebbe it was half a minute off, as you might say.'

'Describe the man.'

Hull did, with more or less accuracy.

'Would you know him if you saw him again?'

'Yes, sir, I sure would.'

The coroner flung a question at the witness as though it were a weapon. 'Ever carry a gun, Mr. Hull?'

The big man on the stand dabbed at his veined face with the bandanna. He answered, with an ingratiating whine. 'I ain't no gunman, sir. Never was.'

'Ever ride the range?'

'Well, yes, as you might say,' the witness answered uneasily.

'Carried a six-shooter for rattlesnakes, didn't you?'

'I reckon, but I never went hellin' around with it.'

'Wore it to town with you when you went, I expect, as the other boys did.'

'Mebbeso.'

'What caliber was it?'

'A .38, sawed-off.'

'Own it now?'

The witness mopped his fat face. 'No, sir.'

'Don't carry a gun in town?'

'No, sir.'

'Ever own an automatic?'

'No sir. Wouldn't know how to fire one.'

'How long since you sold your .38?'

'Five years or so.'

'Where did you carry it?'

'In my hip pocket.'

'Which hip pocket?'

Hull was puzzled at the question. 'Why, this one—the right one, o' course. There wouldn't be any sense in carryin' it where I couldn't reach it.'

'That's so. Mr. Johns, you may take the witness again.'

The young lawyer asked questions about the Dry Valley irrigation project. He wanted to know why there was dissatisfaction among the farmers, and from a reluctant witness drew the information that the water supply was entirely inadequate for the needs of the land under cultivation.

Mrs. Hull, called to the stand, testified that on the evening of the twenty-third a man had knocked at their door to ask in which apartment Mr. Cunningham lived. She had gone to the door, answered his question, and watched him pass upstairs.

'What time was this?'

'9:20.'

Again Kirby felt a tide of excitement running in his arteries. Why were this woman and her husband setting back the clock thirty-five minutes? Was it to divert suspicion from themselves? Was it to show that this stranger must have been in Cunningham's rooms for almost an hour, during which time the

69

millionaire promoter had been murdered?

'Describe the man.'

This tall, angular woman, whose sex the years had seemed to have dried out of her personality, made a much better witness than her husband. She was acid and incisive, but her very forbidding aspect hinted of the 'good woman' who never made mistakes. She described the stranger who had knocked at her door with a good deal of circumstantial detail.

'He was an outdoor man, a rancher, perhaps, or more likely a cattleman,' she concluded.

'You have not seen him since that time?'

She opened her lips to say 'No,' but she did not say it. Her eyes had traveled past the lawyer and fixed themselves on Kirby Lane. He saw the recognition grow in them, the leap of triumph in her as the long, thin arm shot straight toward him.

'That's the man!'

A tremendous excitement buzzed in the courtroom. It was as though some one had exploded a mental bomb. Men and women craned forward to see the man who had been identified, the man who no doubt had murdered James Cunningham. The murmur of voices, the rustle of skirts, the shuffling of moving bodies filled the air.

The coroner rapped for order. 'Silence in the court-room,' he said sharply.

'Which man do you mean, Mrs. Hull?'

70

asked the lawyer.

'The big brown man sittin' at the end of the front bench, the one right behind you.'

Kirby rose. 'Think prob'ly she means me,' he suggested.

An officer in uniform passed down the aisle and laid a hand on the cattleman's shoulder. 'You're under arrest,' he said.

'For what, officer?' asked James Cunningham.

'For the murder of your uncle, sir.'

In the tense silence that followed rose a little throat sound that was not quite a sob and not quite a wail. Kirby turned his head toward the back of the room.

Wild Rose was standing in her place looking at him with dilated eyes filled with incredulity and horror.

CHAPTER THIRTEEN

'ALWAYS, PHYLLIS'

'Chuck' Ellis, reporter, testified that on his way home from the Press Club on the night of the twenty-third, he stopped at an alley on Glenarm Street to strike a light for his cigar. Just as he lit the match he saw a man come out from the window of a room in the Paradox Apartments and run down the fire escape. It

71

struck him that the man might be a burglar, so he waited in the shadow of the building. The runner came down the alley toward him. He stopped the man and had some talk with him. At the request of the district attorney's assistant he detailed the conversation and located on a chart shown him the room from which he had seen the fellow emerge.

'Would you know him again?'

'Yes.'

'Do you see him in this room?'

Ellis, just off his run, had reached the court-room only a second before he stepped to the stand. Now he looked around, surprised at the lawyer's question. His wandering eye halted at Lane.

'There he is.'

'Which man do you mean?'

'The one on the end of the bench.'

'At what time did this take place?'

'Lemme see. About quarter-past ten, maybe.'

'Which way did he go when he left you?'

'Toward Fifteenth Street.'

'That is all.' The lawyer turned briskly toward Kirby. 'Mr. Lane, will you take the stand?'

Every eye focused on the range rider. As he moved forward and took the oath the scribbling reporters found in his movements a pantherish lightness, in his compact figure rippling muscles perfectly under control.

There was an appearance of sunburnt competency about him, a crisp confidence born of the rough-and-tumble life of the outdoor West. He did not look like a cold-blooded murderer. Women found themselves hoping that he was not. The jaded weariness of the sensation-seekers vanished at sight of him. A man had walked upon the stage, one full of vital energy.

The assistant district attorney led him through the usual preliminaries. Lane said that he was by vocation a cattleman, by avocation a rough rider. He lived at Twin Buttes, Wyoming.

One of the reporters leaned toward another and whispered, 'By Moses, he's the same Lane that won the rough-riding championship at Pendleton and was second at Cheyenne last year.'

'Are you related to James Cunningham, the deceased?' asked the lawyer.

'His nephew.'

'How long since you had seen him prior to your visit to Denver this time?'

'Three years.'

'What were your relations with him?'

The coroner interposed. 'You need answer no questions tending to incriminate you, Mr. Lane.'

A sardonic smile rested on the rough rider's lean, brown face. 'Our relations were not friendly,' he said quietly.

A ripple of excitement swept the benches.

'What was the cause of the bad feeling between you?'

'A few years ago my father fell into financial difficulties. He was faced with bankruptcy. Cunningham not only refused to help him, but was the hardest of his creditors. He hounded him to the time of my father's death a few months later. His death was due to a breakdown caused by intense worry.'

'You felt that Mr. Cunningham ought to have helped him?'

'My father helped him when he was young. What my uncle did was the grossest ingratitude.'

'You resented it.'

'Yes.'

'And quarreled with him?'

'I wrote him a letter an' told him what I thought of him. Later, when we met by chance, I told him again face to face.'

'You had a bitter quarrel?'

'That was how long ago?'

'Three years since.'

'In that time did your feelings toward him modify at all?'

'My opinion of him did not change, but I had no longer any feelin' in the matter.'

'Did you write to him or hear from him in that time?'

'No.'

'Had you any expectation of being

remembered in your uncle's will?'

'None whatever.' answered Kirby, smiling. 'Even if he had left me anything I should have declined to accept it. But there was no chance at all that he would.'

'Yet when you came to town you called on him at the first opportunity?'

'Yes.'

'On what business?'

'I reckon we'll not go into that.'

Johns glanced at his notes and passed to another line of questioning. 'You have heard the testimony of Mr. and Mrs. Hull and of Mr. Ellis. Is that testimony true?'

'Except in one point. It lacked only three of four minutes to ten when I knocked at the door an' Mrs. Hull opened it.'

'You're sure of that?'

'Sure. I looked at my watch just before I went into the Paradox Apartments.'

'Will you tell the jury what took place between you and Mrs. Hull?'

' 'Soon as I saw her I knew she was scared stiff about somethin'. So was Hull. He was headin' for a bedroom, so I wouldn't see him.'

The slender, well-dressed woman in the black veil, sitting far over to the left, leaned forward and seemed to listen intently. All over the room there was a stir of quickened interest.

'How did she show her fear?'

'No color in her face, eyes dilated an' full of

terror, hands tremblin'.'

'And Mr. Hull?'

'He was yellow. Color all gone from his face. Looked as though he'd had a shock.'

'What was said, if anything?'

'I asked Mrs. Hull where my uncle's apartment was. That gave her another fright. At least she almost fainted.'

'Did she say anything?'

'She told me where his rooms were. Then she shut the door, right in my face. I went upstairs to Apartment 12.'

'Where your uncle lived?'

'Where my uncle lived. I rang the bell twice an' didn't get an answer. Then I noticed the door was ajar. I opened it, called, an' walked in, shuttin' it behind me. I guessed he must be around an' would be back in a few minutes.'

'Just exactly what did you do?'

'I waited by the table in the living-room for a few minutes. There was a note there signed by S. Horikawa.'

'We have that note. What happened next? Did your uncle return?'

'No. I had a feelin' that somethin' was wrong. I looked into the bedroom an' then opened the door into the small smoking-room. The odor of chloroform met me. I found the button an' flashed on the light.'

Except the sobbing breath of an unnerved woman no slightest sound could be hear in the court-room but Lane's quiet, steady voice. It

76

went on evenly, clearly, dominating the crowded room by the drama of its undramatic timbre.

'My uncle was sittin' in a chair, tied to it. His head was canted a little to one side an' he was lookin' up at me. There was a bullet hole in his forehead. He was dead.'

The veiled woman in black gasped for air. Her head sank forward and her slender body swayed.

'Look out!' called the witness to the woman beside her. Before Kirby could reach her, the fainting woman had slipped to the floor. He stood to lift her head from the dusty planks— and the odor of violet perfume met his nostrils.

'If you'll permit me,' a voice said.

The cattleman looked up. His cousin James, white to the lips, was beside him unfastening the veil.

The face of the woman in black was the original of the photograph Kirby had seen in his uncle's room, the one upon which had been written the words, 'Always, Phyllis.'

CHAPTER FOURTEEN

A FRIEND IN NEED

The rest of the coroner's inquest was anticlimax. Those who had come to tickle their palates with excitement tasted only one other moment of it.

'According to your own story you must have been in your uncle's apartment at least a quarter of an hour, Mr. Lane,' said the prosecuting attorney. 'What were you doing there all that time?'

'Most of the time I was waitin' for him to return.'

'Why did you not call up the police at once, as soon as you found the crime had been committed?'

'I suppose I lost my head an' went panicky. I heard some one at the door, an' I did not want to be found there. So I ran into the bedroom, put out the light, an' left by the fire escape.'

'Was that the conduct one would expect of an innocent man?'

'It was the action of an innocent man.'

'You don't look like a man that would lose his head, Mr. Lane.'

A smile lit the brown face of the witness. 'Perhaps I wouldn't where I come from, but I'm not used to city ways. I didn't know what to do. So I followed my instinct an' bolted. I was unlucky enough to be seen.'

'Carry a gun, Mr. Lane?'

'No.' He corrected himself. 'Sometimes I do on the range.'

'Own one, I suppose?'

'Two. A .45 and a .38.'

'Bring either of them to Denver?'

'No, sir.'

'Did you see any gun of any kind in your uncle's rooms—either a revolver or an automatic?'

'I did not.'

'That's all, sir.'

The jury was out something more than an hour. The news of the verdict was brought to Kirby at the city jail by his cousin James.

'Jury finds that Uncle James came to his death from the effect of either a blow on the head by some heavy instrument or a bullet fired at close quarters by some unknown person,' James said.

'Good enough. Might have been worse for me,' replied Kirby.

'Yes. I've talked with the district attorney and think I can arrange for bond. We're going to take it up with the court tomorrow. My opinion is that the Hulls did this. All through his testimony the fellow sweated fear. I've put it in the hands of a private detective agency to keep tabs on him.'

The cattleman smiled ruefully. 'Trouble is

I'm the only witness to their panic right after the murder. Wish it had been some one else. I'm a prejudiced party whose evidence won't count for much. You're right. They've somethin' to do with it. In their evidence they shifted the time back thirty-five minutes so as to get me into Apartment 12 that much earlier. Why? If I could answer that question, I could go a long way toward solvin' the mystery of who killed Uncle James an' why he did it.'

'Probably. As I see it, we have three leads to go on. One is that the guilty man is Hull. A second possibility is the unknown man from Dry Valley. A third is Horikawa.'

'How about Horikawa? Did you know him well?'

'One never knows an Oriental. Perhaps I'm prejudiced because I used to live in California, but I never trust a Japanese fully. His sense of right and wrong is so different from mine. Horikawa is a quiet little fellow whose thought processes I don't pretend to understand.'

'Why did he run away if he had nothin' to conceal?'

'Looks bad. By the way, a Japanese housecleaner was convicted recently of killing a woman for whom he was working. He ran away, too, and was brought back later.'

'Well, I don't know a thing about Japs except that they're good workers. But there's one thing about this business that puzzles me. This murder doesn't look to me like a white man's job. An American bad man kills an' is done with it. But whoever did this aimed to torture an' then kill, looks like. If not, why did they tie him up first?'

James nodded, reflectively. 'Maybe something in what you say. Orientals strike me as being kind of unhuman, if you know what I mean. Maybe they have the red Indian habit of torture in Japan.'

'Never heard of it if they have, but I've got a kinda notion—picked it up in my readin'—that Asiatics will go a long way to square a grudge. If this Horikawa had anything against Uncle James he might have planned this revenge an' taken the two thousand dollars to help his getaway.'

'Yes, he might.'

'Anyhow, I've made up my mind to one thing. You can 'most always get the truth when you go after it good an' hard. I'm goin' to find out who did this thing an' why.'

James Cunningham looked into his cousin's face. A strong man himself, he recognized strength in another. Into the blue-gray eyes of the man from Twin Buttes had come a cold steely temper that transformed the gay, boyish face. The oil broker knew Lane had no love for his uncle. His resolution was probably based on a desire to clear his own name.

'I'm with you in that,' he said quietly, and his own dark eyes were hard as jade. 'We'll work this out together if you say so, Kirby.'

The younger man nodded. 'Suits me fine.' His face softened. 'You mentioned three leads. Most men would have said four. On the face of it, of the evidence at hand, the guilty man is sittin' right here talkin' with you. You know that the dead man an' I had a bitter feelin' against each other. You know there was a new cause of trouble between us, an' that I told you I was goin' to get justice out of him one way or another. I'm the only man known to have been in his rooms last night. Accordin' to the Hulls I must 'a' been there when he was killed. Then, as a final proof of my guilt, I slide out by the fire escape to get away without bein' seen. I'll say the one big lead points straight to Kirby Lane.'

'Yes, but there's such a thing as character,' James answered. 'It's written in your face that you couldn't have done it. That's why the jury said a person unknown.'

'Yes, but the jury didn't know what you knew, that I had a fresh cause of quarrel with Uncle James. Do you believe me absolutely? Don't you waver at all?'

'I don't think you had any more to do with it than I had myself,' answered the older cousin instantly, with conviction.

Kirby gave him his hand impulsively. 'You'll sure do to ride the river with, James.'

CHAPTER FIFTEEN

A GLOVE AND THE HAND IN IT

As Rose saw the hand of the law closing in on Kirby, she felt as though an ironic fate were laughing in impish glee at this horrible climax of her woe. He had sacrificed a pot of gold and his ambition to be the champion rough rider of the world in order to keep her out of trouble. Instead of that he had himself plunged into it head first.

She found herself entangled in a net from which there was no easy escape. Part, at least, of the evidence against Kirby, or at least the implication to be drawn from it, did not fit in with what she knew to be the truth. He had not been in the apartment of James Cunningham from 9:20 until 10:15. He might have been there at both times, but not for the whole interval between. Rose had the best reason in the world for knowing that.

But what was she to do? What ought she to do? If she went with her story to the district attorney, her sister's shame must inevitably be dragged forth to be flaunted before the whole world. She could not do that. She could not make little Esther the scapegoat of her conscience. Nor could she remain silent and let Kirby stay in prison. That was unthinkable.

If her story would free him she must tell it. But to whom?

She read in the *Post* that James Cunningham was endeavoring to persuade the authorities to accept bond for his cousin's appearance. Swiftly Rose made up her mind what she would do. She looked up in the telephone book the name she wanted and made connections on the line.

'Is this Mr. Cunningham?' she asked.

'Mr. Cunningham talking,' came the answer.

'I want to see you on very important business. Can I come this morning?'

'I think I didn't catch your name, madam.'

'My name doesn't matter. I have information about—your uncle's death.'

There was just an instant's pause. Then, 'Ten o'clock, at the office here,' Rose heard.

A dark, good-looking young man rose from a desk in the inner office when Rose entered exactly at ten. In his eyes there sparked a little flicker of surprised appreciation. Jack Cunningham was always susceptible to the beauty of women. This girl was lovely both of feature and of form. The fluent grace of the slender young body was charming, but the weariness of grief was shadowed under the long-lashed eyes.

She looked around, hesitating. 'I have an appointment with Mr. Cunningham,' she explained.

'My name,' answered the young man.

'Mr. James Cunningham?'

'Afraid you've made a mistake. I'm Jack Cunningham. This is my uncle's office. I'm taking charge of his affairs. You called his number instead of my brother's. People are always confusing the two.'

'I'm sorry.'

'If I can be of any service to you,' he suggested.

'I read that your brother was trying to arrange bond for Mr. Lane. I want to see him about that. I am Rose McLean. My sister worked for your uncle in his office.'

'Oh!' A film of wary caution settled over his eyes. It seemed to Rose that what she had said transformed him into a potential adversary. 'Glad to meet you, Miss McLean. If you'd rather talk with my brother I'll make an appointment with him for you.'

'Perhaps that would be best,' she said.

'Of course he's very busy. If it's anything I could do for you—'

'I'd like you both to hear what I have to say.'

For the beating of a pulse his eyes thrust at her as though they would read her soul. Then he was all smiling urbanity.

'That seems to settle the matter. I'll call my brother up and make an appointment.'

Over the wire Jack put the case to his brother. Presently he hung up the receiver. 'We'll go right over, Miss McLean.'

They went down the elevator and passed

through the lower hall of the building to Sixteenth Street. As they walked along Stout to the Equitable Building, Rose made an explanation.

'I saw you and Mr. James Cunningham at the inquest.'

His memory stirred. 'Think I saw you, too. 'Member your bandaged arm. Is it broken?'

'Yes.'

He felt the need of talking against an inner perturbation he did not want to show. What was this girl, the sister of Esther McLean, going to tell him and his brother? What did she know about the murder of his uncle? Excitement grew in him and he talked at random to cover it.

'Fall down?'

'A horse threw me and trod on my arm.'

'Girls are too venturesome nowadays.' In point of fact he did not think so. He liked girls who were good sportsmen and played the game hard. But he was talking merely to bridge a mental stress. 'Think they can do anything a man can. 'Fess up, Miss McLean. You'd try to ride any horse I could, no matter how mettlesome it was. Now wouldn't you?'

'I wouldn't go that far,' she said dryly. For an instant the thought flickered through her mind that she would like to get this spick-and-span riding-school model on the back of Wild Fire and see how long he would stick to the saddle.

James Cunningham met Rose with a suave courtesy, but with reserve. Like his brother he knew of only one subject about which the sister of Esther McLean could want to talk with him. Did she intend to be reasonable? Would she accept a monetary settlement and avoid the publicity that could only hurt her sister as well as the reputation of the name of Cunningham? Or did she mean to try to impose impossible conditions? How much did she know and how much guess? Until he discovered that he meant to play his cards close.

Characteristically, Rose came directly to the point after the first few words of introduction.

'You know my sister, Esther McLean, a stenographer of your uncle?' she asked.

The girl was standing. She had declined a chair. She stood straight-backed as an Indian, carrying her head with fine spirit. Her eyes attacked the oil broker, would not yield a thousandth part of an inch to his impassivity.

'I—have met her,' he answered.

'You know . . . about her trouble?'

'Yes. My cousin mentioned it. We—my brother and I—greatly regret it. Anything in reason that we can do we shall, of course, hold ourselves bound for.'

He flashed a glance at Jack who murmured a hurried agreement. The younger man's eyes were busy examining a calendar on the wall.

'I didn't come to see you about that now,'

87

the young woman went on, cheeks flushed, but chin held high. 'Nor would I care to express my opinion of the . . . the creature who could take advantage of such a girl's love. I intend to see justice is done my sister, as far as it can now be done. But not today. First, I'm here to ask you if you're friends of Kirby Lane. Do you believe he killed his uncle?'

'No,' replied James promptly. 'I am quite sure he didn't kill him. I am trying to get him out on bond. Any sum that is asked I'll sign for.'

'Then I want to tell you something you don't know. The testimony showed that Kirby went to his uncle's apartment about 9:20 and left nearly an hour later. That isn't true.'

'How do you know it isn't?'

'Because I was there myself part of the time.'

Jack stared at her in blank dismay. Astonishment looked at her, too, from the older brother's eyes.

'You were in my uncle's apartment—on the night of the murder?' James said at last.

'I was. I came to Denver to see him—to get justice for my sister. I didn't intend to let the villain escape scot free for what he had done.'

'Pardon me,' interrupted Jack, and the girl noticed his voice had a queer note of anxiety in it. 'Did your sister ever tell you that my uncle was responsible for—?' He left the sentence in air.

'No, she won't talk yet. I don't know why. But I found a note signed with his initials. He's the man. I know that.'

James looked at his brother. 'I think we may take that for granted, Jack. We'll accept such responsibilities on us as it involves. Perhaps you'd better not interrupt Miss McLean till she has finished her story.'

'I made an appointment with him after I had tried all day to get him on the 'phone or to see him. That was Thursday, the day I reached town.'

'He was in Colorado Springs all that day,' explained James.

'Yes, he told me so when I reached him finally at the City Club. He didn't want to see me, but I wouldn't let him off till he agreed. So he told me to come to the Paradox and he would give me ten minutes. He told me not to come till nearly ten, as he would be busy. I think he hoped that by putting it so late and at his rooms he would deter me from coming. But I intended to see him. He couldn't get away from me so easily as that. I went.'

Jack moistened dry lips. His debonair ease had quite vanished. 'When did you go?'

'It was quite a little past a quarter to ten when I reached his rooms.'

'Did you meet any one going up or coming down?' asked James.

'A man and a woman passed me on the stairs.'

'A man and a woman,' repeated Jack, almost in a whisper. His attitude was tense. His eyes burned with excitement.

'Was it light enough to tell who they were?' James asked. His cold eyes did not lift from hers until she answered.

'No. It was entirely dark. The woman was on the other side of the man. I wouldn't have been sure she was a woman except for the rustle of her skirts and the perfume.'

'Sure it wasn't the perfume you use yourself that you smelled?'

'I don't use any.'

'You stick to it that you met a man and a woman, but couldn't possibly recognize either of them,' James Cunningham said, still looking straight at her.

She hesitated an instant. Somehow she did not quite like the way he put this. 'Yes,' she said steadily.

'You didn't take the elevator up, then?'

'No. I'm not used to automatic elevators. I rang when I got to the door. Nobody answered, but the door was wide open. I rang again, then went in and switched on the light. There didn't seem to be anybody in. I didn't feel right about it. I wanted to go. But I wouldn't because I thought maybe he—your uncle—was trying to dodge me. I looked into the bedroom. He wasn't there. So after a little I went to a door into another room that was shut and knocked on it. I don't know why I opened it when no answer came. Something seemed to move my hand to the knob. I switched the light on there.'

'Yes?' James asked, gently.

The girl gulped. She made a weak, small gesture with her hand, as though to push from her mind the horrible sight her eyes had looked upon. 'He was dead, in the chair, tied to it. I think I screamed. I'm not sure. But I switched off the light and shut the door. My knees were weak, and I felt awf'lly queer in the head. I was crazy to get away from the place, but I couldn't seem to have the power to move. I leaned against the door, weak and limp as a small puppy. Then I heard some one comin' up the stairs, and I knew I mustn't be caught there. I switched off the lights just as some one came to the landing outside.'

'Who was it? Did he come in?' asked Jack.

'He rang and knocked two or three times. Then he came in. I was standing by the table with my hand on some kind of heavy metal paperweight. His hand was groping for the light switch. I could tell that. He must have heard me, for he called out, "Who's there?". In the darkness there I was horribly frightened. He might be the murderer come back. If not, of course he'd think I had done it. So I tried to slip by him. He jumped at me and caught me by the hand. I pulled away from him and hit hard at his face. The paperweight was still in my hand and he went down just as though a hammer had hit him. I ran out of the room, downstairs, and out into the street.'

'Without meeting anybody?'

'You don't know who it was you struck?'

'Unless it was Kirby.'

'Jove! That explains the bruise on his chin,' Jack cried out. 'Why didn't he tell us that?'

The color flushed the young woman's cheeks. 'We're friends, he and I. If he guessed I was the one that struck him he wouldn't tell.'

'How would he guess it?' asked James.

'He knew I meant to see your uncle—meant to make him do justice to Esther. I suppose I'd made wild threats. Besides, I left my glove there—on the table, I think. I'd taken it off with some notion of writing a note telling your uncle I had been there and that he had to see me next day.'

'The police didn't find a woman's glove in the room, did they?' James asked his brother.

'Didn't hear of it if they did,' Jack replied.

'That's it, you see,' explained Rose. 'Kirby would know my glove. It was a small riding-gauntlet with a rose embroidered on it. He probably took it with him when he left. He kept still about the whole thing because I was the woman and he was afraid of gettin' me into trouble.'

'Sounds reasonable,' agreed James.

'That's how it was. Kirby's a good friend. He'd never tell on me if they hanged him for it.'

'They won't do that, Miss McLean,' the older brother assured her. 'We're going to find who did this thing. Kirby and I have shaken hands on that. But about your story. I don't quite see how we're going to use it. We must protect your sister, too, as well as my cousin. If we go to the police with your evidence and ask them to release Kirby, they'll want to arrest you.'

'I know,' she nodded wisely, 'and of course they'd find out about Esther then and the papers would get it and scatter the story everywhere.'

'Exactly. We must protect her first. Kirby wouldn't want anything done that would hurt her. Suppose we put it up to him and see what he wants to do.'

'But we can't have him kept in jail,' she protested.

'I'll get him out on bond: if not today, tomorrow.'

'Well,' she agreed reluctantly. 'If that's the best we can do.'

Rose would have liked to have paid back Kirby's generosity in kind. If her sister had not been a factor of the equation she would have gone straight to the police with her story and suffered arrest gladly to help her friend. But the circumstances did not permit a heroic gesture. She had to take and not give.

CHAPTER SIXTEEN

THE LADY WITH THE VIOLET PERFUME

'I won't have it,' Kirby said flatly. 'If Miss McLean tells her story to the district attorney he'll probably arrest her. It'll come out about her sister an' the papers will run scare-heads. No need of it a-tall. Won't hurt me to stay here a few days if I have to.'

Jack, dapper and trim, leaned on his cane and watched his cousin. He felt a reluctant admiration for this virile cousin so picturesquely competent, so clean-cut and four-square of mind. Was he in love with the Wild Rose from Wyoming, whose spirit also was like a breath from the sweet hill pines? Or was his decision only the expression of a native chivalry that went out to all his friends and perhaps to all women?

'They'd certainly arrest her,' Jack commented. 'From a lawyer's point of view there's every reason why they should. Motive for the crime, sufficient; intention to force the victim to make reparation or punish him, declared openly; opportunity to commit it, confessed; presence on scene and eagerness to escape being seen there, admitted. The case against her is stronger than the one against you.' He offered this last with a smile decorously but not wholly concealed.

'Yet she couldn't possibly have done it!' the cattleman replied.

'Couldn't she? I wonder.' The Beau Brummel stroked his bit of mustache, with the hint of insolence his manner often suggested.

'Not possible,' said Lane forcefully. 'Uncle James was a big, two-fisted fighter. No slip of a girl could have overpowered him an' tied him. It's not within reason.' He spoke urgently, though still in the low murmur both the cousins were using in order not to be overheard.

Jack put a neat, highly polished boot on the desk of the sergeant of police. 'Ever hear of a lady called Delilah?' he asked lightly.

'What about her?' In Kirby's quiet eye there was a warning.

The man-about-town shrugged his well-tailored shoulders. 'They have a way, the ladies. Guile, my son, is more potent than force.'

'Meaning?'

'Delilah chloroformed Samson's suspicions before she sheared his locks.'

Kirby repressed an anger that he knew was worse than futile. 'If you knew Miss McLean you couldn't misjudge her so. She thinks an' acts as straight as a man.'

'I don't say she did it, old top. I'm merely pointing out that it's possible she did. Point of fact your friend made a hit with me. I'd say she's a game little thoroughbred.'

'You an' James will regard what she told you as confidential, of course.'

'Of course. We're of your mind, too, though I put her proposition to you. Can't see anything to be gained by airing her story unless it's absolutely necessary on your account. By the way, James wants me to tell you that he thinks you won't have to spend another night at this delightful hotel the city keeps for its guests. Bond has been practically agreed on.'

'Fine. Your brother's a brick. We're goin' to run down this business, he an' I, an' drag the truth to light.'

A glitter of sardonic mockery shone out of the dark eyes of Cunningham. 'You'll work together fine and Sherlock-Holmes this thing till it's as clear as mud,' he predicted.

By the middle of the afternoon Kirby was free. After he had talked over with James a plan of campaign, he called Rose up on the telephone and told her he would be right out to Cherokee Street.

She came to meet him in the stuffy parlor of the boarding-house with hand outstretched.

'Oh, Kirby, I'm so glad to see you and so sorry I was such a horrid little beast last time we met. I'm ashamed of myself. My temper explodes so—and after you came to Denver to help me and gave up so much for me. You'll forgive me, won't you?'

96

'You know it, Rose,' he said, smiling.

'Yes, I do know it,' she cried quickly. 'That makes it worse for me to impose on you. Now you're in trouble because of me. I should think you'd pretty near hate me.'

'We're in trouble together,' he corrected. 'I thought that was supposed to bring friends closer an' not to drive them apart.'

She flashed a quick look at him and changed the subject of conversation. Just now she could not afford to be emotional. 'Are you going back to Twin Buttes?'

'No. I'm goin' to find out who killed James Cunningham an' bring the man to justice. That's the only way to clear us both before the world.'

'Yes!' she cried eagerly. 'Let me help you. Let's be partners in it, Kirby.'

He already had one partner, but he threw him overboard instantly. James Cunningham was retired to the position of an adviser.

'Bully! We'll start this very minute. Tell me all you know about what happened the evenin' of the murder.'

She told again the story she had confessed to his cousins. He asked questions, pushed home inquiries. When she mentioned the woman who had passed her on the stairs he showed a keen interest.

'You say you knew it was a woman with the man by the perfume. What kind of perfume was it?'

'Violet.'

'Did you notice a violet perfume any other place that night?'

'In your uncle's living-room.'

'Sure?'

'Yes.'

'So did I.'

'The woman I met on the stairs, then, had just come from your uncle's rooms.'

'Looks like it,' he nodded in agreement.

'Then we've got to find her. She must have been in his apartment when he was killed.' The thought came to Rose as a revelation.

'Or right after.'

'All we've got to do is to find her and the man with her, and we've solved the mystery,' the girl cried eagerly.

'That's not quite all,' said Kirby, smiling at the way her mind leaped gaps. 'We've got to induce them to talk, an' it's not certain they know any more than we do.'

'Her skirts rustled like silk and the perfume wasn't cheap. I couldn't really see her, but I knew she was well dressed,' Rose told him.

'Well, that's somethin',' he said with the whimsical quirk to his mouth she knew of old. 'We'll advertise for a well-dressed lady who uses violet perfume. Supposed to be connected with the murder at the Paradox Apartments. Generous reward an' many questions asked.'

His badinage was of the surface only. The subconscious mind of the rough rider was preoccupied with a sense of a vague groping. The thought of violet perfume associated itself with something else in addition to the darkness of his uncle's living-room, but he did not find himself able to localize the nebulous memory. Where was it his nostrils had whiffed the scent more recently?

'Don't you think we ought to see all the tenants at the Paradox and talk with them? Some of them may have seen people going in or out. Or they may have heard voices,' she said.

'That's a good idea. We'll make a canvass of the house.'

Her eyes sparkled. 'We'll find who did it! When two people look for the truth intelligently they're bound to find it. Don't you think so?'

'I think we'll sure round up the wolf that did this killin',' he drawled. 'Anyhow, we'll sleep on his trail for a moon or two.'

They shook hands on it.

CHAPTER SEVENTEEN

IN DRY VALLEY

If Kirby had been a properly authenticated detective of fiction he would have gone to his uncle's apartment, locked the door, measured

99

the rooms with a tape-line, found imprints of fingers on a door panel, and carefully gathered into an envelope the ashes from the cigar his uncle had been smoking. The data obtained would have proved conclusively that Cunningham had come to his death at the hands of a Brahmin of high caste on account of priceless gems stolen from a temple in India. An analysis of the cigar ashes would have shown that a subtle poison, unknown to the Western world, had caused the victim's heart to stop beating exactly two minutes and twelve seconds after taking the first puff at the cigar.

Thus the fictional ethics of the situation would have been correctly met.

But Kirby was only a plain, outdoors Westerner. He did not know the conventional method of procedure. It did not even occur to him at first that Apartment 12 might still have secrets to tell him after the police and the reporters had pawed over it for several days. But his steps turned back several times to the Paradox as the center from which all clues must emanate. He found himself wandering around in that vicinity trying to pick up some of the pieces of the Chinese puzzle that made up the mystery of his uncle's death.

It was on one of these occasions that he and Rose met his cousin James coming out of the apartment house. Cunningham was a man of admirable self-control, but he looked shaken this morning. His hand trembled as it met that of his cousin. In his eyes was the look of a man who has suffered a shock.

'I've been sitting alone for an hour in the room where Uncle James met his death—been arranging his papers,' he explained. 'It began to get my nerve. I couldn't stand it any longer. The horrible thing kept jumping to my mind.' He drew his right hand heavily across his eyes, as though to shut out and brush away the sight his imagination conjured.

His left arm hung limp. Kirby's quick eyes noticed it. 'You've hurt yourself,' Lane said.

'Yes,' admitted James. 'My heel caught on the top step as I started to walk down. I've wrenched my arm badly. Maybe I've broken it.'

'Oh, I hope not,' Rose said quickly, a warm sympathy in her vibrant young voice. 'A broken arm's no fun. I find it an awful nuisance.'

The janitor of the Paradox came out and joined them. He was a little Japanese well on toward middle life, a small-featured man with small, neat feet.

'You feelum all right yes now?' he asked, directing his slant, oval eyes toward Cunningham.

'Yes, I've got over the nausea, thanks, Shibo.' James turned to the others. 'Shibo was at the foot of the stairs when I caught my heel. He gathered up the pieces. I guess I was all in, wasn't I, Shibo?'

The Japanese nodded agreement. 'You

heap sick for minute.'

'I've been worrying a good deal about this business of Uncle James, I suppose. Anyhow, I've had two or three dizzy spells lately. Nothing serious, though.'

'I don't wonder. You sit at a desk too much, James. What you need is exercise. If you'd get in the saddle a couple o' hours a day an' do some stiff ridin' you'd quit havin' dizzy spells. Sorry you're hurt, old man. I'll trail along with you to a doctor's.'

'Not necessary. I'll be all right. It's only a few blocks to his office. Fact is, I'm feeling quite myself again.'

'Well, if you're sure. Prob'ly you've only sprained your arm. By the way, I'd kinda like to go over Uncle's apartment again. Mind if I do? I don't reckon the police missed anything, but you can never tell.'

James hesitated. 'I promised the Chief of Police not to let anybody else in. Tell you what I'll do. I'll see him about it and get a permit for you. Say, Kirby, I've been thinking one of us ought to go up to Dry Valley and check things up there. We might find out who wrote that note to Uncle. Maybe some one has been making threats in public. We could see who was in town from there last week. Could you go? Today? Train leaves in half an hour.'

Kirby could and would. He left Rose to talk with the tenants of the Paradox Apartments, entrained for Dry Valley at once, and by noon was winding over the hilltops far up in the Rockies.

He left the train at Summit, a small town which was the center of activities for Dry Valley. Here the farmers bought their supplies and here they marketed their butter and eggs. In the fall they drove in their cattle and loaded them for Denver at the chutes in the railroad yard.

There had been times in the past when Summit ebbed and flowed with a rip-roaring tide of turbulent life. This had been after the round-ups in the golden yesterday when every other store building had been occupied by a saloon and the rattle of chips lasted far into the small hours of night. Now Colorado was dry and the roulette wheel had gone to join memories of the past. Summit was quiet as a Sunday afternoon on a farm. Its busiest inhabitant was a dog which lay in the sun and lazily poked over its own anatomy for fleas.

Kirby registered at the office of the frame building which carried on its false front the word HOTEL. This done, he wandered down to the shack which bore the inscription, 'Dry Valley Enterprise.' The owner of the paper, who was also editor, reporter, pressman, business manager, and circulator, chanced to be in printing some dodgers announcing a dance at Odd Fellows' Hall. He desisted from his labors to chat with the stranger.

The editor was a fat, talkative little man.

Kirby found it no trouble at all to set him going on the subject of James Cunningham, Senior. In fact, during his stay in the valley the Wyoming man could always use that name as an 'Open Sesame.' It unlocked all tongues. Cunningham and his mysterious death were absorbing topics. The man was hated by scores who had been brought close to ruin by his chicanery. Dry Valley rejoiced openly in the retribution that had fallen upon him.

'Who killed him?' the editor asked rhetorically. 'Well, sir, I'll be dawged if I know. But if I was guessin' I'd say it was this fellow Hull, the slicker that helped him put through the Dry Valley steal. 'Course it might 'a' been the Jap, or it might 'a' been the nephew from Wyoming, but I'll say it was Hull. We know that cuss Hull up here. He's one bad package, that fat man is, believe me. Cunningham held out on him, an' he laid for the old crook an' got him. Don't that look reasonable to you? It sure does to me. Put a rope round Hull's neck an' you'll hang the man that killed old J. C.'

Lane put in an hour making himself *persona grata*, then read the latest issue of the *Enterprise* while the editor pulled off the rest of the dodgers. In the local news column he found several items that interested him. These were:

Jim Harkins is down in Denver on business and won't be home till Monday.

104

Have a good time, Jim.

T. J. Lupton is enjoying a few days vacation in the Queen City. He expects to buy some fancy stock at the yards for breeding purposes. Dry Valley is right in the van of progress.

Art Jelks and Brad Mosely returned from Denver today after a three day's visit in the capital. A good time was had by both. You want to watch them, girls. The boys are both live ones.

Oscar Olson spent a few days in Denver this week. Oscar owns a place three miles out of town on the Spring Creek road.

Casually Kirby gathered information. He learned that Jim Harkins was the town constable and not interested in land; that Lupton was a very prosperous cattleman whose ranch was nowhere near the district promoted by Cunningham; and that Jelks and Mosely were young fellows more or less connected with the garage. The editor knew Olson only slightly.

'He's a Swede—big, fair fellow—got caught in that irrigation fake of Hull and Cunningham. Don't know what he was doin' in Denver.' the newspaperman said.

Lane decided that he would see Olson and have a talk with him. Incidentally, he meant to see all the Dry Valley men who had been in Denver at the time Cunningham was killed. But the others he saw only to eliminate them from suspicion. One glance at each of them was enough to give them a clean bill so far as the mystery went. They knew nothing whatever about it.

Lane rode out to Olson's place and found him burning brush. The cattleman explained that he was from Wyoming and wanted to sell some registered Herefords.

Olson looked over his dry, parched crops with sardonic bitterness. 'Do I look like I could buy registered stock?' he asked sourly.

Kirby made a remark that set the ranchman off. He said that the crops looked as though they needed water. Inside of five minutes he had heard the story of the Dry Valley irrigation swindle. Olson was not a foreigner. He had been born in Minnesota and attended the public schools. He spoke English idiomatically and without an accent. The man was a tall, gaunt, broad-shouldered Scandinavian of more than average intelligence.

The death of Cunningham had not apparently assuaged his intense hatred of the man or the bitterness which welled out of him toward Hull.

'Cunningham got his! Suits me fine! Now all I ask is that they hang Hull for it!' he cried vindictively.

'Seems to be some doubt whether Hull did it,' suggested Kirby, to draw him on.

'That so? Mebbe there's evidence you don't know about.' The words had come out in the heat of impulse, shot at Kirby tensely and breathlessly. Olson looked at the man on the horse and Lane could see caution grow on him. A film of suspicion spread over the pupils beneath the heavy, ragged eyebrows. 'I ain't sayin' so. All I'm dead sure of is that Hull did it.'

Kirby fired a shot point-blank at him. 'Nobody can be dead sure of that unless he saw him do it.'

'Mebbe some one saw him do it. Folks don't tell all they know.' Olson looked across the desert beyond the palpitating heat waves to the mountains in the distance.

'No. That's tough sometimes on innocent people, too.'

'Meanin' this nephew of old Cunningham. He'll get out all right.'

'Will he? There's a girl under suspicion, too. She had no more to do with it than I had, but she's likely to get into mighty serious trouble just the same.'

'I ain't read anything in the papers about any girl,' Olson answered sullenly.

'No, it hasn't got to the papers yet. But it will. It's up to every man who knows anything about this to come clean.'

'Is it?' The farmer looked bleakly at his visitor. 'Seems to me you take a lot of interest in this. Who are you, anyhow?'

'My name is Kirby Lane.'

'Nephew of the old man?'

'Yes.'

Olson gave a snort of dry, splenetic laughter. 'And you're out here sellin' registered Herefords.'

'I have some for sale. But that's not why I came to see you.'

'Why did you come, then?' asked the Scandinavian, his blue eyes hard and defiant.

'I wanted to have a look at the man who wrote the note to James Cunningham threatenin' to dry-gulch him if he ever came to Dry Valley again.'

It was a center shot. Kirby was sure of it. He read it in the man's face before anger began to gather in it.

'I'm the man who wrote that letter, am I?' The lips of Olson were drawn back in a vicious snarl.

'You're the man.'

'You can prove that, o' course.'

'Yes.'

'How?'

'By your handwritin'. I've seen three specimens of it today.'

'Where?'

'One at the court-house, one at the bank that holds your note, an' the third at the office

108

of the *Enterprise*. You wrote an article urgin' the Dry Valley people to fight Cunningham. That article, in your own handwritin', is in my pocket right now.'

'I didn't tell them to gun him, did I?'

'That's not the point. What I'm gettin' at is that the same man wrote the article that wrote the letter to Cunningham.'

'Prove it! Prove it!'

'The paper used in both cases was torn from the same tablet. The writin' is the same.'

'You've got a nerve to come out here an' tell me I'm the man that killed Cunningham,' Olson flung out, his face flushing darkly.

'I'm not sayin' that.'

'What are you sayin', then? Shoot it at me straight.'

'If I thought you had killed Cunningham I wouldn't be here now. What I thought when I came was that you might know somethin' about it. I didn't come out here to trap you. My idea is that Hull did it. But I've made up my mind you're hidin' somethin'. I'm sure of it. You as good as told me so. What is it?' Kirby, resting easy in the saddle with his weight on one stirrup, looked straight into the rancher's eyes as he asked the question.

'I'd be likely to tell you if I was, wouldn't I?' jeered Olson.

'Why not? Better tell me than wait for the police to third-degree you. If you're not in this killin' why not tell what you know? I've told my story.'

'After they spotted you in the court-room,' the farmer retorted. 'An' how do I know you told all you know? Mebbe you're keepin' secrets, too.'

Kirby took this without batting an eye. 'An innocent man hasn't anything to fear,' he said.

'Hasn't he?' Olson picked up a stone and flung it at a pile of rocks he had gathered fifty yards away. He was left-handed. 'How do you know he hasn't? Say, just for argument, I do know somethin'. Say I practically saw Cunningham killed an' hadn't a thing to do with it. Could I get away with a story like that? You know darned well I couldn't. Wouldn't the lawyers want to know howcome I to be so handy to the place where the killin' was, right at the very time it took place, me who is supposed to have threatened to bump him off myself? Sure they would. I'd be tyin' a noose round my own neck.'

'Do you know who killed my uncle?' demanded Lane point-blank. 'Did you see it done?'

Olson's eyes narrowed. A crafty light shone through the slitted lids. 'Hold yore hawsses. I ain't said I knew a thing. Not a thing. I was stringin' you.'

Kirby knew he had overshot the mark. He had been too eager and had alarmed the man. He was annoyed at himself.

It would take time and patience and finesse

110

to recover lost ground. Shrewdly he guessed at the rancher's state of mind. The man wanted to tell something, was divided in mind whether to come forward as a witness or keep silent. His evidence, it was clear enough, would implicate Hull; but, perhaps indirectly, it would involve himself, too.

'Well, whatever it is you know, I hope you'll tell it,' the cattleman said. 'But that's up to you, not me. If Hull is the murderer, I want the crime fastened on him. I don't want him to get off scot free. An' that's about what's goin' to happen. The fellow's guilty, I believe, but we can't prove it.'

'Can't we? I ain't sure o' that.' Again, through the narrowed lids, wary guile glittered. 'Mebbe we can when the right time comes.'

'I doubt it.' Lane spoke casually and carelessly. 'Any testimony against him loses force if it's held out too long. The question comes up, why didn't the witness come right forward at once. No, I reckon Hull will get away with it—if he really did it.'

'Don't you think it,' Olson snapped out. 'They've pretty nearly got enough now to convict him.'

The rough rider laughed cynically. 'Convict him! They haven't enough against him even to make an arrest. They've got a dozen times as much against me an' they turned me loose. He's quite safe if he keeps his mouth shut—an' he will.'

Olson flung a greasewood shrub on a pile of brush. His mind, Kirby could see, was busy with the problem before it. The man's caution and his vindictive desire for vengeance were at war. He knew something, evidence that would tend to incriminate Hull, and he was afraid to bring it to the light of day. He worked automatically, and the man on horseback watched him. On that sullen face Kirby could read fury, hatred, circumspection, suspicion, the lust for revenge.

The man's anger barked at Lane. 'Well, what you waitin' for?' he asked harshly.

'Nothin'. I'm goin' now.' He wrote his Denver address on a card. 'If you find there is any evidence against Hull an' want to talk it over, perhaps you'd rather come to me than the police. I'm like you. If Hull did it I want him found guilty. So long.'

He handed Olson his card. The man tossed it away. Kirby turned his horse toward town. Five minutes later he looked back. The settler had walked across to the place where he had thrown the card and was apparently picking it up.

The man from Wyoming smiled. He had a very strong hunch that Olson would call on him within a week or ten days. Of course he was disappointed, but he knew the game had to be played with patience. At least he had learned something. The man had in his possession evidence vitally important. Kirby

112

meant to get that evidence from him somehow by hook or crook.

What was it the man knew? Was it possible he could have killed Cunningham himself and be trying to throw the blame of it on Hull? Was that why he was afraid to come out in the open with what testimony he had? Kirby could not forget the bitter hatred of Cunningham the farmer cherished. That hatred extended to Hull. What a sweet revenge to kill one enemy and let the other one hang for the crime!

A detail jumped to his mind. Olson had picked up a stone and thrown it to the rock piles with his left hand.

CHAPTER EIGHTEEN

'BURNIN' A HOLE IN MY POCKET'

Cole Sanborn passed through the Welcome Arch at the station carrying an imitation-leather suitcase. He did not take a car, but walked up Seventeenth Avenue as far as the Markham Hotel. Here he registered, left his luggage, and made some inquiries over the telephone.

Thirty minutes later he was shaking hands with Kirby Lane.

'You dawg-goned old hellamile, what you mean comin' down here an' gettin' throwed in the calaboose?' he demanded, thumping his friend on the shoulder with a heavy brown fist.

'I'm sure enough glad to see you, Mr. Champeen-of-the-World,' Kirby answered, falling into the easy venacular of the outdoor country. 'Come to the big town to spend that thousand dollars you won the other day?'

'Y'betcha; it's burnin' a hole in my pocket. Say, you blamed ol' horntoad, howcome you not to stay for the finals? Folks was plumb disappointed we didn't ride it off.'

'Tell you about that later. How long you figurin' to stay in Denver, Cole?'

'I dunno. A week, mebbe. Fellow at the Empress wants me to go on that circuit an' do stunts, but I don't reckon I will. Claims he's got a trained bronc I can show on.'

'Me, I'm gonna be busy as a dog with fleas,' said Kirby. 'I got to find out who killed my uncle. Suspicion rests on me, on a man named Hull, on the Jap servant, an' on Wild Rose.'

'On Wild Rose!' exclaimed Cole, in surprise. 'Have they gone crazy?'

'The police haven't got to her yet, old-timer. But their suspicions will be headed that way right soon if I don't get busy. She thinks her evidence will clear me. It won't. It'll add a motive for me to have killed him. The detectives will figure out we did it together, Rose an' me'

'Hell's bells! Ain't they got no sense a-tall?'

Kirby looked at his watch. 'I'm headed right

114

now for the apartment where my uncle was killed. Gonna look the ground over. Wanta come along?'

'Surest thing you know. I'm in this to a fare-you-well. Go ahead. I'll take yore dust.'

The lithe, long-bodied man from Basin, Wyoming, clumped along in his high-heeled boots beside his friend. Both of them were splendid examples of physical manhood. The sun tan was on their faces, the ripple of health in their blood. But there was this difference between them, that while it was written on every inch of Sanborn that he lived astride a cowpony, Kirby might have been an irrigation engineer or a mining man from the hills. He had neither the bow legs nor the ungraceful roll of the man who rides most of his waking hours. His clothes were well made and he knew how to carry them.

As they walked across to Fourteenth Street, Kirby told as much of the story as he could without betraying Esther McLean's part in it. He trusted Sanborn implicitly, but the girl's secret was not his to tell.

From James Cunningham Kirby had got the key of his uncle's apartment. His cousin had given it to him a little reluctantly.

'The police don't want things moved about,' he had explained. 'They would probably call me down if they knew I'd let you in.'

'All I want to do is to look the ground over a bit. What the police don't know won't worry

115

'em any,' the cattleman had suggested.

'All right.' James had shrugged his shoulders and turned over the key. 'If you think you can find out anything I don't see any objection to your going in.'

Sanborn applied his shrewd common sense to the problem as he listened to Kirby.

'Looks to me like you're overlookin' a bet, son,' he said. 'What about this Jap fellow'? Why did he light out so *pronto* if he ain't in this thing?'

'He might 'a' gone because he's a foreigner an' guessed they'd throw it on him. They would, too, it they could.'

'Shucks! He had a better reason than that for cuttin' his stick. Sure had. He's in this somehow.'

'Well, the police are after him. They'll likely run him down one o' these days. Far as I'm concerned I've got to let his trail go for the present. There are possibilities right here on the ground that haven't been run down yet. For instance. Rose met a man an' a woman comin' down the stairs while she was goin' up. Who were they?'

'Might 'a' been any o' the tenants here.'

'Yes, but she smelt a violet perfume that both she an' I noticed in the apartment. My hunch is that the man an' the woman were comin' from my uncle's rooms.'

'Would she recognize them? Rose, I mean?' asked Sanborn.

'No; it was on the dark stairs.'

'Hmp! Queer they didn't come forward an' tell they had met a woman goin' up. That is, if they hadn't anything to do with the crime.'

'Yes. Of course there might be other reasons why they must keep quiet. Some love affair, for instance.'

'Sure. That might be, an' that would explain why they went down the dark stairs an' didn't take the elevator.'

'Just the same I'd like to find out who that man an' woman are.' Kirby said. He lifted his hand in a small gesture. 'This is the Paradox Apartments.'

A fat man rolled out of the building just as they reached the steps. He pulled up and stared down at Kirby. 'What—what—?' His question hung poised.

'What am I doin' out o' jail, Mr. Hull? I'm lookin' for the man that killed my uncle,' Kirby answered quietly, looking straight at him.

'But—'

'Why did you lie about the time when you saw me that night?'

Hull got excited at once. His eyes began to dodge. 'I ain't got a word to say to you—not a word—not a word!' He came puffing down the steps and went waddling on his way.

'What do you think of that prize package, Cole?' asked Lane, his eyes following the man.

'Guilty as hell,' said the bronco buster crisply.

'I'd say so too,' agreed Kirby. 'I don't know as we need to look much farther. My vote is for Mr. Cass Hull—with reservations.'

CHAPTER NINETEEN

A DISCOVERY

The men from Wyoming stepped into the elevator and Kirby pressed the button numbered 3. At the third floor they got out and turned to the right. With the Yale key his cousin had given him Kirby opened the door of Apartment 12.

He knew that there was not an inch of space in the rooms that the police and the newspaper reporters had not raked as with a fine-tooth comb for clues. The desk had been ransacked, the books and magazines shaken, the rugs taken up. There was no chance that he would discover anything new unless it might be by deduction.

Wild Rose had reported to him the result of her canvass of the tenants. One or two of them she had missed, but she had managed to see all the rest. Nothing of importance had developed from these talks. Some did not care to say anything. Others wanted to gossip a whole afternoon away, but knew no more than what the newspapers had told them. The single fact that stood out from her inquiries was that those who lived in the three apartments nearest to Number 12 had all been out of the house on the evening of the twenty-third. The man who rented the rooms next those of Cunningham had left for Chicago on the twenty-second and had not yet returned to Denver.

Cole took in the easy-chairs, the draperies, and the soft rugs with an appreciative eye. 'The old boy believed in solid comfort. You wouldn't think to look at this that he'd spent years on a bronc's back buckin' blizzards. Some luxury, I'll say! Looks like one o' them palaces of the vamp ladies the movies show.'

Kirby wasted no time in searching the apartment for evidence. What interested him was its entrances and its exits, its relation to adjoining rooms and buildings. He had reason to believe that, between nine o'clock and half-past ten on the night of the twenty-third, not less than eight persons in addition to Cunningham had been in the apartment. How had they all managed to get in and out without being seen by each other?

Lane talked aloud, partly to clear his own thought and partly to put the situation before his friend.

'O' course I don't *know* every one of the eight was here. I'm guessin' from facts I do know, makin' inferences, as you might say. To begin with, I was among those present. So was

Rose. We don't need to guess any about that.'

Cole, still almost incredulous at the mention of Rose as a suspect, opened his lips to speak and closed them again with no word uttered. He was one of those loyal souls who can trust without asking for explanations.

'The lady of the violet perfume an' her escort were here,' Kirby went on. 'At least she was—most prob'ly he was, too. It's a cinch the Hulls were in the rooms. They were scared stiff when I saw 'em a little later. They lied on the witness stand so as to clear themselves an' get me into trouble in their place. Olson backs up the evidence. He good as told me he'd seen Hull in my uncle's rooms. If he did he must 'a' been present himself. Then there's the Jap Horikawa. He'd beat it before the police went to his room to arrest him at daybreak the mornin' after the murder. How did he know my uncle had been killed? It's not likely any one told him between half-past ten an' half-past five the next mo'nin'. No, sir. He knew it because his eyes had told him so.'

'I'll say he did,' agreed Sanborn.

'Good enough. That makes eight of us that came an' went. We don't need to figure on Rose an' me. I came by the door an' went by the fire escape. She walked upstairs an' down too. The violet lady an' the man with her took the stairs down. We know that. But how about Hull an' Olson an' the Jap? Here's another point. Say it was 9:50 when Rose got here. My

120

uncle didn't reach his rooms before nine o'clock. He changed his shoes, put on a smokin'-jacket, an' lit a cigar. He had it half smoked before he was tied to the chair. That cuts down to less than three quarters of an hour the time in which he was chloroformed, tied up to the chair, an' shot, an' in which at least six people paid a visit here, one of the six stayin' long enough to go through his desk an' look over a whole lot o' papers. Some o' these people were sure enough treadin' close on each other's heels an' I reckon some were makin' quick getaways.'

'Looks reasonable,' Cole admitted.

'I'll bet I wasn't the only man in a hurry that night an' not the only one trapped here. The window of the den was open when I came. Don't you reckon some one else beat it by the fire escape?'

'Might've.'

They passed into the small room where James Cunningham had met his death. Broad daylight though it was, Kirby felt for an instant a tightening at his heart. In imagination he saw again the gargoyle grin on the dead face upturned to his. With an effort he pushed from him the grewsome memory.

The chair in which the murdered man had been found was gone. The district attorney had taken it for an exhibit at the trial of the man upon whom evidence should fasten. The littered papers had been sorted and most

121

of them removed, probably by James Cunningham, Junior. Otherwise the room remained the same.

The air was close. Kirby stepped to the window and threw it up. He looked out at the fire escape and at the wall of the rooming-house across the alley. Denver is still young. It offers the incongruities of the West. The Paradox Apartments had been remodeled and were modern and up to date. Adjoining it was the Wyndham Hotel, a survival of earlier days which could not long escape the march of progress.

Lane and his friend stepped out to the platform of the fire escape. Below them was the narrow alleyway, directly in front the iron frame of the Wyndham fire escape.

A discovery flashed across Kirby's brain and startled him. 'See here, Cole. If a man was standin' on that platform over there, an' if my uncle had been facin' him in a chair, sittin' in front of the window, he could 'a' rested his hand on that railin' to take aim an' made a dead-center shot.'

Cole thought it out. 'Yes, he could, if yore uncle had been facin' the window. But the chair wasn't turned that way, you told me.'

'Not when I saw it. But some one might 'a' moved the chair afterward.'

The champion of the world grinned. 'Seems to me, old man, you're travelin' a wide trail this trip. If some one tied up the old man an' chloroformed him an' left him here convenient, then moved him back to the wall after he'd been shot, then some one on the fire escape could 'a' done it. What's the need of all them *ifs?* Since some one in the room had to be in the thing, we can figure he fired the shot, too, whilst he was doin' the rest. Besides, yore uncle's face was powder-marked, showin' he was shot from right close.'

'Yes, that's so,' agreed Lane, surrendering his brilliant idea reluctantly. A moment, and his face brightened. 'Look, Cole! The corridor of that hotel runs back from the fire escape. If a fellow had been standin' there he could 'a' seen into the room if the blind wasn't down.'

'Sure enough,' agreed Sanborn. 'If the murderer had give him an invite to a grand-stand scat. But prob'ly he didn't.'

'No, but it was hot that night. A man roomin' at the Wyndham might come out to get a breath of air, say, an' if he had he might 'a' seen somethin'.'

'Some more of them *ifs,* son. What are you drivin' at anyhow?'

'Olson. Maybe it was from there he saw what he did.'

Sanborn's face lost its whimsical derision. His blue eyes narrowed in concentration of thought. 'That's good guessin', Kirby. It may be 'way off; then again it may be absolutely correct. Let's find out if Olson stayed at the Wyndham whilst he was in Denver. He'd be

123

more apt to hang out nearer the depot.'

'Unless he chose the Wyndham to be near my uncle.'

'Mebbeso. But if he did it wasn't because he meant the old man any good. Prove to me that the Swede stayed there an' I'll say he's as liable as Hull to be guilty. He could 'a' throwed a rope round that stone curlycue stickin' out up there above us, swung acrost to the fire escape here, an' walked right in on Cunningham'

Lane's quick glance swept the abutment above the distance between the buildings.

'You're shoutin', Cole. He could 'a' done just that. Or he might have been waitin' in the room for my uncle when he came home.'

'Yes. More likely that was the way of it—if we're on a hot trail a-tall.'

'We'll check up on that first. Chances are ten to one we're barkin' up the wrong tree. Right away we'll have a look at the Wyndham register.'

They did. The Wyndham was a rooming-house rather than a hotel, but the landlady kept a register for her guests. She brought it out into the hall from her room for the Wyoming men to look at.

There, under date of the twenty-first, they found the name they were looking for. Oscar Olson had put up at the Wyndham. He had stayed three nights, checking out on the twenty-fourth.

The friends walked into the street and back

toward the Paradox without a word. As they stepped into the elevator again, Lane looked at his friend and smiled.

'I've a notion Mr. Olson had a right interestin' trip to Denver,' he said quietly.

'I'll say he had,' answered Sanborn. 'An' that ain't but half of it either. He's mighty apt to have another interestin' one here one o' these days.'

CHAPTER TWENTY

THE BRASS BED

The rough riders gravitated back to the fire escape. Kirby had studied the relation of his uncle's apartment to the building opposite. He had not yet examined it with reference to the adjoining rooms.

'While we're cuttin' trail might as well be thorough,' he said to his friend. 'The miscreant that did this killin' might 'a' walked out the door or he might 'a' come through the window here. If he did that last, which fork of the road did he take? He could go down the ladder or swing across to the Wyndham an' slip into the corridor. Let's make sure we've got all the prospects figured out at that.'

Before he had finished the sentence, Lane saw another way of flight. The apartment in front of Cunningham's was out of reach of the fire escape. But the nearest window of the one to the rear was closer. Beneath it ran a stone ledge. An active man could swing himself from the railing of the platform to the coping and force an entrance into that apartment through the window.

Kirby glanced up and down the alley. A department store delivery auto was moving out of sight. Nobody was in the line of vision except an occasional pedestrian passing on the sidewalk at the entrances to the alley.

'I'm gonna take a whirl at it,' Lane said, nodding toward the window.

'How much do they give for burglary in this state?' asked Sanborn, his eyes dancing. 'I'd kinda hate to see you do twenty years.'

'They have to catch the rabbit before they cook it, old-timer. Here goes. Keep an eye peeled an' gimme the office if any cop shows up.'

'Mebbe the lady's at home. I don't allow to rescue you none if she massacres you,' the world's champion announced, grinning.

'Wrong guess, Cole. The boss of this hacienda is a man, an' he's in Chicago right now.'

'You're the dawg-gonedest go-getter I ever threw in with.' Sanborn admitted. 'All right. Go to it. If I gotta go to the calaboose I gotta go, that's all.'

Kirby stepped lightly to the railing, edged

far out with his weight on the ledge, and swung to the window-sill. The sash yielded to the pressure of his hands and moved up. A moment later he disappeared from Sanborn's view into the room.

It was the living-room of the apartment into which Lane had stepped. The walls were papered with blue and the rug was a figured yellow and blue. The furniture was of fumed oak, the chairs leather-padded.

The self-invited guest met his first surprise on the table. It was littered with two or three newspapers. The date of the uppermost caught his eye. It was a copy of the *Post* of the twenty-fifth. He looked at the other papers. One was the *Times* and another the *News,* dated respectively the twenty-fourth and the twenty-sixth. There was an *Express* of the twenty-eighth. Each contained long accounts of the developments in the Cunningham murder mystery.

How did these papers come here? The apartment was closed, its tenant in Chicago. The only other persons who had a key and the right of entry were Horikawa and the Paradox janitor, and the house servant had fled to parts unknown. Who, then, had brought these papers here? And why? Some one, Lane guessed, who was vitally interested in the murder. He based his presumption on one circumstance. The sections of the newspapers which made no reference to the Cunningham affair had been jammed into the waste-paper basket close to an adjoining desk.

The apartment held two rooms, a buffet kitchen and a bathroom. Kirby opened the door into the bedroom.

He stood paralyzed on the threshold. On the bed, fully dressed, his legs stretched in front of him and his feet crossed, was the missing man Horikawa. His torso was propped up against the brass posts of the bedstead. A handkerchief encircled each arm and bound it to the brass upright behind.

In the forehead, just above the slant, oval eyes, was a bullet hole. The man had probably been dead for a day, at least for a good many hours.

The cattleman had no doubt that it was Horikawa. His picture, a good snapshot taken by a former employer at a picnic where the Japanese had served the luncheon, had appeared in all the papers and on handbills sent out by James Cunningham, Junior. There was a scar, V-shaped and ragged, just above the left eye, that made identification easy.

Kirby stepped to the window of the living-room and called to his friend.

'Want me to help you gather the loot?' chaffed Cole.

'Serious business, old man,' Kirby told him, and the look on his face backed the words.

Sanborn swung across to the window and came through. 'What is it?' he asked quickly.

128

'I've found Horikawa.'

'Found him—where?'

The eyes of the men met and Cole guessed that grim tragedy was in the air. He followed Kirby to the bedroom.

'God!' he exclaimed.

His gaze was riveted to the bloodless, yellow face of the Oriental. Presently he broke the silence to speak again.

'The same crowd that killed Cunningham must 'a' done this, too.'

'Prob'ly.'

'Sure they must. Same way exactly.'

'Unless tyin' him up here was an afterthought—to make it look like the other,' suggested Lane. He added, after a moment, 'Or for revenge, because Horikawa killed my uncle. If he did, fate couldn't have sent a retribution more exactly just.'

'Sho, that's a heap unlikely. You'd have to figure there were *two* men that are Apache killers, both connected with this case, both with minds just alike, one of 'em a Jap an' the other prob'ly a white man. A hundred to one shot. I'd call it. No, sir. Chances are the same man bossed both jobs.'

'Yes,' agreed Kirby. 'The odds are all that way.'

He stepped closer and looked at the greenish-yellow flesh. 'May have been dead a couple o' days,' he continued.

'What was the sense in killin' him? What

for? How did he come into it?' Cole's boyish face wrinkled in perplexity. 'I don't make head or tail of this thing. Cunningham's enemies couldn't be his enemies, too, do you reckon?'

'More likely he knew too much an' had to be got out of the road.'

'Yes, but—' Sanborn stopped, frowning, while he worked out what he had to say. 'He wasn't killed right after yore uncle. Where was he while the police were huntin' for him everywhere? If he knew somethin' why didn't he come to bat with it? What was he waitin' for? An' if the folks that finally bumped him off knew he didn't aim to tell what he knew, whyfor did they figure they had to get rid of him?'

'I can't answer your questions right off the reel, Cole. Mehbe I could guess at one or two answers, but they likely wouldn't be right. F'r instance, I could guess that he was here in this room from the time my uncle was killed till he met his own death.'

'In this room?'

'In these apartments. Never left 'em, most likely. What's more, some one knew he was here an' kept him supplied with the daily papers.'

'Who?'

'If I could tell you that I could tell you who killed him,' answered Kirby with a grim, mirthless smile.

'How do you know all that?'

Lane told him of the mute testimony of the newspapers in the living-room. 'Some one brought those papers to him every day,' he added.

'And then killed him. Does that look reasonable to you?'

'We don't know the circumstances. Say, to make a long shot, that the Jap had been hired to kill my uncle by this other man, and say he was beginnin' to get ugly an' make threats. Or say Horikawa knew about the killin' of my uncle an' was hired by the other man to keep away. Then he learns from the papers that he's suspected, an' he gets anxious to go to the police with what he knows. Wouldn't there be reason enough then to kill him? The other man would have to do it to save himself.'

'I reckon.' Cole harked back to a proceding suggestion. 'The revenge theory won't hold water. If some friend of yore uncle knew the Jap had killed him he'd sick the law on him. He wouldn't pull off any private execution like this.'

Kirby accepted this. 'That's true. There's another possibility. We've been forgettin' the two thousand dollars my uncle drew from the bank the day he was killed. If Horikawa an' some one else are guilty of the murder an' the theft, they might have quarreled later over the money. Perhaps the accomplice saw a chance to get away with the whole of it by gettin' rid of Horikawa.'

131

'Mebbeso. By what you tell me yore uncle was a big, two-fisted scrapper. It was a two-man job to handle him. This li'l' Jap never in the world did it alone. What it gets back to is that he was prob'ly in on it an' later for some reason his pardner gunned him.'

'Well, we'd better telephone for the police an' let them do some of the worryin'.'

Kirby stepped into the living-room followed by his friend. He was about to reach for the receiver when an exclamation stopped him. Sanborn was standing before a small writing-desk, of which he had just let down the top. He had lifted idly a piece of blotting-paper and was gazing down at a sheet of paper with writing on it.

'Looky here. Kirby,' he called.

In three strides Lane was beside him. His eyes, too, fastened on the sheet and found there the pothooks we have learned to associate with Chinese and Japanese chirography.

'Shows he'd been makin' himself at home,' the champion rough rider said.

Lane picked up the paper. There were two or three sheets of the writing. 'Might be a letter to his folks—or it might be—' His sentence flickered out. He was thinking. 'I reckon I'll take this along with me an' have it translated, Cole.'

He put the sheets in his pocket after he had folded them. 'You never can tell. I might as well know what this Horikawa was thinkin' about first off as the police. There's just an off chance he might 'a' seen Rose that night an' tells about it here.'

A moment later he was telephoning to the City Hall for the police.

There was the sound of a key in the outer door. It opened, and the janitor of the Paradox stood in the doorway. 'What you do here?' asked the little Japanese quickly.

'We came in through the window,' explained Kirby. 'Thought mebbe the man that killed my uncle slipped in here.'

'I hear you talk. I come in. You no business here.'

'True enough, Shibo. But we're not burglars an' we're here. Lucky we are too. We've found somethin'.'

'Mr. Jennings he in Chicago. He no like you here.'

'I want to show you somethin', Shibo. Come.'

Kirby led the way into the bedroom. Shibo looked at his countryman without a muscle of his impassive face twitching. 'Some one killum plenty dead,' he said evenly.

'Quite plenty,' Kirby agreed, watching his imperturbable Oriental face.

The cattleman admitted to himself that what he did not know about Japanese habits of mind would fill a great many books.

133

CHAPTER TWENTY-ONE

JAMES LOSES HIS TEMPER

Cole grinned whimsically at his friend.

'Do we light out now or wait for the cops?' he asked.

'We wait. They'd probably find out, anyhow, that we'd been here.'

Five minutes later a patrol wagon clanged up to the Paradox. A sergeant of police and two plainclothes men took the elevator. The sergeant, heading the party, stopped in the doorway of the apartment and let a hard, hostile eye travel up and down Lane's six feet.

'Oh, it's you,' he said suspiciously.

Kirby smiled. 'That's right, officer. We've met before, haven't we?'

They had. The sergeant was the man who had arrested him at the coroner's inquest. It had annoyed him that the authorities had later released the prisoner on bond.

'Have you touched the body or moved anything since you came?' the sergeant demanded.

'No, sir, to both questions, except the telephone when I used it to reach headquarters.'

The officer made no answer. He and the detectives went into the bedroom, examined the dead valet's position and clothes, made a tour of the rooms. and came back to Lane.

'Who's your friend?' asked the sergeant superciliously.

'His name is Cole Sanborn.'

'The champion bronco buster?'

'Yes.'

The sergeant looked at Sanborn with increased respect. His eyes went back to Kirby sullenly.

'What you doing here?'

'We were in my uncle's apartment lookin' things over. We stepped out on the fire escape an' happened to notice this window here was open a little. It just came over me that mebbe we might discover some evidence here. So I got in by the window, saw the body of the Jap, an' called my friend.'

'Some one hire you to hunt up evidence?' the officer wanted to know with heavy sarcasm.

'I hired myself. My good name is involved. I'm goin' to see the murderer is brought to justice.'

'You are, eh?'

'Yes.'

'Well, I'll say you could find him if anybody could.'

'You're entitled to your opinion, sergeant, just as I am to mine, but before we're through with this case you'll have to admit you've been wrong.' Lane turned to his friend. 'We'll go

135

now, Cole, if you're ready.'

The sergeant glared at this cool customer who refused to be appalled at the position in which he stood. He had half a mind to arrest the man again on the spot, but he was not sure enough of his ground. Not very long since he had missed a promotion by being overzealous. He did not want to make the same mistake twice.

The Wyoming men walked across to Seventeenth Street and down it to the Equitable Building. James Cunningham was in his office.

He looked up as they entered, a cold smile on his lips.

'Ah, my energetic cousin,' he said, with his habitual touch of irony. 'What's in the wind now?'

Kirby told him. Instantly James became grave. His irony vanished. In his face was a flicker almost of consternation at this follow-up murder. He might have been asking himself how much more trouble was coming.

'We'll get the writing translated. You have it with you?' he said.

His eyes ran over the pages Lane handed him. 'I know a Jap we can get to read it for us, a reliable man, one who won't talk if we ask him not to.'

The broker's desk buzzer rang. He talked for a moment over the telephone, then hung up again.

'Sorry,' Cunningham said, 'I'm going to be busy for an hour or two. Going to lunch with Miss Phyllis Harriman. She was Uncle James's fiancée, perhaps you know. There are some affairs of the estate to be arranged. I wonder if you could come back later this afternoon. Say about four o'clock. We'll take up then the business of the translation. I'll get in touch with a Japanese in the meantime.'

'Suits me. Shall I leave the writing here?'

'Yes, if you will. Doesn't matter, of course, but since we have it I'll put it in the safe.'

'How's the arm?' Kirby asked, glancing at the sling his cousin wore.

'Only sprained. The doctor thinks I must have twisted it badly as I fell. I couldn't sleep a wink all night. The damned thing pained so.'

James looked as though he had not slept well. His eyes were shadowed and careworn.

They walked together as far as the outer office. A slender, dark young woman, beautifully gowned, was waiting there. James introduced her to his cousin and Sanborn as Miss Harriman. She was, Kirby knew at once. the original of the photograph he had seen in his uncle's rooms.

Miss Harriman was a vision of sheathed loveliness. The dark, long-lashed eyes looked out at Kirby with appealing wistfulness. When she moved, the soft lines of her body took on a sinuous grace. From her personality there seemed to emanate an enticing aura of sex mystery.

She gave Kirby her little gloved hand. 'I'm glad to meet you, Mr. Lane,' she said, smiling at him. 'I've heard all sorts of good things about you from James—and Jack.'

She did not offer her hand to Sanborn, perhaps because she was busy buttoning one of the long gloves. Instead, she gave him a flash of her eyes and a nod of the carefully coiffured head.

Kirby said the proper things, but he said them with a mind divided. For his nostrils were inhaling again the violet perfume, that associated itself with his first visit to his uncle's apartment. He did not start. His eyes did not betray him. His face could be wooden on occasion, and it told no stories now. But his mind was filled with racing thoughts. Had Phyllis Harriman been the woman Rose had met on the stairs? What had she been doing in Cunningham's room? Who was the man with her? What secret connected with his uncle's death lay hidden back of the limpid innocence of those dark, shadowed eyes? She was one of those women who are forever a tantalizing mystery to men. What was she like behind the inscrutable, charming mask of her face?

Lane carried this preoccupation with him throughout the afternoon. It was still in the hinterland of his thoughts when he returned to his cousin's office.

His entrance was upon a scene of agitated

storm. His cousin was in the outer office facing a clerk. In his eyes there was a cold fury of anger that surprised Kirby. He had known James always as self-restrained to the point of chilliness. Now his anger seemed to leap out and strike savagely.

'Gross incompetence and negligence, Hudson. You are discharged, sir. I'll not have you in my employ an hour longer. A man I have trusted and found wholly unworthy.'

'I'm sorry, Mr. Cunningham,' the clerk said humbly. 'I don't see how I lost the paper, if I did, sir. I was very careful when I took the deeds and leases out of the safe. It seems hardly possible—'

'But you lost it. Nobody else could have done it. I don't want excuses. You can go, sir.' Cunningham turned abruptly to his cousin. 'The sheets of paper with the Japanese writing have been lost. This man, by some piece of inexcusable carelessness, took them with a bundle of other documents to my lawyer's office. He must have taken them. They were lying with the others. Now they can't be found anywhere.'

'Have you 'phoned to your lawyer?' asked Kirby.

''Phoned and been in person. They are nowhere to be found. They ought to turn up somewhere. This clerk probably dropped them. I've sent an advertisement to the afternoon papers.'

Kirby was taken aback at this unexpected mischance, but there was no use wasting nerve energy in useless fretting. He regretted having left the papers with James, for he felt that in them might be the key to the mystery of the Cunningham case. But he had no doubt that his cousin was more distressed about the loss than he was. He comforted himself with the reflection that a thorough search would probably restore them, anyhow.

He asked Hudson a few questions and had the man show them exactly where he had picked up the papers he took to the lawyer. James listened, his anger still simmering.

Kirby took his cousin by the arm and led him into the inner office.

'Frankly, James, I think you were partly to blame,' he said. 'You must have laid the writing very close in the safe to the other papers. Hadn't you better give Hudson another chance before you fire him?' His disarming smile robbed both the criticism and the suggestion of any offense they might otherwise have had.

In the end he persuaded Cunningham to withdraw his discharge of the clerk.

'He doesn't deserve it.' James grumbled. 'He's maybe spoiled our chance of laying hands on the man who killed Uncle. I can't get over my disappointment.'

'Don't worry, old man.' Lane said quietly. 'We're goin' to rope an' hogtie that wolf even

140

if Horikawa can't point him out to us with his dead hand.'

Cunningham looked at him, and again the faint, ironic smile of admiration was in evidence. 'You're confident, Kirby.'

'Why wouldn't I be? With you an' Rose McLean an' Cole Sanborn an' I all followin' the fellow's trail, he can't double an' twist enough to make a getaway. We'll ride him down sure.'

'Maybe we will and maybe we won't,' the oil broker replied. 'I'd give odds that he goes scot free.'

'Then you'd lose.' Kirby answered, smiling easily.

CHAPTER TWENTY-TWO

'ARE YOU WITH ME OR AGAINST ME?'

Miss Phyllis Harriman had breakfasted earlier than usual. Her luxuriant, blue-black hair had been dressed and she was debating the important question as to what gown she would wear. The business of her life was to make an effective carnal appeal, and she had a very sure sense of how to accomplish this.

A maid entered with a card at which Miss Harriman glanced indolently. A smile twitched at the corners of her mouth, but it was not wholly one of amusement. In the dark eyes a hint of adventure sparked. Her pulses beat with a little glow of triumph. For this young woman was of the born coquettes. She could no more resist alluring an attractive man and playing with him to his subsequent mental discomfort than she could refrain from bridge drives and dinner dances. This Wild Man from Wyoming, so strong of stride, so quietly competent, whose sardonic glance had taken her in so directly and so keenly, was a foeman worthy of her weapons.

'Good gracious!' she murmured, 'does he usually call in the middle of the night, I wonder? And does he really expect me to see him now?'

The maid waited. She had long ago discovered that Miss Phyllis did not always regulate her actions by her words.

'Take him into the red room and tell him I'll be down in a minute,' Miss Harriman decided.

After which there was swift action in the lady's boudoir.

The red room was scarcely more than a cozy alcove set off the main reception-room, but it had a note of warmth, of friendly and seductive intimacy. Its walls whispered of tête-à-têtes, the cushions hinted at interesting secrets they were forever debarred from telling. In short, when Miss Harriman was present, it seemed, no less than the clothes she wore, an expression of her personality.

142

After a very few minutes Miss Phyllis sauntered into the room and gave her hand to the man who rose at her entrance. She was simply but expensively gowned. Her smile was warm for Kirby. It told him, with a touch of shy reluctance, that he was the one man in the world she would rather meet just now. He did not know that it would have carried the same message to any one of half a dozen men.

'I'm so glad you cane to see me.' she said, just as though she were in the habit of receiving young men at eleven in the morning. 'Of course I want to know you better. James thinks so much of you.'

'And Jack,' added Lane, smilingly.

'Oh, yes, Jack, too,' she said, and laughed outright when their eyes met.

'I'm sure Jack's very fond of me. He can't help showing it occasionally.'

'Jack's—impulsive,' she explained. 'But he's amenable to influence.'

'Of the right sort. I'm sure he would be.'

He found himself the object of a piquant, amused scrutiny under her long lashes. It came to him that this Paris-gowned, long-limbed young sylph was more than willing to let him become intrigued by her charms. But Kirby Lane had not called so early in the day to fall in love.

'I came to see you, Miss Harriman, about the case.' he said. 'My good name is involved. I must clear it. I want you to help me.'

143

He saw a pulse of excitement flutter in her throat. It seemed to him that her eyes grew darker, as though some shadow of dread had fallen over them. The provocative smile vanished.

'How can *I* help you?' she asked.

'If you would answer a few questions—'

'What questions?' All the softness had gone from her voice. It had become tense and sharp.

'Personal ones. About you and my uncle. You were engaged to him, were you not?'

'Yes.'

'There wasn't any quarrel between you recently, was there?'

A flash of apprehension filled her eyes. Then, resolutely, she banished fear and called to her aid hauteur.

'There was not, though I quite fail to see how this can concern you. Mr. Lane.'

'I don't want to distress you,' he said gently. 'Just now that question must seem to you a brutal one. Believe me, I don't want to hurt you.'

Her eyes softened, grew wistful and appealing. 'I'm sure you don't. You couldn't. It's all so—so dreadful to think about.' There was a little catch in her throat as the voice broke. 'Let's talk of something more cheerful. I want to forget it all.'

'I'm sure you do. We all want to do that. The surest way to get it out of our minds is to solve the mystery and find out who is guilty.

That's why I want you to tell me a few things to clear up my mind.'

'But I don't know anything about it—nothing at all. Why should you come to me?'

'When did you last see my uncle alive?'

'What a dreadful question! It was—let me think—in the afternoon—the day before—'

'And you parted from him on the best of terms?'

'Of course.'

He leaned toward her ever so little, his eyes level with hers and steadily fastened upon her. 'That's the last time you saw him—until you went to his rooms at the Paradox the night he was killed?'

She had lifted her hand to pat into place an escaping tendril of hair. The hand remained lifted. The dark eyes froze with horror. They stared at him, as though held by some dreadful fascination. From her cheeks the color ebbed. Kirby thought she was going to faint.

But she did not. A low moan of despair escaped from the ashen lips. The lifted arm fell heavily to her lap.

Then Kirby discovered that the two in the red room had become three. Jack Cunningham was standing in the doorway.

His glance flashed to Lane accusingly. 'What's up? What are you doing here?' he demanded abruptly.

The Wyoming man rose. 'I've been asking Miss Harriman a question.'

145

'A question. What business have you to ask her questions?' demanded Jack hotly.

His cousin tried a shot in the dark. 'I was asking her,' he said, his voice low and even, 'about that visit you and she paid to Uncle James's rooms the night he was killed.'

Kirby knew instantly he had scored a hit. The insolence, the jaunty confidence, were stricken from him as by a buffet in the face. For a moment body and mind alike were lax and stunned. Then courage flowed back into his veins. He came forward, blustering.

'What do you mean? What visit? Its a damned lie.'

'Is it? Then why is the question such a knockout to you and Miss Harriman? She almost fainted, and it certainly crumpled you up till you got second breath.'

Jack flushed angrily. 'Of course it shocked her for you to make such a charge against her. It would frighten any woman. By God, it's an outrage. You come here and try to brow-beat Miss Harriman when she's alone. You ask her impudent questions, as good as tell her she— she—'

Kirby's eyes were like a glittering rapier probing for the weakness of his opponent's defense. 'I say that she and you were in the rooms of Uncle James at 9:50 the evening he was killed. I say that you concealed the fact at the inquest. Why?' He shot his question at the other man with the velocity of a bullet.

146

Cunningham's lip twitched, his eye wavered. How much did his cousin know? How much was he merely guessing?

'Who told you we were there? How do you know it? I don't propose to answer every wild accusation nor to let Miss Harriman be insulted by you. Who are you, anyhow? A man accused of killing my uncle, the man who found his valet dead and is suspected of that crime, too, a fellow who would be lying behind the bars now if my brother hadn't put up the money to save the family from disgrace. If we tell all we know, the police will grab you again double-quick. Yet you have the nerve to come here and make insinuations against the lady who is mourning my uncle's death. I've a good mind to 'phone for the police right now.'

'Do,' suggested Kirby, smiling. 'Then we'll both tell what we know and perhaps things will clear up a bit.'

It was a bluff pure and simple. He couldn't tell what he knew any more than his cousin could. The part played by Rose and Esther McLean in the story barred him from the luxury of truth-telling. Moreover, he had no real evidence to back his suspicions. But Jack did not know how strong the restraining influence was.

'I didn't say I was going to 'phone. I said I'd a jolly good mind to,' Cunningham replied sulkily.

'I'd advise you not to start anything you

147

can't finish. Jack. I'll give you one more piece of advice, too. Come clean with what you know. I'm goin' to find out, anyhow. Make up your mind to that. I'm goin' through with this job till it's done.'

'You'll pull off your Sherlock-Holmes stuff in jail, then, for I'm going to ask James to get off your bond,' Jack retorted vindictively.

'As you please about that,' Lane said quietly.

'He'll choose between you or me. I'll be damned if I'll stand for his keeping a man out of jail to try and fasten on me a murder I didn't do.'

'I haven't said you did it. What I say is that you and Miss Harriman know somethin' an' are concealin' it. What is it? I'm not a fool. I don't think you killed Uncle any more than I did. But you an' Miss Harriman have a secret. Why don't you go to James an' make a clean breast of it? He'll tell you what to do.'

'The devil he will! I tell you we haven't any secret. We weren't in Uncle's rooms that night.'

'Can you prove an alibi for the whole evening—both of you?' the range rider asked curtly.

'None of your business. We're not in the prisoner's dock. It's you that is likely to be there,' Jack tossed out petulantly.

Phyllis Harriman had flung herself down to sob with her head in the pillows. But Kirby noticed that one small pink ear was in the open to take in the swift sentences passing between the men.

'I'm intendin' to make it my business,' Lane said, his voice ominously quiet.

'You're laying up trouble for yourself,' Jack warned blackly. 'If you want me for an enemy you're going at this the right way.'

'I'm not lookin' for enemies. What I want is the truth. You're concealin' it. We'll see if you can make it stick.'

'We're not concealing a thing.'

'Last call for you to show down your cards, Jack. Are you with me or against me?' asked Kirby.

'Against you, you meddling fool!' Cunningham burst out in a gust of fury. 'Don't you meddle with my affairs, unless you want trouble right off the bat. I'm not going to have a Paul Pry nosing around and hinting slanders about me and Miss Harriman. What do you think I am? I'll protect my good name and this lady's if I have to do it with a gun. Don't forget that, Mr. Lane.'

Kirby's steady gaze appraised him coolly. 'You're excited an' talkin' foolishness. I'm not attackin' anybody's good name. I'm lookin' for the man who killed Uncle James. I'm expectin' to find him. If anybody stands in the way, I'm liable to run against him.'

The man from Twin Buttes bowed toward the black hair and pink ear of his hostess. He turned on his heel and walked from the room.

CHAPTER TWENTY-THREE

COUSINS DISAGREE

It was essential to Kirby's plans that he should be at liberty. If he should be locked up in prison even for a few days the threads that he had begun to untangle from the snarl known as the Cunningham mystery would again be ensnared. He was not sure what action James would take at his brother's demand that he withdraw from the bond. But Lane had no desire to embarrass him by forcing the issue. He set about securing a new bond.

He was, ten minutes later, in the law offices of Irwin, Foster & Warren, attorneys who represented the cattle interests in Wyoming with which Kirby was identified. Foster, a stout, middle-aged man with only a few locks of gray hair left, heard what the rough rider had to say.

'I'll wire to Caldwell and to Norman as you suggest, Mr. Lane,' he said. 'If they give me instructions to stand back of you, I'll arrange a new bond as soon as possible.'

'Will it take long? I can't afford to be tied up behind the bars right now.'

'Not if I can get it accepted. I'll let you know at once.'

Kirby rose. He had finished his business.

'Just a moment, Mr. Lane.' Foster leaned back in his swivel-chair and looked out of the window. His eyes did not focus on any detail of the office building opposite. They had the far-away look which denotes a preoccupied mind. 'Ever been to Golden?' he asked at last abruptly, swinging back in his seat and looking at his client.

'No. Why?'

'Golden is the Gretna Green of Denver, you know. When young people elope they go to Golden. When a couple gets married and doesn't want it known they choose Golden. Very convenient spot.'

'I'm not figuring on gettin' married right now,' the cattleman said, smiling.

'Still you might find a visit to the place interesting and useful. I was there on business a couple of weeks ago.'

The eyes of the men fastened. Lane knew he was being given a hint that Foster did not want to put more directly.

'What are the interestin' points of the town?' asked the Twin Buttes man.

'Well, sir, there are several. Of course, there's the School of Mines, and the mountains right back of the town. Gold was discovered there somewhere about fifty-seven, I think. Used to be the capital of the territory before Denver found her feet.'

'I'm rather busy.'

'Wouldn't take you long to run over on the

151

interurban.' The lawyer began to gather toward him the papers upon which he had been working when the client was shown in. He added casually: 'I found it quite amusing to look over the marriage licenses of the last month or two. Found the names there of some of our prominent citizens. Well, I'll call you up as soon as I know about the bond.'

Lane was not entirely satisfied with what he had been told, but he knew that Foster had said all he meant to say. One thing stuck in his mind as the gist of the hint. The attorney was advising him to go to the court-house and check up the marriage licenses.

He walked across to the Equitable Building and dropped in on his cousin James. Cunningham rose to meet him a bit stiffly. The cattleman knew that Jack had already been in to see him or had got him on the wire.

Kirby brushed through any embarrassment there might be and told frankly why he had come.

'I've had a sort of row with Jack. Under the circumstances I don't feel that I ought to let you stay on my bond. It might create ill-feelin' between you an' him. So I'm arrangin' to have some Wyoming friends put up whatever's required. You'll understand I haven't any bad feeling against you, or against him for that matter. You've been bully all through this thing, an' I'm certainly in your debt.'

'What's the trouble between you about?'

asked James.

'I've found out that he an' Miss Harriman were in Uncle James's rooms the night he was killed. I want them to come through an' tell what they know.'

'How did you find that out?'

The eyes of the oil broker were hard as jade. They looked straight into those of his cousin.

'I can't tell you that exactly. Put two an' two together.'

'You mean you *guess* they were there. You don't *know* it.'

A warm, friendly smile lit the brown face of the rough rider. He wanted to remain on good terms with James if he could. 'I don't know it in a legal sense. Morally, I'm convinced of it.'

'Even though they deny it.'

'Practically they admitted rather than denied.'

'Do you think it was quite straight, Kirby, to go to Miss Harriman with such a trumped-up charge? I don't. I confess I'm surprised at you.' In voice and expression James showed his disappointment.

'It isn't a trumped-up charge. I wanted to know the truth from her.'

'Why didn't you go to Jack, then?'

'I didn't know at that time Jack was the man with her.'

'You don't know it now. You don't know she was there. In point of fact the idea is

153

ridiculous. You surely don't think for a moment that she had anything to do with Uncle James's death.'

'No; not in the sense that she helped bring it about. But she knows somethin' she's hidin'.'

'That's absurd. Your imagination is too active, Kirby.'

'Can't agree with you.' Lane met him eye to eye.

'Grant for the sake of argument that she was in Uncle's room that night. Your friend Miss Rose McLean was there, too—by her own confession. When she came to Jack and me with her story, we respected it. We did not insist on knowing why she was there, and it was of her own free will she told us. Yet you go to our friend and distress her by implications that must shock and wound her. Was that generous? Was it even fair?'

The cattleman stood convicted at the bar of his own judgment. His cousins had been magnanimous to Esther and Rose, more so than he had been to Miss Harriman. Yet, even while he confessed fault, he felt uneasily that there was a justification he could not quite lay hold of and put into words.

'I'm sorry you feel that way, James. Perhaps I was wrong. But you want to remember that I wasn't askin' about what she knew with any idea of makin' it public or tellin' the police. I meant to keep it under my own hat to help run down a cold-blooded murderer.'

154

'You can't want to run him down any more than we do—and in that 'we' I include Jack and Miss Harriman as well as myself,' the older man answered gravely. 'Rut I'm sure you're entirely wrong. Miss Harriman knows nothing about it. If she had she would have confided in us.'

'Perhaps she has confided in Jack.'

'Don't you think that obsession of yours is rather—well, unlikely, to put it mildly? Analyze it and you'll find you haven't a single substantial fact to base it on.'

This was true. Yet Kirby's opinion was not changed. He still believed that Jack and Miss Harriman had been in his uncle's rooms just before Wild Rose had been there.

He returned to the subject of the bond. It seemed to him best, he said, in view of Jack's feeling, to get other bondsmen. He hoped James would not interpret this to mean that he felt less friendly toward him.

His cousin bowed, rather formally. 'Just as you please. Would you like the matter arranged this afternoon?'

Lane looked at his watch. 'I haven't heard from my new bondsmen yet. Besides, I want to go to Golden. Would tomorrow morning suit you?'

'I dare say.' James stifled a yawn. 'Did you say you were going to Golden?'

'Yes. Some one gave me a tip. I don't know what there's in it, but I thought I'd have a look at the marriage-license registry.'

Cunningham flashed a startled glance at him that asked a peremptory question. 'Probably waste of time. I've been in the oil business too long to pay any attention to tips.'

'Expect you're right, but I'll trot out there, anyhow. Never can tell.'

'What do you expect to find among the marriage licenses?'

'Haven't the slightest idea. I'll tell you tomorrow what I do find.'

James made one dry, ironic comment. 'I rather think you have too much imagination for sleuthing. You let your wild fancies gallop away with you. If I were you I'd go back to bronco busting.'

Kirby laughed. 'Dare say you're right. I'll take your advice after we get the man we're after.'

CHAPTER TWENTY-FOUR

REVEREND NICODEMUS RANKIN FORGETS AND REMEMBERS

By appointment Kirby met Rose at Graham & Osborne's for luncheon. She was waiting in the tower room for him.

'Where's Esther?' he asked.

Rose mustered a faint smile. 'She's eating

lunch with a handsomer man.'

'You can't throw a stone up Sixteenth Street without hittin' one,' he answered gayly.

They followed the head waitress to a small table for two by a window. Rose walked with the buoyant rhythm of perfect health. Her friend noticed, as he had often done before, that she had the grace of movement which is a corollary to muscles under perfect response. Seated across the table from her, he marveled once more at the miracle of her soft skin and the peach bloom of her complexion. Many times she had known the sting of sleet and the splash of sun on her face. Yet incredibly her cheeks did not tan nor lose their firmness.

'You haven't told me who this handsomer man is,' Kirby suggested.

'Cole Sanborn.' She flushed a little, but looked straight at him. 'Have you told him—about Esther?'

'No. But from somethin' he said I think he guesses.'

Her eyes softened. 'He awf'ly good to Esther. I can see he likes her and she likes him. Why couldn't she have met him first? She's so lovable.' Tears brimmed to her eyes. 'That's been her ruin. She was ready to believe any man who said he cared for her. Even when she was a little bit of a trick when people liked her, she was grateful to them for it and kinda snuggled up to them. I never saw a more cuddly baby.'

157

'Have you found out anything more yet about the man?' he asked, his voice low and gentle.

'No. It's queer how stubborn she can be for all her softness. But she almost told me last night. I'll find out in a day or two now. Of course it was your uncle. The note I found was really an admission of guilt. Your cousins feel that some settlement ought to be made on Esther out of the estate. I've been trying to decide what would be fair. Will you think it over and let me know what seems right to you?'

The waitress came, took their order, and departed.

'I'm goin' out to Golden today on a queer wild-goose chase.' Kirby said. 'A man gave me a hint. He didn't want to tell me the information out an' out, whatever it is. I don't know why. What he said was for me to go to Golden an' look over the list of marriage licenses for the past month or two.'

Her eyes flashed an eager question at him. 'You don't suppose—it couldn't he that Esther was married to your uncle secretly and that she promised not to tell.'

'I hadn't thought of that. It might be.' His eyes narrowed in concentration. 'And if Jack an' Miss Harriman had just found it out, that would explain why they called on Uncle James the night he was killed. Do you want to go to Golden with me?'

She nodded, eagerly. 'Oh, I do, Kirby! I believe we'll find out something there. Shall we go by the interurban?'

'As soon as we're through lunch.'

They walked across along Arapahoe Street to the loop and took a Golden car. It carried them by the viaduct over the Platte River and through the North Side into the country. They rushed past truck farms and apple orchards into the rolling fields beyond, where the crops had been harvested and the land lay in the mellow bath of a summer sun. They swung round Table Mountain into the little town huddled at the foot of Lookout.

From the terminus of the line they walked up the steep hill to the court-house. An automobile, new and of an expensive make, was standing by the curb. Just as Kirby and Rose reached the machine a young man ran down the steps of the court-house and stepped into the car. The man was Jack Cunningham. He took the driver's seat. Beside him was a veiled young woman in a leather motoring-coat. In spite of the veil Lane recognized her as Phyllis Harriman.

Cunningham caught sight of his cousin and anger flushed his face. Without a word he reached for the starter, threw in the clutch, and gave the engine gas.

The rough rider watched the car move down the hill. 'I've made a mistake,' he told his companion. 'I told James I was comin' here today. He let Jack know, an' he's beat us to it.'

'What harm will that do?' asked Rose. 'The information will be there for us, too, won't it?'

'Mebbe it will. Mebbe it won't. We'll soon find out.'

Rose caught her friend's arm as they were passing through the hall. 'Kirby, do you suppose your cousins really know Esther was married to your uncle? Do you think they can be trying to keep it quiet so she can't claim the estate?'

He stopped in his stride. James had deprecated the idea of his coming to Golden and had ridiculed the possibility of his unearthing any information of value. Yet he must have called up Jack as soon as he had left the office. And Jack had hurried to the town within the hour. It might be that Rose had hit on the reason for the hostility he felt on the part of both cousins to his activities. There was something they did not want brought to the light of day. What more potent reason could there be for concealment than their desire to keep the fortune of the millionaire in their own hands?

'I shouldn't wonder if you haven't rung the bull's-eye, pardner,' he told her. 'We ought to know right soon now.'

The clerk in the recorder's office smiled when Kirby said he wanted to look through the license register. He swung the book round toward them.

'Help yourself. What's the big idea? Another young fellow was in lookin' at the licenses only a minute ago.'

The clerk moved over to another desk where he was typewriting. His back was turned toward them. Kirby turned the pages of the book. He and Rose looked them over together. They covered the record for three months without finding anything of interest. Patiently they went over the leaves again.

Kirby stepped over to the clerk. 'Do you happen to remember whether you made out any license application for a man named Cunningham any time in the past two months?' he asked.

'For a marriage license?'

'Yes.'

'Don't think I have. Can't remember the name. I was on my vacation two weeks. Maybe it was then. Can't you find it in the book?'

'Know the date?'

Kirby shook his head.

The voice of Rose, high with excitement, came from across the room. 'Look, here.'

Her finger ran down the book, close to the binding. A page had been cut out with a sharp penknife, so deftly that they had passed it twice without noticing.

'Who did that?' demanded the clerk angrily.

'Probably the young man who was just in here. His name is Jack Cunningham,' Lane answered.

'What in time did he want to do that for? If he wanted it why didn't he take a copy? The boss'll give me Hail Columbia. That's what a fellow gets for being accommodating.'

'He did it so that we wouldn't see it. Is there any other record kept of the marriages?'

'Sure there is. The preachers and the judges who perform marriages have to turn back to us the certificate within thirty days and we make a record of 'em.'

'Can I see that book?'

'I'll do the lookin',' the clerk said shortly. 'Whose marriage is it? And what date?'

Lane gave such information as he could. The clerk mellowed when Rose told him it was very important to her, as officials have a way of doing when charming young women smile at them. But he found no record of any marriage of which they knew either of the contracting parties.

'Once in a while some preacher forgets to turn in his certificate,' the clerk said as he closed the book. 'Old Rankin is the worst that way. He forgets. You might look him up.'

Kirby slipped the clerk a dollar and turned away. Rankin was a forlorn hope, but he and Rose walked out to a little house in the suburbs where the preacher lived.

He was a friendly, white-haired old gentleman, and he made them very much at home under the impression they had come to get married. A slight deafness was in part

162

responsible for this mistake.

'May I see the license?' he asked after Kirby had introduced himself and Rose.

For a moment the cattleman was puzzled. His eyes went to Rose, seeking information. A wave of color was sweeping into her soft cheeks. Then Lane knew why, and the hot blood mounted into his own. His gaze hurriedly and in embarrassment fled from Miss McLean's face.

'You don't quite understand,' he explained to the Reverend Nicodemus Rankin. 'We've come only to—to inquire about some one you married—or rather to find out if you did marry him. His name is Cunningham. We have reason to think he was married a month or two ago. But we're not sure.'

The old man stroked his silken white hair. At times his mind was a little hazy. There were moments when a slight fog seemed to descend upon it. His memory in recent years had been quite treacherous. Not long since he had forgotten to attend a funeral at which he was to conduct the services.

'I dare say I did marry your friend. A good many young people come to me. The license clerk at the court is very kind. He sends them here.'

'The man's name was Cunningham—James Cunningham,' Kirby prompted.

'Cunningham—Cunningham! Seems to me I did marry a man by that name. Come to

163

think of it I'm sure I did. To a beautiful young woman,' the old preacher said.

'Do you recall her name? I mean her maiden name,' Rose said. excitement drumming in her veins.

'No-o. I don't seem quite to remember it. But she was a charming young woman—very attractive, I might say. My wife and daughter mentioned it afterward.'

'May I ask if Mrs. Rankin and your daughter are at present in the house?' asked Lane.

'Unfortunately. no. They have gone to spend a few days visiting in Idaho Springs. If they were here they could re-enforce any gaps in my memory, which is not all it once was.' The Reverend Nicodemus smiled apologetically.

'Was her name Esther McLean?' asked Rose eagerly.

The old parson brought his mind back to the subject with a visible effort. 'Oh, yes! The young lady who was married to your friend—' He paused, at a loss for the name.

'—Cunningham,' Kirby supplied.

'Quite so—Cunningham. Well, it might have been McLeod. I—I rather think it did sound like that.'

'McLean. Miss Esther McLean,' corrected the cattleman patiently.

'The fact is I'm not sure about the young lady's name. Mother and Ellen would know.

I'm sorry they're not here. They talked afterward about how pleasant the young lady was.'

'Was she fair or dark?'

The old preacher smiled at Rose benevolently. 'I really don't know. I'm afraid, my dear young woman, that I'm a very unreliable witness.'

'You don't recollect any details. For instance, how did they come and did they bring witnesses with them?'

'Yes. I was working in the garden—weeding the strawberry-patch, I think. They came in an automobile alone. Wife and daughter were the witnesses.'

'Do you know when Mrs. Rankin and your daughter will be home?'

'By next Tuesday, at the latest. Perhaps you can call again. I trust there was nothing irregular about the marriage.'

'Not so far as we know. We were anxious about the young lady. She is a friend of ours,' Kirby said. 'By the way, the certificate of the marriage is not on record at the court-house. Are you sure you returned it to the clerk?'

'Bless my soul, did I forget that again?' exclaimed the Reverend Nicodemus. 'I'll have my daughter look for the paper as soon as she returns.'

'You couldn't find it now, I suppose,' Lane suggested.

The old gentleman searched rather

helplessly among the papers overflowing his desk. He did not succeed in finding what he looked for.

Kirby and Rose walked back to the court-house. They had omitted to arrange with the license clerk to forward a copy of the marriage certificate when it was filed.

The rough rider left the required fee with the clerk and a bank note to keep his memory jogged up.

'Soon as Mrs. Rankin comes home, will you call her up and remind her about lookin' for the certificate?' he asked.

'Sure I will. I've got to have it, anyhow, for the records. And say, what's the name of that fresh guy who came in here and cut the page from the register? I'm going after him right, believe you me.'

Kirby gave his cousin's name and address. He had no animosity whatever toward him, but he thought it just as well to keep Jack's mind occupied with troubles of his own during the next few days. Very likely then he would not get in his way so much.

They were no sooner clear of the court-house than Rose burst out with what was in her mind.

'It's just as I thought. Your uncle married Esther and got her to keep quiet about the marriage for some reason. Your cousins are trying to destroy the evidence so that the estate won't all go to her. I'll bet we get an

166

offer of a compromise right away.'

'Mebbe.' Kirby's mind was not quite satisfied. Somehow, this affair did not seem to fit in with what he knew of his uncle. Cunningham had been always bold and audacious in his actions, a law to himself. Yet if he were going to marry the stenographer he had wronged, he might do it secretly to conceal the date on account of the unborn child.

The eyes of Rose gleamed with determination. Her jaw set. 'I'm gonna get the whole story out of Esther soon as I get back to town,' she said doggedly. But she did not—not for many days after.

CHAPTER TWENTY-FIVE

A CONFERENCE OF THREE

Kirby heard his name being paged as he entered his hotel.

'Wanted at the telephone, sir,' the bell-hop told him.

He stepped into a booth and the voice of Rose came excited and tremulous. It was less than ten minutes since he had left her at the door of her boarding-house.

'Something's happened, Kirby. Can you come here—right away?' she begged. Then.

unable to keep back any longer the cry of her heart, she broke out with her tidings. 'Esther's gone.'

'Gone where?' he asked.

'I don't know. She left a letter for me. If you'll come to the house—Or shall I meet you downtown?'

'I'll come. Be there in five minutes.'

He more than kept his word. Catching a car on the run at the nearest corner, he dropped from it as it crossed Broadway and walked to Cherokee.

Rose opened the house door when he rang the bell and drew him into the parlor. With a catch of the breath she blurted out again the news.

'She was gone when I got home. I found—this letter.' Her eyes sought his for comfort.

He read what Esther had written.

I can't stand it any longer, dearest. I'm going away where I won't disgrace you. Don't look for me. I'll be taken care of till—afterward.

And, oh, Rose, don't hate me, darling. Even if I am wicked, love me. And try some time to forgive your little sister

ESTHER

'Did anybody see her go?' Lane asked.

'I don't know. I haven't talked with anybody but the landlady. She hasn't seen Esther this

168

afternoon, she said. I didn't let on I was worried.'

'What does she mean that she'll be taken care of till afterward? Who'll take care of her?'

'I don't know.'

'Have you any idea where she would be likely to go—whether there is any friend who might have offered her a temporary home?'

'No.' Rose considered. 'She wouldn't go to any old friend. You see she's awf'ly sensitive. And she'd have to explain. Besides, I'd find out she was there.'

'That's true.'

'I ought never to have left her last spring. I should have found work here and not gone gallumpin' all over the country.' Her chin trembled. She was on the verge of tears.

'Nonsense. You can't blame yourself. We each have to live our own life. How could you tell what was comin'? Betcha we find her right away. Mebbe she let out somethin' to Cole. She doesn't look to me like a girl who could play out a stiff hand alone.'

'She isn't. She's dependent—always has leaned on some one.' Rose had regained control of herself quickly. She stood straight and lissom, mistress of her emotions, but her clear cheeks were colorless. 'I'm worried, Kirby, dreadfully. Esther hasn't the pluck to go through alone. She-she might—'

No need to finish the sentence. Her friend understood.

His strong hand went out and closed on hers. 'Don't you worry, pardner. It'll be all right. We'll find her an' take her somewhere into the country where folks don't know.'

Faintly she smiled. 'You're such a comfort.'

'Sho! We'll get busy right away. Denver ain't such a big town that we can't find one li'l' girl *muy pronto*.' His voice was steady and cheerful, almost light. 'First off, we'll check up an' see if any one saw her go. What did she take with her?'

'One suitcase.'

'How much money? Can you make a guess?'

'She had only a dollar or two in her purse. She had money in the bank. I'll find out if she drew any.'

'Lemme do that. I'll find Cole, too. You make some inquiries round the house here, kinda easylike. Meet you here at six o'clock. Or mebbe we'd better meet downtown. Say at the Boston Chop House.'

Cole was with Kirby when he met Rose at the restaurant.

'We'll go in an' get somethin' to eat,' Lane said. 'We'll talk while we're waitin'. That way we'll not lose any time.'

They found a booth and Kirby ordered the dinner. As soon as the waiter had gone he talked business.

'Find out anything, Rose?'

'Yes. A girl at the house who works for the telephone company saw Esther get into an

170

automobile a block and a half from the house. A man helped her in. I pretended to laugh and asked her what sort of a lookin' man he was. She said he was a live one, well-dressed and handsome. The car was a limousine.'

'Good. Fits in with what I found out,' Kirby said. 'The bank was closed, but I got in the back door by pounding at it. The teller at the K-R window was still there, working at his accounts. Esther did not draw any money today or yesterday.'

'Why do you say good?' Cole wanted to know. 'Is it good for our li'l' friend to be in the power of this good-lookin' guy with the big car, an' her without a bean of her own? I don't get it. Who is the man? Howcome she to go with him? She sure had no notion of goin' when we was eatin' together an hour before.'

'I don't see who he could be. She never spoke of such a man to me,' Rose murmured, greatly troubled.

'I don't reckon she was very well acquainted with him,' Lane said, shaking out his napkin.

The talk was suspended while he ladled the soup into the plates and the waiter served them. Not till the man's back was turned did Rose fling out her hot challenge to Kirby.

'Why would she go with a man she didn't know very well? Where would she be going with him?' The flame in her cheeks, the stab of her eyes, dared him to think lightly of her sister. It was in her temperament to face all

171

slights with high spirit.

His smile reassured. 'Mebbe she didn't know where she was goin'. That was his business. Let's work this out from the beginnin'.'

Kirby passed Rose the crackers. She rejected them with a little gesture of impatience.

'I don't want to eat. I'm not hungry.'

Lane's kind eyes met hers steadily. 'But you must eat. You'll be of no help if you don't keep up your strength.' Rather than fight it out, she gave up.

'We know right off the reel Esther didn't plan this,' he continued. 'Before we knew the man was in it you felt it wasn't like her to run away alone, Rose. Didn't you?'

'Yes.'

'She hadn't drawn any money from her account. So she wasn't makin' any plans to go. The man worked it out an' then persuaded Esther. It's no surprise to me to find a Mr. Man in this thing. I'd begun to guess it before you told me. The question is, what man.'

The girl's eyes jumped to his. She began to see what he was working toward. Cole, entirely in the dark, stirred uneasily. His mind was still busy with a possible love tangle.

'What man or men would benefit most if Esther disappeared for a time? We know of two it might help,' the man from Twin Buttes

172

went on.

'Your cousins!' she cried, almost in a whisper.

'Yes, if we've guessed rightly that Esther was married to Uncle James. That would make her his heir. With her in their hands and away from us, they would be in a position to drive a better bargain. They know that we're hot on the trail of the marriage. If they're kind to her—and no doubt they will be—they can get anything they want from her in the way of an agreement as to the property. Looks to me like the fine Italian hand of Cousin James. We know Jack wasn't the man. He was busy at Golden right then. Kinda leaves James in the spotlight, doesn't it?'

Rose drew a long, deep breath. 'I'm so glad! I was afraid—thought maybe she would do something desperate. But if she's being looked after it's a lot better. We'll soon have her back. Until then they'll be good to her, won't they?'

'They'll treat her like a queen. Don't you see? That's their game. They don't want a lawsuit. They're playin' for a compromise.'

Kirby leaned back and smiled expansively on his audience of two. He began to fancy himself tremendously as a detective.

CHAPTER TWENTY-SIX

CUTTING TRAIL

Kirby's efforts to find James Cunningham after dinner were not successful. He was not at his rooms, at the Country Club, or at his office. Nor was he at a dinner dance where he was among the invited guests, a bit of information Rose had gathered from the society columns of the previous Sunday's *News*. His cousin reached him at last next morning by means of his business telephone. An appointment was arranged in five sentences.

If James felt any surprise at the delegation of three which filed in to see him he gave no sign of it. He bowed, sent for more chairs from the outer office and seated his visitors, all with a dry, close smile hovering on the edge of irony.

Kirby cut short preliminaries. 'You know why we're here and what we want,' he said abruptly.

'I confess I don't, unless to report on your trip to Golden,' James countered suavely. 'Was it successful, may I ask?'

'If it wasn't, you know why it wasn't.'

The eyes of the two men met. Neither of them dodged in the least or gave to the rigor of the other's gaze.

'Referring to Jack's expedition, I presume.'

'You don't deny it, then.'

'My dear Kirby, I never waste breath in useless denials. You saw Jack. Therefore he must have been there.'

'He was. He brought away with him a page cut from the marriage-license registry.'

James lifted a hand of protest. 'Ah! There we come to the parting of the ways. I can't concede that.'

'No, but you know it's true,' said Kirby bluntly.

'Not at all. He surely would not mutilate a public record.'

'We needn't go into that. He did. But that didn't keep us from getting the information we wanted.'

'No?' James murmured the monosyllable with polite indifference. But he watched, lynx-eyed, the strong, brown face of his cousin.

'We know now the secret you wanted to keep hidden in the court-house at Golden.'

'I grant you energy in ferreting out other people's business, dear cousin. If you're always so—so altruistic, let us say—I wonder how you have time to devote to your own affairs.'

'We intend to see justice done Miss Esther McLean—Mrs. James Cunningham, I should say. You can't move us from that intention or—'

The expression on the oil broker's face was either astonishment or the best counterfeit of it Kirby had ever seen.

'I beg pardon. *What* did you say?'

'I told you, what you already know, that Esther McLean was married to Uncle James at Golden on the twenty-first of last month.'

'Miss McLean and Uncle James married— at Golden—on the twenty-first of last month? Are you sure?'

'Aren't you? What did you think we found out?'

Cunningham's eyes narrowed. A film of caution spread over them. 'Oh, I don't know. You're so enterprising you might discover almost anything. It's really a pity with your imagination that you don't go into fiction.'

'Or oil promotin',' suggested Cole with a grin. 'Or is that the same thing.'

'Let's table our cards, James,' his cousin said. 'You know now why we're here.'

'On the contrary, I'm more in the dark than ever.'

Kirby was never given to useless movements of his limbs or body. He had the gift of repose, of wonderful poise. Now not even his eyelashes flickered.

'We want to know what you've done with Esther McLean.'

'But, my dear fellow, why should I do anything with her?'

'You know why as well as I do. Somehow you've persuaded her to go somewhere and hide herself. You want her in your power, to

176

force or cajole her into a compromise of her right to Uncle James's estate. We won't have it.'

A satiric smile touched the face of Cunningham without warming it. 'That active imagination of yours again. You do let it run away with you.'

'You were seen getting into a car with Miss McLean.'

'Did she step in of her own free will?'

'We don't claim an abduction.'

'On your own statement of the case, then, you have no ground of complaint whatever.'

'Do you refuse to tell us where she is?' Kirby asked.

'I refuse to admit that I know where the young lady is.'

'We'll find her. Don't make any mistake about that.' Kirby rose. The interview was at an end.

Cole Sanborn strode forward. He leaned over the desk toward the oil broker, his blue eyes drilling into those of the broker.

'We sure will, an' if you've hurt our li'l friend—if she's got any grievance against you an' the way you treat her—I'll certainly wreck you proper, Mr. Cunningham.'

James flushed angrily. 'Get out of here—all of you! Or I'll send for the police and have you swept out. I'm fed up on your interference.'

'Is it interference for Miss McLean here to want to know where her sister is?' asked Kirby quietly.

'Why should you all assume I know?'

'Because the evidence points to you.'

'Absurd. You come down here from Wyoming and do nothing but make trouble far me and Jack even though we try to stand your friend. I've had about enough of you.'

'Sorry you look at it that way.' Kirby's smile was friendly. It was even wistful. 'I appreciate what you did for me, but I've got to go through with what I've started. I can't quit on the job because I'm under an obligation to you. By the way, I've arranged the matter of the bond. We're to take it up at the district attorney's office at eleven this morning.'

'Glad to hear it. I want to be quit of you,' snapped Cunningham tartly.

Outside, Kirby gave directions to his lieutenants.

'It's up to you two to dig up some facts. I'm gonna be busy all mornin' with this bond business so's I can keep outa jail. Rose, you go up to the Secretary of State's office and find the number of the license of my cousin's car and the kind of machine it is. Then you'd better come back an' take a look at all the cars parked within three or four blocks of here. He may have driven it down when he came to work this mornin'. Look at the speedometer an' see what the mileage record is of the last trip taken. Cole, you go to this address. That's where my cousin lives. Find out at what garage

178

he keeps his car. If they don't know, go to all the garages within several blocks of the place. See if it's a closed car. Get the make an' the number an' the last trip mileage. Meet me here at twelve o'clock, say. Both of you.'

'Suits me,' said Cole. 'But wise me up. What's the idea in the mileage?'

'Just this. James was outa town last night probably. We couldn't find him anywhere. My notion is that he's taken Esther somewhere into the mountains. If we can get the mileage of the last trip, all we have to do is to divide it by two to know how far away Esther is. Then we'll draw a circle round Denver at that distance an'—'

Cole slapped his thigh with his hat. 'Bully! You're sure the white-haired lad in this deteckative game.'

'Maybe he didn't set the speedometer for the trip,' suggested Rose.

'Possible. Then again more likely he did. James is a methodical chap. Another thing, while you're at the private hotel where he lives, Cole. Find out if you can where James goes when he fishes or drives into the mountains. Perhaps he's got a cottage of his own or some favorite spot.'

'I'm on my way, old-timer!' Cole announced with enthusiasm.

At luncheon the committee reported progress. Cole had seen James Cunningham's car. It was a sedan. He had had it out of the garage all afternoon and evening and had brought it back just before midnight. The trip record on the speedometer registered ninety-two miles.

From his pocket Kirby drew an automobile map and a pencil. He notched on the pencil a mark to represent forty-six miles from the point, based on the scale of miles shown at the foot of the map. With the pencil as a radius he drew a semicircle from Denver as the center. The curved line passed through Loveland, Long's Peak, and across the Snow Range to Tabernash. It included Georgetown, Gray's Peak, Mount Evans, and Cassell's. From there it swept on to Palmer Lake.

'I'm not includin' the plains country to the east,' Kirby explained. 'You'll have enough territory to cover as it is, Cole. By the way, did you find anything about where James goes into the hills?'

'No.'

'Well, we'll make some more inquiries. Perhaps the best thing for you to do would be to go out to the small towns around Denver an' find out if any of the garage people noticed a car of that description passin' through. That would help a lot. It would give us a line on whether he went up Bear Canon, Platte Cañon, into Northern Colorado, or south toward the Palmer Lake country.'

'You've allowed forty-six miles by an air line,' Rose pointed out. 'He couldn't have

180

gone as far as Long's Peak or Evans—nowhere nearly as far, because the roads are so winding when you get in the hills. He could hardly have reached Estes Park.'

'Right. You'll have to check up the road distances from Denver, Cole. Your job's like lookin' for a needle in a hay-stack. I'll put a detective agency on James. He might take a notion to run out to the cache any fine evenin'. He likely will, to make sure Esther is contented.'

'Or he'll send Jack,' Rose added.

'We'll try to keep an eye on him, too.'

'This is my job, is it?' Cole asked, rising.

'You an' Rose can work together on it. My job's here in town on the murder mystery.'

'If we work both of them out—finding Esther and proving who killed your uncle—I think we'll learn that it's all the same mystery, anyhow,' Rose said, drawing on her gloves.

Cole nodded sagely. 'You've said somethin', Rose.'

'Say *when,* not *if,* we work 'em out. Well be cuttin' hot trail *poco tempo,*' Kirby prophesied, smiling up at them.

CHAPTER TWENTY-SEVEN

THE DETECTIVE GETS TWO SURPRISES

Kirby stared down at the document in front of him. He could scarcely believe the evidence flashed by his eyes to his brain. It was the document he had asked the county recorder at Golden to send him—and it certified that, on July 21, *James Cunningham and Phyllis Harriman had been united in marriage* at Golden by the Reverend Nicodemus Rankin.

This knocked the props from under the whole theory he had built up to account for the disappearance of Esther McLean. If Esther were not the widow of his uncle, then the motive of James in helping her to vanish was not apparent. Perhaps he told the truth and knew nothing about the affair whatever.

But Kirby was puzzled. Why had his uncle, who was openly engaged to Phyllis Harriman, married her surreptitiously and kept that marriage a secret? It was not in character, and he could see no reason for it. Foster had sent him to Golden on the tacit hint that there was some clue in the license register to the mystery of James Cunningham's death. What bearing had this marriage on it, if any?

It explained, of course, the visit of Miss

Harriman to his uncle's apartments on the night he was murdered. She had an entire right to go there at any time, and if they were keeping their relation a secret would naturally go at night when she could slip in unobserved.

But Kirby's mind wandered up and down blind alleys. The discovery of this secret seemed only to make the tangle more difficult.

He had a hunch that there was a clue at Golden he had somehow missed, and that feeling took him back there within three hours of the receipt of the certificate.

The clerk in the recorder's office could tell him nothing new except that he had called up Mrs. Rankin by telephone and she had brought up the delayed certificate at once. Kirby lost no time among the records. He walked to the Rankin house and introduced himself to an old lady sunning herself on the porch. She was a plump, brisk little person with snapping eyes younger than her years.

'I'm sorry I wasn't at home when you called. Can I help you now?' she asked.

'I don't know. James Cunningham was my uncle. We thought he had married a girl who is a sister of the friend with me the day I called. But it seems we were mistaken. He married Phyllis Harriman, the young woman to whom he was engaged.'

Mrs. Rankin smiled, the placid, motherly smile of experience 'I've noticed that men sometimes do marry the girls to whom they are

183

engaged.'

'Yes, but—' Kirby broke off and tried another tack. 'How old was the lady? And was she dark or fair?'

'Miss Harriman? I should think she may be twenty-five. She is dark, slender, and beautifully dressed. Rather an—an expensive sort of young lady, perhaps.'

'Did she act as though she were much—well, in love with—Mr. Cunningham?'

The bright eyes twinkled. 'She's not a young woman who wears her heart on her sleeve, I judge. I can't answer that question. My opinion is that he was very much in love with her. Why do you ask?'

'You have read about his death since, of course,' he said.

'Is he dead? No, I didn't know it.' The birdlike eyes opened wider. 'That's strange too.'

'It's on account of the mystery of his death that I'm troubling you, Mrs. Rankin. We want it cleared up, of course.'

'But—two James Cunninghams haven't died mysteriously, have they?' she asked. 'The nephew isn't killed, too, is he?'

'Oh, no. Just my uncle.'

'Then we're mixed up somewhere. How old was your uncle?'

'He was past fifty-six—just past.'

'That's not the man my husband married.'

'Not the man! Oh, aren't you mistaken,

Mrs. Rankin? My uncle was strong and rugged. He did not look his age.'

The old lady got up swiftly. 'Please excuse me a minute.' She moved with extraordinary agility into the house. It was scarcely a minute before she was with him again, a newspaper in her hand. In connection with the Cunningham murder mystery several pictures were shown. Among them were photographs of his uncle and two cousins.

'This is the man whose marriage to Miss Harriman I witnessed,' she said.

Her finger was pointing to the likeness of his cousin James Cunningham.

CHAPTER TWENTY-EIGHT

THE FINGER OF SUSPICION POINTS

The words of the preacher's little wife were like a bolt from a sunny heaven. Kirby could not accept them without reiteration. Never in the wildest dreams of the too vivid imagination of which his cousin had accused him had this possibility occurred to him.

'Do you mean that this man—the younger one—is the husband of Phyllis Harriman?' His finger touched the reproduction of his cousin's photograph.

'Yes. He's the man my husband married her

185

to on the twenty-first of July.'

'You're quite sure of that?'

'I ought to be,' she answered rather dryly. 'I was a witness.'

A young woman came up the walk from the street. She was a younger and more modern replica of Mrs. Rankin. The older lady introduced her.

'Daughter, this is Mr. Lane, the gentleman who called on Father the other day while we were away. Mr. Lane, my daughter Ellen.' Briskly she continued, showing her daughter the picture of James Cunningham, Junior. 'Did you ever see this man, dear?'

Ellen took one glance at it. 'He's the man Father married the other day.'

'When?' the mother asked.

'It was—let me see—about the last week in July. Why?'

'Married to who?' asked Mrs. Rankin colloquially.

'To that lovely Miss Harriman, of course.'

The old lady wheeled on Kirby triumphantly. 'Are you satisfied now that I'm in my right mind?' she demanded smilingly.

'Have to ask your pardon if I was rude,' he said, meeting her smile. 'But the fact is it was such a surprise I couldn't take it in.'

'This gentleman is the nephew of the Mr. Cunningham who was killed. He thought it was his uncle who had married Miss Harriman,' the mother explained to Ellen.

186

The girl turned to Kirby. 'You know I've wondered about that myself. The society columns of the papers said it was the older Mr. Cunningham that was going to marry her. And I've seen, since your uncle's death, notices in the paper about his engagement to Miss Harriman. But I thought it must have been a mistake, since it was the younger Mr. Cunningham she did marry. Maybe the reporters got the two mixed. They do sometimes get things wrong in the papers, you know.'

This explanation was plausible, but Kirby happened to have inside information. He remembered the lovely photograph of the young woman in his uncle's rooms and the 'Always, Phyllis' written across the lower part of it. He recalled the evasive comments of both James and his brother whenever any reference had been made to the relation between Miss Harriman and their uncle. No, Phyllis Harriman had been engaged to marry James Cunningham, Senior. He was sure enough of that. In point of fact he had seen at the district attorney's office a letter written by her to the older man, a letter which acknowledged that they were to be married in October. It had been one of a dozen papers turned over to the prosecutor's office for examination. Then she had jilted the land promoter for his nephew.

Did his uncle know of the marriage of his

nephew? That was something Kirby meant to find out if he could. The news he had just heard lit up avenues of thought as a searchlight throws a shaft into the darkness. It brought a new factor into the problem at which he was working. Roughly speaking, the cattleman knew his uncle, the habits of mind that guided him, the savage and relentless passions that swayed him. If the old man knew his favorite nephew and his fiancée had made a mock of him, he would move swiftly to a revenge that would hurt. The first impulse of his mind would be to strike James from his will.

And even if his uncle had not yet discovered the secret marriage, he would soon have done so. It could not have been much longer concealed. This thing was as sure as any contingency in human life can be: *if Cunningham had lived, his nephew James would never have inherited a cent of his millions. The older man had died in the nick of time for James.*

Already Kirby had heard a hint to this effect. It had been at a restaurant much affected by the business men of the city during the lunch hour. Two men had been passing his table on their way out. One, lowering his voice, had said to the other: 'James Cunningham ought to give a medal to the fellow that shot his uncle. Didn't come a day too soon for him. Between you and me, J. C. has been speculating heavy and has been hit hard. He was about due to throw up the sponge. Luck for him, I'll say.'

It was on the way back from Golden, while he was being rushed through the golden fields of summer, that suspicion of his cousin hit Kirby like a blow in the face. Facts began to marshal themselves in his mind, an irresistible phalanx of them. James was the only man, except his brother, who benefited greatly by the death of his uncle. Not only was this true; the land promoter had to die *soon* to help James, just how soon Kirby meant to find out. Phyllis and a companion had been in the victim's apartment either at the time of his death or immediately afterward. That companion *might have been James and not Jack.* James had lost the sheets with the writing left by the Japanese valet Horikawa. The rage he had vented on his clerk might easily have been a blind. When James knew he was going to Golden to look up the marriage register, he had at once tried to forestall him by destroying the information.

Kirby tried to fight off his suspicions. He wanted to believe in his cousin. In his own way he had been kind to him. He had gone on his bond to keep him out of prison after he had tried to conceal the fact of his existence at the coroner's inquest. But doubts began to gnaw at the Wyoming man's confidence in him. Had James befriended him merely to be in a position to keep closer tab on anything he

189

discovered? Had he wanted to be close enough to throw him off the track with the wrong suggestions?

The young cattleman was ashamed of himself for his doubts. But he could not down them. His discovery of the marriage changed the situation. It put his cousin James definitely into the list of the suspects.

As soon as he reached town he called at the law offices of Irwin, Foster & Warren. The member of the firm he wanted to see was in.

'I've been to Golden, Mr. Foster,' he said, when he was alone with that gentleman. 'Now I want to ask you a question.'

The lawyer looked at him, smiling warily. Both of the James Cunninghams had been clients of his.

'I make my living giving legal advice,' he said.

'I don't want legal advice just now,' Kirby answered. 'I want to ask you if you know whether my uncle knew that James and Miss Harriman were married.'

Foster looked out of the window and drummed with his finger-tips on the desk. 'Yes,' he said at last.

'He knew?'

'Yes.'

'Do you know when he found out?'

'I can answer that, too. He found out on the evening of the twenty-first—two days before his death. I told him—after dinner at the City

190

Club.'

'You had just found it out yourself?'

'That afternoon.'

'How did you decide that the James Cunningham mentioned in the license you saw was the younger one?'

'By the age given.'

'How did my uncle take the news when you told him?'

'He took it standing,' the lawyer said. 'Didn't make any fuss, but looked like the Day of Judgment for the man who had betrayed him.'

'What did he do?'

'Wrote a note and called for a messenger to deliver it.'

'Who to?' Kirby asked colloquially.

'I don't know. Probably the company has a record of all calls. If so, you can find the boy who delivered the message.'

'I'll get busy right away.'

Foster hesitated, then volunteered another piece of information. 'I don't suppose you know that your uncle sent for me next day and told me to draft a new will for him and get it ready for his signature.'

'Did you do it?'

'Yes. I handed it to him the afternoon of the day he was killed. It was found unsigned among his papers after his death. The old will still stands.'

'Leaving the property to James and Jack?'

'Yes.'

'And the new will?'

'Except for some bequests and ten thousand for a fountain at the city park, the whole fortune was to go to Jack.'

'So that if he had lived twenty-four hours longer James would have been disinherited.'

Foster looked at him out of eyes that told nothing of what he was thinking. 'That's the situation exactly.'

Kirby made no further comment, nor did the lawyer.

Within two hours the man from Twin Buttes had talked with the messenger boy, refreshed his memory with a tip, and learned that the message Cunningham had sent from the City Club had been addressed to his nephew Jack.

CHAPTER TWENTY-NINE

'COME CLEAN, JACK'

Jack Cunningham, co-heir with James of his uncle's estate, was busy in the office he had inherited settling up one of the hundred details that had been left at loose ends by the promoter's sudden death. He looked up at the entrance of Lane.

'What do you want?' he asked sharply.

'Want a talk with you.'

'Well, I don't care to talk with you. What are you doing here anyhow. I told the boy to tell you I was too busy to see you.'

'That's what he said.' Kirby opened his slow, whimsical smile on Jack. 'But I'm right busy, too. So I brushed him aside an' walked in.'

In dealing with this forceful cousin of his, Jack had long since lost his indolent insolence of manner. 'You can walk out again, then. I'll not talk,' he snapped.

Kirby drew up a chair and seated himself. 'When Uncle James sent a messenger for you to come to his rooms at once on the evening of the twenty-first, what did he want to tell you?' The steady eyes of the cattleman bored straight into those of Cunningham.

'Who said he sent a messenger for me?'

'It doesn't matter who just now. There are two witnesses. What did he want?'

'That's my business.'

'So you say. I'm beginnin' to wonder if it isn't the business of the State of Colorado, too.'

'What do you mean?'

'I mean that Uncle sent for you because he had just found out your brother and Miss Harriman were married.'

Jack flashed a startled look at him. It seemed to him his cousin showed an uncanny knowledge at times. 'You think so.'

'He wanted to tell you that he was goin' to cut your brother out of his will an' leave you sole heir. An' he wanted you to let James know it right away.'

Kirby was guessing, but he judged he had scored. Jack got up and began to pace the room. He was plainly agitated.

'Look here. Why don't you go back to Wyoming and mind your own business? You're not in this. It's none of your affair. What are you staying here for hounding the life out of James and me?'

'None of my business! That's good, Jack. An' me out on bond charged with the murder of Uncle James. I'd say it was quite some of my business. I'm gonna stick to the job. Make up your mind to that.'

'Then leave us alone,' retorted Jack irritably. 'You act as though you thought we were a pair of murderers.'

'If you have nothin' to conceal, why do you block my way? Why aren't you frank an' open? Why did you steal that record at Golden? Why did James lose the Jap's confession—if it was a confession? Why did he get Miss McLean to disappear? Answer those questions to my satisfaction before you talk about me buttin' in with suspicions against you.'

Jack slammed a fist down on the corner of the desk. 'I'm not going to answer any questions! I'll say you've got a nerve! You're the man charged with this crime—the man that's liable to be tried for it. You've got a rope round your neck right this minute—and you go around high and mighty trying to throw suspicion on men that there's no evidence against.'

'You said you had a quarrel with your uncle that night—no, I believe you called it a difference of opinion, at the inquest. What was that disagreement about?'

'Find out! I'll never tell you.'

'Was it because you tried to defend James to him—tried to get him to forgive the treachery of his fiancée and his nephew?'

Again Jack shot at him a look of perplexed and baffled wonder. That brown, indomitable face, back of which was so much strength of purpose and so much keenness of apprehension, began to fill him with alarm. This man let no obstacles stop him. He would go on till he had uncovered the whole tangle they were trying to keep hidden.

'For God's sake, man, stop this snooping around! You'll get off. We'll back you. There's nowhere nearly enough evidence to convict you. Let it go at that,' implored Jack.

'I can't do that. I've got to clear my name. Do you think I'm willin' to go back to my friends with a Scotch verdict hangin' over me? "He did it, but we haven't evidence enough to prove it." Come clean, Jack! Are you and James in this thing? Is that why you want me to drop my investigations?'

'No, of course we're not! But—damn it, do you think we want the name of my brother's wife dragged through the mud?'

'Why should it be dragged through the mud—if you're all innocent?'

'Because gossips cackle—and people never forget. If there was some evidence against her and against James—no matter how little— twenty years from now people would still whisper that they had killed his uncle for the fortune, though it couldn't be proved. You know that.'

'Just as they're goin' to whisper about Rose McLean if I don't clear things up. No, Jack. You've got the wrong idea. What we want to do is for us all to jump in an' find the man who did it. Then all gossip against us stops.'

'That's easy to say. How're you going to find the guilty man?' asked Jack sulkily.

'If you'd tell what you know we'd find him fast enough. How can I get to the bottom of the thing when you an' James won't give me the facts?'

Jack looked across at him doggedly. 'I've told all I'm going to tell.'

The long, lithe body of the man from the Wyoming hills leaned forward ever so slightly. 'Don't you think it! Don't you think it for a minute! You'll come clean whether you want to or not—or I'll put that rope you mentioned round your brother's throat.'

Jack looked at this man with the nerves of chilled steel and shivered. What could he do against a single-track mind with such driving force back of it? Had Kirby got anything of importance on James? Or was he bluffing?

'Talk's cheap,' he sneered uneasily.

'You'll find how cheap it is. James had been speculatin'. He was down an' out. Another week, an' he'd have been a bankrupt. Uncle discovers how he's been tricked by him an' Miss Harriman. He serves notice that he's cuttin' James out of his will an' he sends for a lawyer to draw up a new one. James an' his wife go to the old man's rooms to beg off. There's a quarrel, maybe. Anyhow, this point sticks up like a sore thumb: if Uncle hadn't died that night your brother would 'a' been a beggar. Now he's a millionaire. And James was in his room the very hour in which he was killed.'

'You can't prove that!' Jack cried, his voice low and hoarse. 'How do you know he was there? What evidence have you?'

Kirby smiled, easily and confidently. 'The evidence will be produced at the right time.' He rose and turned to go.

Jack also got up, white to the lips. 'Hold on! Don't—don't do anything in a hurry! I'll—talk with you tomorrow—here—in the forenoon. Or say in a day or two. I'll let you know then.'

His cousin nodded grimly.

The hard look passed from his eyes as he reached the corridor. 'Had to throw a scare into him to make him come through,' he murmured in apology to himself.

CHAPTER THIRTY

KIRBY MAKES A CALL

Kirby had been bluffing when he said he had evidence to prove that James was in his uncle's rooms the very hour of the murder. But he was now convinced that he had told the truth. James had been there, and his brother Jack knew it. The confession had been written in his shocked face when Kirby flung out the charge.

But James might have been there and still be innocent, just as was the case with him and Rose. The cattleman wanted to find the murderer, but he wanted almost as much to find that James had nothing to do with the crime. He eliminated Jack, except perhaps as an accessory after the fact. Jack had a telltale face, but he might be cognizant of guilt without being deeply a party to it. He could be insolent, but faults of manner are not a crime. Besides, all Jack's interests lay in the other direction. If his uncle had lived a day longer, he would have been sole heir to the estate.

As he wandered through the streets Kirby's mind was busy with the problem. Automatically his legs carried him to the Paradox Apartments. He found himself there before he even knew he had been heading in that direction. Mrs. Hull came out and passed him. She was without a hat, and probably was going to the corner grocery on Fifteenth.

'I've been neglecting friend Hull,' he murmured to himself. 'I reckon I'll just drop in an' ask him how his health is.'

He was not sorry that Mrs. Hull was out. She was easily, he judged, the dominant member of the firm. If he could catch the fat man alone he might gather something of importance.

Hull opened the door of the apartment to his knock. He stood glaring at the young man, his prominent eyes projecting, the red capillaries in his beefy face filling.

'Whadjawant?' he demanded.

'A few words with you, Mr. Hull.' Kirby pushed past him into the room, much as an impudent agent does.

'Well, I don't aim to have no truck with you at all,' blustered the fat man. 'You've just naturally wore out yore welcome with me before ever you set down. I'll ask you to go right now.'

'Here's your hat. What's your hurry?' murmured Kirby, by way of quotation. 'Sure I'll go. But don't get on the prod, Hull. I came to make some remarks an' to ask a question. I'll not hurt you any. Haven't got smallpox or anything.'

'I don't want you here. If the police knew you was here, they'd be liable to think we was

199

talkin' about—about what happened upstairs.'

'Then they would be right. That's exactly what we're gonna talk about.'

'No, sir! I ain't got a word to say—not a word!' The big man showed signs of panic.

'Then I'll say it.' The dancing light died out of Kirby's eyes. They became hard and steady as agates. 'Who killed Cunningham, Hull?'

The fishy eyes of the man dodged. A startled oath escaped him. 'How do I know?'

'Didn't you kill him?'

'Goddlemighty, no!' Hull dragged out the red bandanna and gave his apoplectic face first aid. He mopped perspiration from the overlapping roll of fat above his collar. 'I dunno a thing about it. Honest, I don't. You got no right to talk to me thataway.'

'You're a tub of iniquity, Hull. Also, you're a right poor liar. You know a lot about it. You were in my uncle's rooms just before I saw you on the night of his death. You were seen there.

'W-w-who says so?' quavered the wretched man.

'You'll know who at the proper time. I'll tell you one thing. It won't look good for you that you held out all you know till it was a showdown.'

'I ain't holdin' out, I tell you. What business you got to come here devilin' me, I'd like for to know?'

'I'm not devilin' you. I'm tellin' you to come through with what you know, or you'll sure get in trouhle. There's a witness against you. When he tells what he saw—'

'Shibo?' The word burst from the man's lips in spite of him.

Kirby did not bat a surprised eye. He went on quietly. 'I'll not say who. Except this. Shibo is not the only one who can tell enough to put you on trial for your life. If you didn't kill my uncle you'd better take my tip, Hull. Tell what you know. It'll be better for you.'

Mrs. Hull stood in the doorway, thin and sinister. The eyes in her yellow face took in the cattleman and passed to her husband. 'What's he doing here?' she asked, biting off her words sharply.

'I was askin' Mr. Hull if he knew who killed my uncle,' explained Kirby.

Her eyes narrowed. 'Maybe *you* know,' she retorted.

'Not yet. I'm tryin' to find out. Can you give me any help, Mrs. Hull?'

Their eyes crossed and fought it out.

'What do you want to know?' she demanded.

'I'd like to know what happened in my uncle's rooms when Mr. Hull was up there—say about half-past nine, mebbe a little before or a little after.'

'He claims to have a witness,' Hull managed to get out from a dry throat.

'A witness of what?' snapped the woman.

'That—that I—was in Cunningham's

201

rooms.'

For an instant the woman quailed. A spasm of fear flashed over her face and was gone.

'He'll claim anything to get outa the hole he's in,' she said dryly. Then, swiftly, her anger pounced on the Wyoming man. 'You get outa my house. We don't have to stand yore impudence—an' what's more, we won't. Do you hear? Get out, or I'll send for the police. I ain't scared any of you.'

The amateur detective got out. He had had the worst of the bout. But he had discovered one or two things. If he could get Olson to talk, and could separate the fat, flabby man from his flinty wife, it would not be hard to frighten a confession from Hull of all he knew. Moreover, in his fear Hull had let slip one admission. Shibo, the little janitor, had some evidence against him. Hull knew it. Why was Shibo holding it back? The fat man had practically said that Shibo had seen him come out of Cunningham's rooms, or at least that he was a witness he had been in the apartment. Yet he had withheld the fact when he had been questioned by the police. Had Hull bribed him to keep quiet?

The cattleman found Shibo watering the lawn of the parking in front of the paradox. According to his custom, he plunged abruptly into what he wanted to say. He had discovered that if a man is not given time to frame a defense, he is likely to give away something he had intended to conceal.

'Shibo, why did you hide from the police that Mr. Hull was in my uncle's rooms the night he was killed?'

The janitor shot one slant, startled glance at Kirby before the mask of impassivity wiped out expression from his eyes.

'You know heap lot about everything. You busy busy all like honey-bee. Me, I just janitor—mind own business.'

'I wonder, now.' Kirby's level gaze took the man in carefully. Was he as simple as he wanted to appear?

'No talk when not have anything to tell.' Shibo moved the sprinkler to another part of the lawn.

Kirby followed him. He had a capacity for patience. 'Did Mr. Hull ask you not to tell about him?'

Shibo said nothing, but he said it with indignant eloquence.

'Did he give you money not to tell? I don't want to go to the police with this if I can help it, Shibo. Better come through to me.'

'You go police an' say I know who make Mr. Cunningham dead?'

'If I have to.'

The janitor had no more remarks to make. He lapsed into an angry, stubborn silence. For nearly half an hour Kirby stayed by his side. The cattleman asked questions. He suggested that, of course, the police would soon find out

203

the facts after he went to them. He even went beyond his brief and implied that shortly Shibo would be occupying a barred cell.

But the man from the Orient contributed no more to the talk.

CHAPTER THIRTY-ONE

THE MASK OF THE RED BANDANNA

It had come by special delivery, an ill-written little note scrawled on cheap ruled paper torn from a tablet.

If you want to know who killed Cunningham i can tell you. Meet me at the Denmark Bilding, room 419, at eleven tonight. Come alone.

One who knows.

Kirby studied the invitation carefully. Was it genuine? Or was it a plant? He was no handwriting expert, but he had a feeling that it was a disguised script. There is an inimitable looseness of design in the chirography of an illiterate person. He did not find here the awkwardness of the inexpert; rather the elaborate imitation of an amateur ignoramus. Yet he was not sure. He could give no definite reason for this fancy.

And in the end he tossed it overboard. He would keep the appointment and see what came of it. Moreover, he would keep it alone—except for a friend hanging under the left arm at his side. Kirby had brought no revolver with him to Denver. Occasionally he carried one on the range to frighten coyotes and to kill rattlers. But he knew where he could borrow one, and he proceeded to do so.

Not that there was any danger in meeting the unknown correspondent. Kirby did not admit that for a moment. There are people so constituted that they revel in the mysterious. They wrap their most common actions in hints of reserve and weighty silence. Perhaps this man was one of them. There was no danger whatever. Nobody had any reason to wish him serious ill. Yet Kirby took a .45 with him when he set out for the Denmark Building. He did it because that strange sixth sense of his had warned him to do so.

During the day he had examined the setting for the night's adventure. He had been to the Denmark Building and scanned it inside and out. He had gone up to the fourth floor and looked at the exterior of Room 419. The office door had printed on it this design:

THE GOLD HILL MILLING & MINING COMPANY

But when Kirby tried the door he found it

locked.

The Denmark Building is a little out of the heart of the Denver business district. It was built far uptown at a time when real estate was booming. Adjoining it is the Rockford Building. The two dominate a neighborhood of squat two-story stores and rooming-houses. In dull seasons the offices in the two big landmarks are not always filled with tenants.

The elevators in the Denmark had ceased running hours since. Kirby took the narrow stairs which wound round the elevator shaft. He trod the iron treads very slowly, very softly. He had no wish to advertise his presence. If there was to be any explosive surprise, he did not want to be at the receiving end of it.

He reached the second story, crossed the landing, and began the next flight. The place was dark as a midnight pit. At the third floor its blackness was relieved slightly by a ray of light from a transom far down the corridor.

Kirby waited to listen. He heard no faintest sound to break the stillness. Again his foot found the lowest tread and he crept upward. In the daytime he had laughed at the caution which had led him to borrow a weapon from an acquaintance at the stockyards. But now every sense shouted danger. He would not go back, but each forward step was taken with infinite care.

And his care availed him nothing. A lifted foot struck an empty soap box with a clatter to

206

wake the seven sleepers. Instantly he knew it had been put there for him to stumble over. A strong searchlight flooded the stairs and focused on him. He caught a momentary glimpse of a featureless face standing out above the light—a face that was nothing but a red bandanna handkerchief with slits in it for eyes—and of a pair of feet below at the top of the stairway.

The searchlight winked out. There was a flash of lightning and a crash of thunder. A second time the pocket flash found Kirby. It found him crouched low and reaching for the .45 under his arm. The booming of the revolver above reverberated down the pit of the stairway.

Arrow-swift, with the lithe ease of a wild thing from the forest, Kirby ducked round the corner for safety. He did not wait there, but took the stairs down three at a stride. Not till he had reached the ground floor did he stop to listen for the pursuit.

No sound of following footsteps came to him. By some miracle of good luck he had escaped the ambush. It was characteristic of him that he did not fly wildly into the night. His brain functioned normally, coolly. Whoever it was had led him into the trap had lost his chance. Kirby reasoned that the assassin's mind would be bent on making his own safe escape before the police arrived.

The cattleman waited, crouched behind an

outjutting pillar in the wall of the entrance. Every minute he expected to see a furtive figure sneak past him into the street. His hopes were disappointed. It was nearly midnight when two men, talking cheerfully of the last gusher in the Buckburnett field, emerged from the stairway and passed into the street. They were tenants who had stayed late to do some unfinished business.

There was a drug-store in the building, cornering on two streets. Kirby stepped into it and asked a question of the clerk at the prescription desk.

'Is there more than one entrance to the Denmark Building?'

'No, sir.' The clerk corrected himself. 'Well, there's another way out. The Producers & Developers Shale and Oil Company have a suite of offices that run into the Rockford Building. They've built an alley to connect between the two buildings. It's on the fifth floor.'

'Is it open? Could a man get out of the Denmark Building now by way of the Rockford entrance?'

'Easiest in the world. All he'd have to do would be to cross the alley bridge, go down the Rockford stairs, and walk into the street.'

Kirby wasted no more time. He knew that the man who had tried to murder him had long since made good his get-away by means of the fifth-story bridge between the buildings.

As he walked back to the hotel where he was stopping his eyes and ears were busy. He took no dark-alley chances, but headed for the bright lights of the main streets where he would be safe from any possibility of a second ambush.

His brain was as busy as his eyes. Who had planned this attempt on his life and so nearly carried it to success? Of one thing he was sure. The assassin who had flung the shots at him down the narrow stairway of the Denmark was the one who had murdered his uncle. The motive for the ambuscade was fear. Kirby was too hot on the trail that might send him to the gallows. The man had decided to play safe by following the old theory that dead men tell no tales.

CHAPTER THIRTY-TWO

JACK TAKES OFF HIS COAT

Afterward, when Kirby Lane looked back upon the weeks spent in Denver trying to clear up the mysteries which surrounded the whole affair of his uncle's death, it seemed to him that he had been at times incredibly stupid. Nowhere did this accent itself so much as in that part of the tangle which related to Esther McLean.

From time to time Kirby saw Cole. He was in and out of town. Most of his time was spent running down faint trails which spun themselves out and became lost in the hills. The champion rough rider was indomitably resolute in his intention of finding her. There were times when Rose began to fear that her little sister was lost to her for always. But Sanborn never shared this feeling.

'You wait. I'll find her,' he promised. 'An' if I can lay my hands on the man that's done her a meanness, I'll certainly give them hospital sharks a job patchin' him up.' His gentle eyes had frozen, and the cold, hard light in them was almost deadly.

Kirby could not get it out of his head that James was responsible for the disappearance of the girl. Yet he could not find a motive that would justify so much trouble on his cousin's part.

He was at a moving-picture house on Curtis Street with Rose when the explanation popped into his mind. They were watching an old-fashioned melodrama in which the villain's letter is laid at the door of the unfortunate hero.

Kirby leaned toward Rose in the darkness and whispered, 'Let's go.'

'Go where?' she wanted to know in surprise. They had seated themselves not five minutes before.

'I've got a hunch. Come.'

She rose, and on the way to the aisle brushed past several irritated ladies. Not till they were standing on the sidewalk outside did he tell her what was on his mind.

'I want to see that note from my uncle you found in your sister's desk,' he said.

She looked at him and laughed a little. 'You certainly want what you want when you want it! Do your hunches often take you like that—right out of a perfectly good show you've paid your money to see?'

'We've made a mistake. It was seein' that fellow in the play that put me wise. Have you got the note with you?'

'No. It's at home. If you like we'll go and get it.'

They walked up to the Pioneers' Monument and from there over to her boarding-place.

Kirby looked the little note over carefully. 'What a chump I was not to look at this before,' he said. 'My uncle never wrote it.'

'Never wrote it?'

'Not his writin' a-tall.'

'Then whose is it?'

'I can make a darn good guess. Can't you?'

She looked at him, eyes dilated, on the verge of a discovery. 'You mean—?'

'I mean that J. C. might stand for at least two other men we know.'

'Your cousin James?'

'More likely Jack.'

His mind beat back to fugitive memories of

211

Jack's embarrassment when Esther's name had been mentioned in connection with his uncle. Swiftly his brain began to piece the bits of evidence he had not understood the meaning of before.

'Jack's the man. You may depend on it. My uncle hadn't anything to do with it. We jumped at that conclusion too quick,' he went on.

'You think that she's . . . with him?'

'No. She's likely out in the country or in some small town. He's havin' her looked after. Probably an attack of conscience. Even if he's selfish as the devil, he isn't heartless.'

'If we could be sure she's all right. But we can't.' Rose turned on him a wistful face, twisted by emotion. 'I want to find her, Kirby. I'm her sister. She's all I've got. Can't you do something?'

'I'll try.'

She noticed the hardening of the lean jaw, the tightening of the muscles as the back teeth clenched.

'Don't—don't do anything—rash,' she begged.

Her hand rested lightly on his arm. Their eyes met. He smiled grimly.

'Don't worry. Mebbe I'll call you up later tonight and report progress.'

He walked to the nearest drug-store and used the telephone freely. At the end of fifteen minutes he stepped out of the booth. His cousin Jack was doing some evening work at

212

the offices where he was now in charge of settling up his uncle's affairs.

Kirby found him there. A man stenographer was putting on his coat to leave, but Jack was still at his desk. He looked up, annoyed.

'Was that you telephoned me?' he asked.

'Yes.'

'I told you I'd let you know when I wanted to see you.'

'So you did. But you didn't let me know. The shoe's on the other foot now. I want to see you.'

'I'm not interested in anything you have to say.'

The stenographer had gone. Kirby could hear his footsteps echoing down the corridor. He threw the catch of the lock and closed the door.

'I can promise to keep you interested,' he said, very quietly.

Jack rose. He wore white shoes, duck trousers, a white piqué shirt, and a blue serge coat that fitted his graceful figure perfectly. 'What did you do that for?' he demanded. 'Open that door!'

'Not just yet, Jack. I've come for a settlement. It's up to you to say what kind of a one it'll be.'

Cunningham's dark eyes glittered. He was no physical coward. Moreover, he was a trained athlete, not long out of college. He had been the middle-weight champion boxer of the university. If this tough brown cousin wanted a set-to, he would not have to ask twice for it.

'Suits me fine,' he said. 'What's your proposition?'

'I've been a blind idiot. Didn't see what was right before my eyes. I reckon you've had some laughs at me. Well, I hope you enjoyed 'em. There aren't any more grins comin' to you.' Kirby spoke coldly, implacably, his voice grating like steel on steel.

'Meaning, in plain English?'

'That you've let a dead man's shoulders carry your sins. You heard us blame Uncle James for Esther McLean's trouble. An' you never said a word to set us right. Yet you're the man, you damned scoundrel!'

Jack went white to the lips, then flushed angrily. 'You can't ever mind your own business, can you?'

'I want just two things from you. The first is, to know where you've taken her; the second, to tell you that you're goin' to make this right an' see that you do it.'

'When you talk to me like that I've nothing to say. No man living can bully me.'

'You won't come through. Is that it?'

'You may go to the devil for all of me.'

Their stormy eyes clashed.

'The girl you took advantage of hasn't any brother,' the Wyoming man said. 'I'm electin' myself to that job for a while. If I can I'm goin' to whale the life outa you.'

214

Jack slipped out of his coat and tossed it on the desk. Even in that moment, while Kirby was concentrating for the attack, the rough rider found time to regret that so good-looking a youth, one so gallantly poised and so gracefully graceless, should be a black-hearted scamp.

'Hop to it!' invited the college man. Under thick dark lashes his black eyes danced with excitement.

Kirby lashed out with his right, hard and straight. His cousin ducked with the easy grace of a man who has spent many hours on a ballroom floor. The cattleman struck again. Jack caught the blow and deflected it, at the same time uppercutting swiftly for the chin. The counter landed flush on Kirby's cheek and flung him back to the wall.

He grinned, and plunged again. A driving left caught him off balance and flung him from his feet. He was up again instantly, shaking his head to clear it of the dizziness that sang there.

It came to him that he must use his brains against this expert boxer or suffer a knockout. He must wear Jack out, let him spend his strength in attack, watch for the chance that was bound to come if he could weather the storm long enough.

Not at all loath, Jack took the offensive. He went to work coolly to put out his foe. He landed three for one, timing and placing his blows carefully to get the maximum effect. A second time Kirby hit the floor.

Jack hoped he would stay down. The clubman was a little out of condition. He was beginning to breathe fast. His cousin had landed hard two or three times on the body. Back of each of these blows there had been a punishing force. Cunningham knew he had to win soon if at all.

But Kirby had not the least intention of quitting. He was the tough product of wind and sun and hard work. He bored in and asked for more, still playing for his opponent's wind. Kirby knew he was the stronger man, in far better condition. He could afford to wait—and Jack could not. He killed the boxer's attacks with deadly counter-blows, moving in and out lithely as a cat.

The rough rider landed close to the solar plexus. Jack winced and gave ground. Kirby's fist got home again. He crowded Jack, feeling that his man was weakening.

Jack rallied for one last desperate set-to, hoping for a chance blow to knock Kirby out. He scored a dozen times. Lane gave ground, slowly, watchfully, guarding as best he could.

Then his brown fist shot out and up. It moved scarcely six inches, straight for the college boxer's chin. Jack's knees sagged. He went down, rolled over, and lay still.

Kirby found water and brought it back. Jack was sitting up, his back propped against the wall. He swallowed a gulp or two and splashed the rest on his face.

'I'll say you can hit like the kick of a mule,' he said. 'If you'd been a reasonable human, I ought to have got you, at that. Don't you ever stay down?'

Kirby could not repress a little smile. In spite of himself he felt a sneaking admiration for this insouciant youth who could take a beating like a sportsman.

'You're some little mixer yourself,' he said.

'Thought I was, before I bumped into you. Say, gimme a hand up. I'm a bit groggy yet.'

Kirby helped him to his feet. The immaculate shirt and trousers were spattered with blood, mostly Kirby's. The young dandy looked at himself, and a humorous quirk twitched at the corner of his mouth.

'Some scrap. Let's go into the lavatory and do some reconstruction work,' he said.

Side by side at adjoining washbowls, perfectly amicably, they repaired as far as possible the damages of war. Not till they had put on again their coats did Kirby hark back to the purpose of the meeting.

'You haven't told me yet what I want to know.'

Out of a damaged eye Jack looked at him evenly. 'And that's only part of it. I'm not going to, either.'

He had said the last word. Kirby could not begin all over again to thrash him. It was not reasonable. And if he did, he knew quite well he would get nothing out of the man. If he would not talk, he would not.

The bronco buster walked back to his hotel. A special-delivery letter was in his box. It was postmarked Golden. As he handed it to him the clerk looked him over curiously. It had been some time since he had seen a face so badly cut up and swollen.

'You ought to see the other fellow,' Kirby told him with a lopsided grin as he ripped open the envelope.

Before his eyes had traveled halfway down the sheet the cowman gave a modulated whoop of joy.

'Good news?' asked the clerk.

Kirby did not answer. His eyes were staring in blank astonishment at one sentence in the letter. The note was from Cole Sanborn. This is what Kirby read in it:

Well, old-timer, there aint no trail so blamed long but what its got a turn in it somewheres. I done found Esther up Platte Cañon and everything's OK as you might say. I reckon you are wondering howcome this to be postmarked Golden. Well, old pardner, Im sure enough married at last but I had a great time getting Esther to see this my way. Shes one swell little girl and theres only one thing I hate. Before she would marry me I had to swear up and down I wouldnt touch the yellow wolf who got her into trouble. But she didnt say nothing about you so I will just slip you his name. It wasnt your uncle at all but that crooked oil broker nephew of his James Cunningham. If you can muss him up proper for me youll sure be doing a favor to

yours respectably
COLE SANBORN

P.S. Esther sends bushels of love to Rose and will write tomorrow. I'll say Im going to make her one happy kid.

COLE

Kirby laughed in sardonic mirth. He had fought the wrong man.

It was James Cunningham, not Jack. And, of course, Jack had known it all the time and been embarrassed by it. He had stuck loyally to his brother and had taken the whaling of his life rather than betray him.

Kirby took off his hat to Jack. He had stood pat to a fighting finish. He was one good square sport.

Even as he was thinking this, Kirby was moving toward the telephone booth. He had promised to report progress. For once he had considerable to report.

CHAPTER THIRTY-THREE

OLSON TELLS A STORY

When Rose heard from Esther next day she and Kirby took the Interurban for Golden. Esther had written that she wanted to see her sister because Cole was going to take her back to Wyoming at once.

The sisters wept in each other's arms and then passed together into Esther's bedroom for an intimate talk. The younger sister was still happy only in moments of forgetfulness, though she had been rescued from death in life. Cole had found her comfortably situated at a farmhouse a mile or two back from the cañon. She had gone there under the urge of her need, at the instigation of James Cunningham, who could not afford to have the scandal of his relations with her become public at the same time as the announcement of his marriage to Phyllis Harriman. The girl loved Cole and trusted him. Her heart went out to him in a warm glow of gratitude. But the shadow of her fault was a barrier in her mind between them, and would be long after his kindness had melted the ice in her bosom.

'We've got it all fixed up to tell how we was married when I come down to Denver last April only we kep' it quiet because she wanted to hold her job awhile,' Cole explained to his friend. 'Onct I get her back there in God's hills she'll sure enough forget all about this trouble. The way I look at it she was jus' like a li'l' kid that takes a mis-step in the dark an' falls an' hurts itself. You know how a wounded deer can look at a fellow so sorrowful an' hurt. Well, tha's how her brown eyes looked at me when I come round the corner o' the house up Platte Cañon an' seen her sittin' there starin' at hell.'

Kirby shook hands with him in a sudden stress of emotion. 'You'll do to take along, old alkali, you sure enough will.'

'Oh, shucks!' retorted Cole, between disgust and embarrassment. 'I always claimed to be a white man, didn't I? You can't give a fellow credit for doin' the thing he'd rather do than anything else. But prod a peg in this. I'm gonna make that girl plumb happy. She thinks she won't be, that she's lost the right to be. She's 'way off. I can see her perkin' up already. I got a real honest-to-God laugh outa her this mo'nin'.'

Kirby knew the patience, the steadiness. and the kindliness of his friend. Esther had fallen into the best of hands. She would find again the joy of life. He had no doubt of that. Gayety and laughter were of her heritage.

He said as much to Rose on the way home. She agreed. For the first time since she left Cheyenne the girl was her old self. Esther's problem had been solved far more happily than she had dared to hope.

'I'm goin' to have a gay time apologizin' to Jack,' said Kirby, his eyes dancing. 'It's not so blamed funny at that, but I can't help laughin' every time I think of how he must 'a' been grinnin' up his sleeve at me for my fool mistake. I'll say he brought it on himself, though. He was feelin' guilty on his brother's account, an' I didn't get his embarrassment right. James is a pretty cool customer. From first to last he never turned a hair when the subject was mentioned.'

'What about him?' Rose asked.

The cattleman pretended alarm. 'Now, don't you,' he remonstrated. 'Don't you expect me to manhandle James, too. 'I'm like Napoleon. Another victory like the battle of last night would sure put me in the hospital. I'm a peaceable citizen, a poor, lone cowboy far away from home. Where I come from it's as quiet as a peace conference. This wildest-Denver stuff gets my nerve.'

She smiled into his battered face. A dimple nestled in her soft, warm cheek. 'I see it does. It's a pity about you. I didn't suppose your cousin Jack had it in him to spoil your beauty like that.'

'Neither did I,' he said, answering her smile. 'I sure picked on the wrong man. He's one handy lad with his dibs—put me down twice before we decided to call it off. I like that young fellow.'

'Better not like him too much. You may have to work against him yet.'

'True enough,' he admitted, falling grave again. 'As to James, we'll ride close herd on him for a while, but we'll ride wide. Looks to me like he may have to face a jury an' fight for his life right soon.'

'Do you think he killed your uncle?'

'I don't want to think so. He's a bad egg, I'm afraid. But my father's sister was his mother. I'd hate to have to believe it.'

'But in your heart you do believe it,' she said gently.

He looked at her. 'I'm afraid so. But that's a long way from knowing it.'

They parted at her boarding-house.

A man rose to meet Kirby when he stepped into the rotunda of his hotel. He was a gaunt, broad-shouldered man with ragged eyebrows.

'Well, I came,' he said, and his voice was harsh.

'Glad to see you, Mr. Olson. Come up to my room. We can talk there more freely.'

The Scandinavian rancher followed him to the elevator and from there to his room.

'Why don't they arrest Hull?' he demanded as soon as the door was closed.

'Not evidence enough.'

'Suppose I can give evidence. Say I practically saw Hull do it. Would they arrest him—or me?'

223

'They'd arrest him,' Kirby answered. 'They don't know you're the man who wrote the threatening letter.'

'Hmp!' grunted the rancher suspiciously. 'That's what you say, but you're not the whole works.'

Kirby offered a chair and a cigar. He sat down on the bed himself. 'Better spill your story to me, Olson. Two heads are better than one,' he said carelessly.

The Swede's sullen eyes bored into him. Before that frank and engaging smile his doubts lost force. 'I got to take a chance. Might as well be with you as any one.'

The Wyoming man struck a match, held it for the use of his guest, then lit his own cigar. For a few moments they smoked in silence. Kirby leaned back easily against the head of the bed. He did not intend to frighten the rancher by hurrying him.

'When Cunningham worked that crooked irrigation scheme of his on Dry Valley, I reckon I was one of them that hollered the loudest. Prob'ly I talked foolish about what all I was gonna do about it. I wasn't blowin' off hot air either. If I'd got a good chance at him, or at Hull either, I would surely have called for a showdown an' gunned him if I could. But that wasn't what I came to Denver for. I had to arrange about gettin' my mortgage renewed.'

He stopped and took a nervous puff or two at the cigar. Kirby nodded in a friendly fashion without speaking. He did not want by anything he might say to divert the man's mind from the track it was following.

'I took a room at the Wyndham because the place had been recommended to me by a neighbor of mine who knew the landlady. When I went there I didn't know that either Cunningham or Hull lived next door. That's a God's truth. I didn't. Well, I saw Hull go in there the very day I got to town, but the first I knew yore uncle lived there was ten or maybe fifteen minutes before he was killed. I wouldn't say but what it was twenty minutes, come to that. I wasn't payin' no attention to time.'

Olson's eyes challenged those of his host. His suspicion was still smoldering. An unhappy remark, a look of distrust, might still have dried up the stream of his story. But he found in that steady regard nothing more damnatory than a keen, boyish interest.

'Maybe you recollect how hot those days were. Well, in my cheap, stuffy room, openin' on an airshaft, it was hotter 'n hell with the lid on. When I couldn't stand it any longer, I went out into the corridor an' down it to the fire escape outside the window. It was a lot cooler there. I lit a stogie an' sat on the railin' smokin', maybe for a quarter of an hour. By-an'-by some one come into the apartment right acrost the alley from me. I could see the lights come on. It was a man. I saw him step into

225

what must be the bedroom. He moved around there some. I couldn't tell what he was doin' because he didn't switch on the light, but he must 'a' been changin' to his easy coat an' his slippers. I know that because he came into the room just opposite the fire escape where I was sittin' on the rail. He threw on the lights, an' I saw him plain. It was Cunningham, the old crook who had beat me outa fifteen hundred dollars.'

Kirby smoked steadily, evenly. Not a flicker of the eyelids showed the excitement racing through his blood. At last he was coming close to the heart of the mystery that surrounded the deaths of his uncle and his valet.

'I reckon I saw red for a minute,' Olson continued. 'If I'd been carryin' a gun I might 'a' used it right there an' then. But I hadn't one, lucky for me. He sat down in a big easy-chair an' took a paper from his pocket. It looked like some kind of a legal document. He read it through, then stuck it in one o' the cubby-holes of his desk. I forgot to say he was smokin', an' not a stogie like I was, but a big cigar he'd unwrapped from silver paper after takin' it from a boxful.'

'He lighted the cigar after coming into the small room,' Kirby said, in the voice of a question.

'Yes. Didn't I say so? Took it from a box on a stand near the chair. Well, when he got through with the paper he leaned back an' kinda shut his eyes like he was thinkin' somethin' over. All of a sudden I saw him straighten up an' get rigid. Before he could rise from the chair a woman came into the room an' after her a man.

'The man was Cass Hull.'

CHAPTER THIRTY-FOUR

FROM THE FIRE ESCAPE

'The woman—what was she like?'

'She was tall an' thin an' flat-chested. I didn't know her at the time, but it must 'a' been Hull's wife.'

'You said you didn't know what time this was,' Kirby said.

'No. My old watch had quit doin' business an' I hated to spend the money to get it fixed. The main-spring was busted, a jeweler told me.'

'Who spoke first after they came into the room?'

'Yore uncle. He laid the cigar down on the stand an' asked them what they wanted. He didn't rise from the chair, but his voice rasped when he spoke. It was the woman answered. She took the lead all through. 'We've come for a settlement,' she said. 'An' we're goin' to have it right now.' He stiffened up at that. He come back at her with, 'You can't get no shot-gun settlement outa me.' Words just poured from that woman's mouth. She roasted him to a turn, told how he was crooked as a dog's hind leg an' every deal he touched was dirty. Said he couldn't even be square to his own pardners, that he couldn't get a man, woman, or child in Colorado to say he'd ever done a good act. Believe me, she laid him out proper, an' every word of it was true, 'far as I know.

'Well, sir, that old reprobate uncle of yours never batted an eye. He slid down in his chair a little so's he could he comfortable while he listened. He grinned up at her like she was some kind of specimen had broke loose from a circus an' he was interested in the way it acted. That didn't calm her down none. She rip-r'ared right along, with a steady flow of words, mostly adjectives. Finally she quit, an' she was plumb white with anger. 'Quite through?' yore uncle asked with that ice-cold voice of his. She asked him what he intended to do about a settlement. 'Not a thing,' he told her. 'I did aim to give Hull two thousand to get rid of him. But I've changed my mind, ma'am. You can go whistle for it.'

'Two thousand! Did he say two thousand?'

Kirby leaned forward eagerly.

'That's what he said. Two thousand,' answered Olson.

'Then that explains why he drew so much from the bank that day.'

'I had it figured out so. If the woman hadn't come at him with that acid tongue of hers he'd intended to buy Hull off cheap. But she got his gorge up. He wouldn't stand for her line of talk.'

'What took place then?' the cattleman questioned.

'Still without rising from the chair, Cunningham ordered them to get out. Hull was standin' kinda close to him. He had his back to me. Cunningham reached out an' opened a drawer of the stand beside him. The fat man took a step forward. I could see his gun flash in the light. He swung it down on yore uncle's head an' the old man crumpled up.'

'So it was Hull killed him, after all,' Kirby said, drawing a long breath of relief.

Then, to his surprise when he thought about it later, a glitter of malicious cunning lit the eyes of the rancher.

'That's what I'm tellin' you. It was Hull. I stood there an' saw just what I've been givin' you.'

'Was my uncle senseless then?'

'You bet he was. His head sagged clear over against the back of the chair.'

'What did they do then?'

'That's where I drop out. Mrs. Hull stepped straight to the window. I crouched down back of the railin . It was dark an' she didn't see me. She pulled the blind down. I waited there awhile an' afterward there was the sound of a shot. That would be when they sent the bullet through the old man's brain.'

'What did you do?'

'I didn't know what to do. I'd talked a lot of wild talk about how Cunningham ought to be shot or strung up to a pole. If I went to the police with my story, like enough they'd light on me as the killer. I milled the whole thing over. After a while I went into a public booth downtown an' phoned to the police. You recollect maybe the papers spoke about the man who called up headquarters with the news of Cunningham's death.'

'Yes, I recollect that all right.'

Kirby did not smile. He did not explain that he was the man. But he resolved to find out whether two men had notified the police of his uncle's death. If not, Olson was lying in at least one detail. He had a suspicion that the man had not given him the whole truth. He was telling part of it, but he was holding back something. A sly and furtive look in his eyes helped to build this impression in the mind of the man who listened to the story.

'You didn't actually see Hull fire the shot that killed my uncle, then?'

Olson hesitated, a fraction of a second. 'No.'

'You don't know that it was he that fired it.'

'No, it might 'a' been the woman. But it ain't likely he handed her the gun to do it with, is it? For that matter I don't know that the

230

crack over the head didn't kill Cunningham. Maybe it did.'

'That's all you saw?'

Again the almost imperceptible hesitation. Then, 'That's all,' the Dry Valley rancher said sullenly.

'What kind of a gun was it?' Kirby asked.

'Too far away. Couldn't be sure.'

'Big as a .45?'

'Couldn't 'a' been. The evidence was that it was done with an automatic.'

'The evidence was that the wound in the head was probably made by a bullet from an automatic. We're talkin' now about the blow *on* the head.'

'What are you drivin' at?' the rancher asked, scowling. 'He wouldn't bring two different kinds of guns with him. That's a cinch.'

'No; but we haven't proved yet he fired the shot you heard later. The chances are all that he did, but legally we have no evidence that somebody else didn't do it.'

'I guess a jury would be satisfied he fired it all right.'

'Probably. It looks bad for Hull. Don't you think you ought to go to the police with your story? Then we can have Hull arrested. They'll give him the third degree. My opinion is he'll break down under it and confess.'

Olson consented with obvious reluctance, but he made a condition precedent to his acceptance. 'Le's see Hull first, just you 'n' me.

I ain't strong for the police. We'll go to them when we've got an open an' shut case.'

Kirby considered. This story didn't wholly fit the facts as he knew them. For instance, there was no explanation in it of how the room where Cunningham was found murdered had become saturated with the odor of chloroform. Nor was it in character that Hull should risk firing a gun, the sound of which might bring detection on him, while his victim lay helpless before him. Another blow or two on the skull would have served his purpose noiselessly. The cattleman knew from his observation of this case that the authorities had a way of muddling things. Perhaps it would be better to wait until the difficulties had been smoothed out before going to them.

'That suits me,' he said. 'We'll tackle Hull when his wife isn't with him. He goes downtown every day about ten o'clock. We'll pick him up in a taxi, run him out into the country somewhere, an' put him over the jumps. The sooner the quicker. How about tomorrow morning?'

'Suits me, too. But will he go with us?'

'He'll go with us,' Kirby said quietly.

CHAPTER THIRTY-FIVE

LIKE A THIEF IN THE NIGHT

From ten thousand bulbs the moving-picture houses of Curtis Street were flinging a glow upon the packed sidewalks when Kirby came out of the hotel and started uptown.

He walked to the Wyndham, entered, and slipped up the stairs of the rooming-house unnoticed. From the third story he ascended by a ladder to the flat roof. He knew exactly what he had come to investigate. From one of the windows of the fourth floor at the Paradox he had noticed the clothes-line which stretched across the Wyndham roof from one corner to another. He went straight to one of the posts which supported the rope. He made a careful study of this, then walked to the other upright support and examined the knots which held the line fast here.

'I'm some good little guesser,' he murmured to himself as he turned back to the ladder and descended to the floor below.

He moved quietly along the corridor to the fire escape and stepped out upon it. Then, very quickly and expertly, he coiled a rope which he took from a paper parcel that had been under his arm. At one end of the coil was a loop. He swung this lightly round his head once or twice to feel the weight of it. The rope snaked forward and up. Its loop dropped upon the stone abutment he had noticed when he had been examining the exteriors of the buildings with Cole Sanborn. It tightened when he gave a jerk.

Kirby climbed over the railing and swung himself lightly out into space. A moment, and he was swaying beside the fire escape of the Paradox. He caught the iron rail and pulled himself to the platform.

By chance the blind was down. There was no light within, but after his eyes had become used to the darkness he tried to take a squint at the room from the sides of the blind. The shade hung an inch or two from the window frame, so that by holding his eye close he could get more than a glimpse of the interior.

He tapped gently on the glass. The lights inside flashed on. From one viewpoint he could see almost half the room. He could go to the other side of the blind and see most of the other half.

A man sat down in a chair close to the opposite wall, letting his hands fall on the arms. A girl stood in front of him and pointed a paper-knife at his head, holding it as though it were a revolver. The head of the man fell sideways.

Kirby tapped on the window pane again. He edged up the sash and stepped into the room.

The young woman turned to him eagerly, a

234

warm glow in her shell-pink cheeks. 'Well?' she inquired.

'Worked out fine, Rose,' Kirby said. 'I could see the whole thing.'

'Still, that don't prove anything,' the other man put in. He belonged to the staff of the private detective agency with which Kirby was dealing.

The Wyoming man smiled. 'It proves my theory is possible. Knowing Olson, I'm willin' to gamble he didn't sit still on the fire escape an' let that drawn blind shut him off from what was goin' on inside. He was one mighty interested observer. Now he must 'a' known there was a clothes-line on the roof. From the street you can see a washin' hangin' out there any old time. In his place I'd 'a' hopped up to the roof an' got that line. Which is exactly what he did, I'll bet. The line had been tied to the posts with a lot of knots. He hadn't time to untie it. So he cut the rope. It's been spliced out since by a piece of rope of a different kind.'

'How do you know that's been done since?' the detective asked.

'A fair question,' Kirby nodded. 'I don't. I'll find out about that when I talk with the landlady of the Wyndham. If I'm right you can bet that cut rope has puzzled her some. She can't figure out why any one would cut her rope down an' then leave it there.'

'If you can show me her rope was cut that

235

night, I'll say you're right,' the detective admitted. 'And if you are right, then the Swede must 'a' been right here when your uncle was killed.'

'*May* have been,' Kirby corrected. 'We haven't any authentic evidence yet as to exactly when my uncle was killed. We're gettin' the time narrowed down. It was between 9:30 and 9:50. We know that.'

'How do you know that?' the professional sleuth asked. 'Accordin' to your story you didn't get into the apartment until after ten o'clock. It might 'a' been done any time up till then.'

The eyes of Kirby and Rose met. They had private information about who was in the rooms from about 9:55 till 10:10.

The cattleman corrected his statement. 'All right, say between 9:30 and 10:05. During that time Hull may have shot my uncle. Or Olson may have opened the window while my uncle lay there helpless, killed him, stepped outa the window again, an' slipped down by the fire escape. All he'd have to do then would be to walk into the Wyndham, replace the rope on the roof, an' next mornin' leave for Dry Valley.'

The detective nodded. '*If* he cut the rope. Lemme find out from the landlady whether it *was* cut that night.'

'Good. We'll wait for you at the corner.'

Ten minutes later the detective joined them

in front of the drug-store where they were standing. The hard eyes in his cold gambler's face were lit up for once.

'I'll say the man from Missouri has been shown,' he said. 'I let on to the dame at the Wyndham that I was after a gang of young sneak thieves in the neighborhood. Pretty soon I drifted her to the night of the twenty-third—said they'd been especially active that night and had used a rope to get into a second story of a building. She woke up. Her clothes-line on the roof had been cut that very night. She remembered the night on account of its being the one when Mr. Cunningham was killed. Could the boys have used it to get into the store an' then brought it back? I thought likely.'

'Bully! We're one step nearer than we were. We know Olson was lookin' in the window from the fire escape just outside.'

The detective slapped his thigh. 'It lies between Hull and the Swede. That's a cinch.'

'I believe it does,' agreed Rose.

Kirby made no comment. He seemed to be absorbed in speculations of his own. The detective was reasoning from a very partial knowledge of the facts. He knew nothing about the relations of James Cunningham to his uncle, nor even that the younger Cunninghams—or at least one of them—had been in his uncle's apartment the evening of his death. He did not know that Rose had been

237

there. Wherefore his deductions, even though they had the benefit of being trained ones, were of slight value in this case.

'Will you take the key back to the Chief of Police?' Kirby asked him as they separated. 'Better not tell him who was with you or what we were doin'.'

'I'm liable to tell him a whole lot,' the detective answered with heavy irony. 'I'm figurin' on runnin' down this murderer myself if any one asks you.'

'Wish you luck,' Kirby said with perfect gravity.

CHAPTER THIRTY-SIX

A RIDE IN A TAXI

Kirby was quite right when he said that Hull would go with them. He was on his way downtown when the taxi caught him at Fourteenth and Welton. The cattleman jumped out from the machine and touched the fat man on the arm as he was waddling past.

'We want you, Hull,' he said.

A shadow of fear flitted over the shallow eyes of the land agent, but he attempted at once to bluster. 'Who wants me? Whadjawant me for?'

'I want you—in that cab. The man who saw

you in my uncle's room the night he was killed is with me. You can either come with us now an' talk this thing over quietly or I'll hang on to you an' call for a policeman. It's up to you. Either way is agreeable to me.'

Beads of perspiration broke out on the fat man's forehead. He dragged from his left hip pocket the familiar bandanna handkerchief. With it he dabbed softly at his mottled face. There was a faint, a very faint, note of defiance in his voice as he answered.

'I dunno as I've got any call to go with you. I wasn't in Cunningham's rooms. You can't touch me—can't prove a thing on me.'

'It won't cost you anything to make sure of that,' Kirby suggested in his low, even tones. 'I'm payin' for the ride.'

'If you got anything to say to me, right here's a good place to onload it.'

The man's will was wobbling. The cattleman could see that.

'Can't talk here, with a hundred people passin'. What's the matter, man? What are you afraid of? *We're not goin' to hit you over the head with the butt of a six-shooter.*'

Hull flung at him a look of startled terror. What did he mean? Or was there anything significant in the last sentence? Was it just a shot in the dark?

'I'll go on back to the Paradox. If you want to see me, why, there's as good a place as any.'

'We're choosin' the place, Hull, not you.

239

You'll either step into that cab or into a patrol wagon.'

Their eyes met and fought. The shallow, protuberant ones wavered. 'Oh, well, it ain't worth chewin' the rag over. I reckon I'll go with you.'

He stepped into the cab. At sight of Olson he showed both dismay and surprise. He had heard of the threats the Dry Valley man had been making. Was he starting on a journey the end of which would be summary vengeance? A glance at Lane's face reassured him. This young fellow would be no accomplice at murder. Yet the chill at his heart told him he was in for serious trouble.

He tried to placate Olson with a smile and made a motion to offer his hand. The Scandinavian glared at him.

The taxicab swung down Fourteenth, across the viaduct to Lake Place, and from it to Federal Boulevard.

Hull moistened his lips with his tongue and broke the silence. 'Where we goin'?' he asked at last.

'Where we can talk without bein' overheard,' Kirby answered.

The cab ran up the steep slope to Inspiration Point and stopped there. The men got out.

'Come back for us in half an hour,' the cattleman told the driver.

In front and below them lay the beautiful

valley of Clear Creek. Beyond it were the foothills, and back of them the line of the Front Range stretching from Pike's Peak at the south up to the Wyoming line. Grey's and Long's and Mount Evans stood out like giant sentinels in the clear sunshine.

Hull looked across the valley nervously and brought his eyes back with a jerk. 'Well, what's it all about? Whadjawant?'

'I know now why you lied at the inquest about the time you saw me on the night my uncle was killed.' Kirby told him.

'I didn't lie. Maybe I was mistaken. Any man's liable to make a mistake.'

'You didn't make a mistake. You deliberately twisted your story so as to get me into my uncle's apartment forty minutes or so earlier than I was. Your reason was a good one. If I was in his rooms at the time he was shot, that let you out completely. So you tried to lie me into the death cell at Cañon City.'

Hull's bandana was busy. 'Nothin' like that. I wouldn't play no such a trick on any man. No, sir.'

'You wouldn't, but you did. Don't stall, Hull. We've got you right.'

The rancher from Dry Valley broke in venomously. 'You bet we have, you rotten crook. I'll pay you back proper for that deal you an' Cunningham slipped over on me. I'm gonna put a rope around yore neck for it. I sure am. Why, you big fat stiff, I was standin' watchin' you when you knocked out Cunningham with the butt of yore gun.'

From Hull's red face the color fled. He teetered for a moment on the balls of his feet, then sank limply to the cement bench in front of him. He tried to gasp out a denial, but the words would not come. In his throat there was only a dry rattle.

He heard, as from a long distance, Lane's voice addressing him.

'We've got it on you, Hull. Come through an' come clean.'

'I-I-I swear to God I didn't do it—didn't kill him,' he gasped at last.

'Then who did—yore wife?' demanded Olson.

'Neither of us. I—I'll tell you—all the whole story.'

'Do you know who did kill him?' Kirby persisted.

'I come pretty near knowin', but I didn't see it done.'

'Who, then?'

'Yore cousin—James Cunningham.'

CHAPTER THIRTY-SEVEN

ON THE GRILL

In spite of the fact that his mind had at times moved toward his cousin James as the murderer, Kirby experienced a shock at this accusation. He happened to glance at Olson, perhaps to see the effect of it upon him.

The effect was slight, but it startled Kirby. For just an instant the Dry Valley farmer's eyes told the truth—shouted it as plainly as words could have done. He had expected that answer from Hull. He had expected it because he, too, had reason to believe it the truth. Then the lids narrowed, and the man's lip lifted in a sneer of rejection. He was covering up.

'Pretty near up to you to find someone else to pass the buck to, ain't it?' he taunted.

'Suppose you tell us the whole story, Hull,' the Wyoming man said.

The fat man had one last flare of resistance. 'Olson here says he seen me crack Cunningham with the butt of my gun. How did he see me? Where does he claim he was when he seen it?'

'I was standin' on the fire escape of the Wyndham across the alley—about ten or fifteen feet away. I heard every word that was said by Cunningham an' yore wife. Oh, I've got you good.'

Hull threw up the sponge. He was caught and realized it. His only chance now was to make a clean breast of what he knew.

'Where shall I begin?' he asked weakly, his voice quavering.

'At the beginning. We've got plenty of time,' Kirby replied.

'Well, you know how yore uncle beat me in that Dry Valley scheme of his. First place, I didn't know he couldn't get water enough. If he give the farmers a crooked deal, I hadn't a thing to do with that. When I talked up the idea to them I was actin' in good faith.'

'Lie number one,' interrupted Olson bitterly.

'Hadn't we better let him tell his story in his own way?' Kirby suggested. 'If we don't start any arguments he ain't so liable to get mixed up in his facts.'

'By my way of figurin' he owed me about four to six thousand dollars he wouldn't pay,' Hull went on. 'I tried to get him to see it right, thinkin' at first he was just bull-headed. But pretty soon I got wise to it that he plain intended to do me. O' course I wasn't going to stand for that, an' I told him so.'

'What do you mean when you say you weren't goin' to stand for it. My uncle told a witness that you said you'd give him two days, then you'd come at him with a gun.'

The fat man mopped a perspiring face with

his bandanna. His eyes dodged. 'Maybe I told him so. I don't recollect. When he's sore a fellow talks a heap o' foolishness. I wasn't lookin' for trouble, though.'

'Not even after he threw you downstairs?'

'No, sir. He didn't exactly throw me down. I kinda slipped. If I'd been expectin' trouble would I have let Mrs. Hull go up to his rooms with me?'

Kirby had his own view on that point, but he did not express it. He rather thought that Mrs. Hull had driven her husband upstairs and had gone along to see that he stood to his guns. Once in the presence of Cunningham, she had taken the bit in her own teeth, driven to it by temper. This was his guess. He knew he might be wrong.

'But I knew how violent he was,' the fat man went on. 'So I slipped my six-gun into my pocket before we started.'

'What kind of a gun?' Kirby asked.

'A sawed-off .38.'

'Do you own an automatic?'

'No, sir. Wouldn't know how to work one. Never had one in my hands.'

'You'll get a chance to prove that,' Olson jeered.

'He doesn't have to prove it. His statement is assumed to be true until it is proved false,' Kirby answered.

Hull's eyes signaled gratitude. He was where he needed a friend badly. He would be

245

willing to pay almost any price for Lane's help.

'Cunningham had left the door open, I reckon because it was hot. I started to push the bell, but Mrs. Hull she walked right in an' of course then I followed. He wasn't in the sittin'-room, but we seen him smokin' in the small room off'n the parlor. So we just went in on him.

'He acted mean right from the start-hollered at Mrs. Hull what was we doin' there. She up an' told him, real civil, that we wanted to talk the business over an' see if we couldn't come to some agreement about it. He kep' right on insultin' her, an' one thing led to another. Mrs. Hull she didn't get mad, but she told him where he'd have to head in at. Fact is, we'd about made up our minds to sue him. Well, he went clean off the handle then, an' said he wouldn't do a thing for us, an' how we was to get right out.'

Hull paused to wipe the small sweat beads from his forehead. He was not enjoying himself. A cold terror constricted his heart. Was he slipping a noose over his own head? Was he telling more than he should? He wished his wife were here to give him a hint. She had the brains as well as the courage and audacity of the family.

'Well, sir, I claim self-defense,' Hull went on presently. 'A man's got no call to stand by an' see his wife shot down. Cunningham reached for a drawer an' started to pull out an

246

automatic gun. Knowin' him, I was scared. I beat him to it an' lammed him one over the head with my gun. My idea was to head him off from drawin' on Mrs. Hull, but I reckon I hit him harder than I'd aimed to. It knocked him senseless.'

'And then?' Kirby said, when he paused.

'I was struck all of a heap, but Mrs. Hull she didn't lose her presence of mind. She went to the window an' pulled down the curtain. Then we figured, seein' as how we'd got in bad so far, we might as well try a bluff. We tied yore uncle to the chair, intendin' for to make him sign a check before we turned him loose. Right at that time the telephone rang.'

'Did you answer the call?'

'Yes, sir. It kept ringing. Finally the wife said to answer it, pretendin' I was Cunningham. We was kinda scared some one might butt in on us. Yore uncle had said he was expectin' some folks.'

'What did you do?'

'I took up the receiver an' listened. Then I said, "Hello!" Fellow at the other end said, "This you, Uncle James?" Kinda grufflike, I said, "Yes." Then, "James talkin'," he said. "We're on our way over now." I was struck all of a heap, not knowin' what to say. So I called back, "Who?" He came back with, "Phyllis an' I." I hung up.'

'And then?'

'We talked it over, the wife an' me. We

247

didn't know how close James, as he called himself, was when he was talkin'. He might be at the drug-store on the next corner for all we knew. We were in one hell of a hole, an' it didn't look like there was any way out. We decided to beat it right then. That's what we did.'

'You left the apartment?'

'Yes, sir.'

'With my uncle still tied up?'

Hull nodded. 'We got panicky an' cut our stick.'

'Did anybody see you go?'

'The Jap janitor was in the hall fixin' one of the windows that was stuck.'

'Did he say anything?'

'Not then.'

'Afterward?'

'He come to me after the murder was discovered—next day, I reckon it was, in the afternoon, just before the inquest and said could I lend him five hundred dollars. Well, I knew right away it was a hold-up, but I couldn't do a thing. I dug up the money an' let him have it.'

'Has he bothered you since?'

Hull hesitated. 'Well—no.'

'Meanin' that he has?'

Hull flew the usual flag of distress, a red bandana mopping a perspiring, apoplectic face. 'He kinda hinted he wanted more money.'

'Did you give it to him?'

'I didn't have it right handy. I stalled.'

'That's the trouble with a blackmailer. Give way to him once an' he's got you in his power,' Kirby said. 'The thing to do is to tell him right off the reel to go to Halifax.'

'If a fellow can afford to,' Olson put in significantly. 'When you've just got through a little private murder of yore own, you ain't exactly free to tell one of the witnesses against you to go very far.'

'Tell you I didn't kill Cunningham,' Hull retorted sullenly. 'Some one else must 'a' come in an' did that after I left.'

'Sounds reasonable,' Olson murmured with heavy sarcasm.

'Was the hall lit when you came out of my uncle's rooms?' Kirby asked suddenly.

'Yes. I told you Shibo was workin' at one of the windows.'

'So Shibo saw you and Mrs. Hull plainly?'

'I ain't denyin' he saw us,' Hull replied testily.

'No, you don't deny anything we can prove on you,' the Dry Valley man jeered.

'And Shibo didn't let up on you. He kept annoyin' you afterward,' the cattleman persisted.

'Well, he—I reckon he aims to be reasonable now,' Hull said uneasily.

'Why now? What's changed his views?'

The fat man looked again at this brown-faced youngster with the single-track mind who never quit till he got what he wanted. Why was he shaking the bones of Shibo's blackmailing. Did he know more than he had told? It was on the tip of Hull's tongue to tell something more, a damnatory fact against himself. But he stopped in time. He was in deep enough water already. He could not afford to tell the dynamic cattleman anything that would make an enemy of him.

'Well. I reckon he can't get blood from a turnip, as the old sayin' is,' the land agent returned.

Kirby knew that Hull was concealing something material, but he saw he could not at the present moment wring it from him. He had not, in point of fact, the faintest idea of what it was. Therefore he could not lay hold of any lever with which to pry it loose. He harked back to another point.

'Do you know that my cousin and Miss Harriman came to see my uncle that night? I mean do you know of your own eyesight that they ever reached his apartment?'

'Well, we know they reached the Paradox an' went up in the elevator. Me an' the wife watched at the window. Yore cousin James wasn't with Miss Harriman. The dude one was with her.'

'Jack!' exclaimed Kirby, astonished.

'Yep.'

'How do you know? How did you recognize

them?'

'Saw 'em as they passed under the street light about twenty feet from our window. We couldn't 'a' been mistook as to the dude fellow. O' course we don't know Miss Harriman, but the woman walkin' beside the young fellow surely looked like the one that fainted at the inquest when you was testifyin' how you found yore uncle dead in the chair. I reckon when you said it she got to seein' a picture of one of the young fellows gunnin' their uncle.'

'One of them. You just said James wasn't with her.'

'No, he come first. Maybe three-four minutes before the others.'

'What time did he reach the Paradox?'

'It might 'a' been ten or maybe only five minutes after we left yore uncle's room. The wife an' me was talkin' it over whether I hadn't ought to slip back upstairs and untie yore uncle before they got here. Then he come an' that settled it. I couldn't go.'

'Can you give me the exact time he reached the apartment house?'

'Well, I'll say it was a quarter to ten.'

'Do you know or are you guessin'?'

'I know. Our clock struck the quarter to whilst we looked at them comin' down the street.'

'At them or at him?'

'At him, I mean.'

251

'Can't stick to his own story,' Olson grunted.

'A slip of the tongue. I meant him.'

'And Jack and the lady were three or four minutes behind him?' Kirby reiterated.

'Yes.'

'Was your clock exactly right?'

'May be five minutes fast. It gains.'

'You know they turned in at the Paradox?'

'All three of 'em. Mrs. Hull she opened the door a mite an' saw 'em go up in the elevator. It moves kinda slow, you know. The heavy-set young fellow went up first. Then two-three minutes later the elevator went down an' the dude an' the young lady went up.'

Kirby put his foot on the cement bench and rested his forearm on his knee. The cattleman's steady eyes were level with those of the unhappy man making the confession.

'Did you at any time hear the sound of a shot?'

'Well, I-I heard somethin'. At the time I thought maybe it was a tire in the street blowin' out But come to think of it later we figured it was a shot.'

'You don't know for sure.'

'Well, come to that I—I don't reckon I do. Not to say for certain sure.'

A tense litheness had passed into the rough rider's figure. It was as though every sense were alert to catch and register impressions.

'At what time was it you thought you heard this shot?'

252

'I dunno, to the minute.'

'Was it before James Cunningham went up in the elevator? Was it between the time he went up an' the other two went up? Or was it after Jack Cunningham an' Miss Harriman passed on the way up?'

'Seems to me it was—'

'Hold on.' Kirby raised a hand in protest. 'I don't want any guesses. You know or you don't. Which is it?'

'I reckon it was between the time yore cousin James went up an' the others followed.'

'You reckon? I'm askin' for definite information. A man's life may hang on this.' The cattleman's eyes were ice-cold.

Hull swallowed a lump in his fat throat before he committed himself. 'Well, it was.'

'Was between the two trips of the elevator, you mean?'

'Yes.'

'Your wife heard this sound, too?'

'Yep. We spoke of it afterward.'

'Do you know anything else that could possible have had any bearing on my uncle's death?'

'No, sir. Honest I don't.'

Olson shot a question at the man on the grill. 'Did you kill the Jap servant, too, as well as his boss?'

'I didn't kill either the one or the other, so help me.'

'Do you know anything at all about the Jap's

death? Did you see anything suspicious going on at any time?' Kirby asked.

'No, sir. Nothin' a-tall.'

The rough rider signaled the taxicab, which was circling the lake at the foot of the hill. Presently it came up the incline and took on its passengers.

'Drive to the Paradox Apartments,' Kirby directed.

He left Hull outside in the cab while he went in to interview his wife. The lean woman with the forbidding countenance opened the door.

Metaphorically speaking, Kirby landed his knockout instantly. 'I've come to see you on serious business, Mrs. Hull. Your husband has confessed how he did for my uncle. Unless you tell the whole truth he's likely to go to the death cell.'

She gasped, her fear-filled eyes fastened on him. Her hand moved blindly to the side of the door for support.

CHAPTER THIRTY-EIGHT

A FULL MORNING

But only for an instant. A faint color dribbled back into her yellow cheeks. He could almost see courage flowing again into her veins.

'That's a lie,' she said flatly.

'I don't expect you to take my word. Hull is in front of the house here under guard. Come an' see if you doubt it.'

She took him promptly at his suggestion. One look at her husband's fat, huddled figure and stricken face was enough.

'You chicken-hearted louse,' she spat at him scornfully.

'They had evidence. A man saw us,' he pleaded.

'What man?'

'This man.' His trembling hand indicated Olson. 'He was standin' on the fire escape acrost the alley.'

She had nothing to say. The wind had died out the sails of her anger.

'We're not goin' to arrest Hull yet—not technically,' Kirby explained to her. 'I'm arrangin' to hire a private detective to be with him all the time. He'll keep him in sight from mornin' till night. Is that satisfactory, Hull? Or do you prefer to be arrested?'

The wretched man murmured that he would leave it to Lane.

'Good. Then that's the way it'll be.' Kirby turned to the woman. 'Mrs. Hull, I want to ask you a few questions. If you'll kindly walk into the house, please.'

She moved beside him. The shock of the surprise still palsied her will.

In the main her story corroborated that of

Hull. She was not quite sure when she had heard the shot in its relation to the trips of the elevator up and down. The door was closed at the time. They had heard it while standing at the window. Her impression was that the sound had come after James Cunningham had ascended to the floor above.

Kirby put one question to the woman innocently that sent the color washing out of her cheeks.

'Which of you went back upstairs to untie my uncle after you had run away in a fright?'

'N-neither of us,' she answered, teeth chattering from sheer funk.

'I understood Mr. Hull to say—'

'He never said that. Y-you must be mistaken.'

'Mebbe so. You didn't go back, then?'

The monosyllable 'No' came quavering from her yellow throat.

'I don't want you to feel that I'm here to take an advantage of you, Mrs. Hull,' Kirby said. 'A good many have been suspected of these murders. Your husband is one of these suspects. I'm another. I mean to find out who killed Cunningham an' Horikawa. I think I know already. In my judgment your husband didn't do it. If he did, so much the worse for him. No innocent person has anything to fear from me. But this is the point I'm makin' now. If you like I'll leave a statement here signed by me to the effect that neither you nor your husband has confessed killing James Cunningham. It might make your mind a little easier to have it.'

She hesitated. 'Well, if you like.'

He stepped to a desk and found paper and pen. 'I'll dictate it if you'll write it, Mrs. Hull.'

Not quite easy in her mind, the woman sat down and took the pen he offered.

'This is to certify—' Kirby began, and dictated a few sentences slowly.

She wrote the statement, word for word as he gave it, *using her left hand.* The cattleman signed it. He left the paper with her.

After the arrangement for the private detective to watch Hull had been made, Olson and Lane walked together to the hotel of the latter.

'Come up to my room a minute and let's talk things over,' Kirby suggested.

As soon as the door was closed, the man from Twin Buttes turned on the farmer and flung a swift demand at him. 'Now, Olson, I'll hear the rest of your story.'

The eyes of the Swede grew hard and narrow. 'What's bitin' you? I've told you my story.'

'Some of it. Not all of it.'

'Whadja mean?'

'You told me what you saw from the fire escape of the Wyndham, but *you didn't tell what you saw from the fire escape of the Paradox.*'

257

'Who says I saw anything from there?'

'I say so.'

'You tryin' to hang this killin' on me?' demanded Olson angrily.

'Not if you didn't do it.' Kirby looked at him quietly, speculatively, undisturbed by the heaviness of his frown. 'But you come to me an' tell the story of what you saw. So you say. Yet all the time you're holdin' back. Why? What's your reason?'

'How do you know I'm holdin' back?' the ranchman asked sulkily.

Kirby knew that in his mind suspicion, dread, fear, hatred, and the desire for revenge were once more at open war.

'I'll tell you what you did that night,' answered Kirby, without the least trace of doubt in voice or manner. 'When Mrs. Hull pulled down the blind, you ran up to the roof an' cut down the clothes-line. You went back to the fire escape, fixed up some kind of a lariat, an' flung the loop over an abutment stickin' from the wall of the Paradox. You swung across to the fire escape of the Paradox. There you could see into the room where Cunningham was tied to the chair.'

'How could I if the blind was down?'

'The blind doesn't fit close to the woodwork of the window. Lookin' in from the right, you can see the left half of the room. If you look in from the other side, you see the other part of it. That's just what you did.'

258

For the moment Olson was struck dumb. How could this man know exactly what he had done unless some one had seen him?

'You know so much I reckon I'll let you tell the rest,' the Scandinavian said with uneasy sarcasm.

'Afraid you'll have to talk, Olson. Either to me or to the Chief at headquarters. You've become a live suspect. Figure it out yourself. You threaten Cunningham by mail. You make threats before people orally. You come to Denver an' take a room in the next house to where he lives. On the night he's killed, by your own admission, you stand on the platform a few feet away an' raise no alarm while you see him slugged. Later, you hear the shot that kills him an' still you don't call the officers. Yet you're so interested in the crime that you run upstairs, cut down the clothes-line, an' at some danger swing over to the Paradox. The question the police will want to know is whether the man who does this an' then keeps it secret may not have the best reason in the world for not wanting it known.'

'What you mean—the best reason in the world?'

'They'll ask what's to have prevented you from openin' the window an' steppin' in while my uncle was tied up, from shootin' him an' slippin' down the fire excape, an' from walkin' back upstairs to your own room at the Wyndham.'

259

'Are you claimin' that I killed him?' Olson wanted to know.

'I'm tellin' you that the police will surely raise the question.'

'If they do I'll tell 'em who did,' the rancher blurted out wildly.

'I'd tell 'em first, if I were in your place. It'll have a lot more weight than if you keep still until your back's against the wall.'

'When I do you'll sit up an' take notice. The man who shot Cunningham is yore own cousin,' the Dry Valley man flung out vindictively.

'Which one?'

'The smug one—James.'

'You saw him do it?'

'I heard the shot while I was on the roof. When I looked round the edge of the blind five minutes later, he was goin' over the papers in the desk—and an automatic pistol was there right by his hand.'

'He was alone?'

'At first he was. In about a minute his brother an' Miss Harriman came into the room. She screamed when she saw yore uncle an' most fainted. The other brother, the young one, kinda caught her an' steadied her. He was struck all of a heap himself. You could see that. He looked at James, an' he said, 'My God, you didn't—' That was all. No need to finish. O' course James denied it. He'd jumped up to help support Miss Harriman outa the

260

room. Maybe a coupla minutes later he came back alone. He went right straight back to the desk, found inside of three seconds the legal document I told you I'd seen his uncle readin', glanced it over, turned to the back page, jammed the paper back in the cubby-hole, an' then switched off the light. A minute later the light was switched off in the big room, too. Then I reckoned it was time to beat it down the fire escape. I did. I went back into the Wyndham carryin' the clothes-line under my coat, walked upstairs without meetin' anybody, left the rope on the roof, an' got outa the house without being seen.'

'That's the whole story?' Kirby said.

'The whole story. I'd swear it on a stack of Bibles.'

'Did you fix the rope for a lariat up on the roof or wait till you came back to the fire escape?'

'I fixed it on the roof—made the loop an' all there. Figured I might be seen if I stood around too long on the platform.'

'So that you must 'a' been away quite a little while.'

'I reckon so. Prob'ly a quarter of an hour or more.'

'Can you locate more definitely the exact time you heard the shot?'

'No, I don't reckon I can.'

Kirby asked only one more question.

'You left next mornin' for Dry Valley, didn't

261

you?'

'Yes. None o' my business if they stuck Hull for it. He was guilty as sin, anyhow. If he didn't kill the old man, it wasn't because he didn't want to. Maybe he did. The testimony at the inquest, as I read the papers, left it that maybe the blow on the head had killed Cunningham. Anyhow, I wasn't gonna mix myself in it.'

Kirby said nothing. He looked out of the window of his room without seeing anything. His thoughts were focused on the problem before him.

The other man stirred uneasily. 'Think I did it?' he asked.

The cattleman brought his gaze back to the Dry Valley settler. 'You? Oh, no! You didn't do it.'

There was such quiet certainty in his manner that Olson drew a deep breath of relief. 'By Jupiter, I'm glad to hear you say so. What made you change yore mind?'

'Haven't changed it. Knew that all the time—well, not all the time. I was millin' you over in my mind quite a bit while you were holdin' out on me. Couldn't be dead sure whether you were hidin' what you knew just to hurt Hull or because of your own guilt.'

'Still, I don't see how you're sure yet. I might 'a' gone in by the window an' gunned Cunningham like you said.'

'Yes, you might have, but you didn't. I'm not goin' to have you arrested, Olson, but I want

262

you to stay in Denver for a day or two until this is settled. We may need you as a witness. It won't be long. I'll see your expenses are paid while you're here.'

'I'm free to come an' go as I please?'

'Absolutely.' Kirby looked at him with level eyes. He spoke quite as a matter of course. 'You're no fool, Olson. You wouldn't stir up suspicion against yourself again by runnning, analyzing, classifying. Some one had once remarked that did it.'

The Swede started. 'You mean—now?'

'Not this very minute,' Kirby laughed. 'I mean I've got the person spotted, at least I think I have. I've made a lot of mistakes since I started roundin' up this fellow with the brand of Cain. Maybe I'm makin' another. But I've a hunch that I'm ridin' herd on the right one this time.'

He rose. Olson took the hint. He would have liked to ask some questions, for his mind was filled with a burning curiosity. But his host's manner did not invite them. The rancher left.

Up and down his room Kirby paced a beat from the window to the door and back again. His mind was busy dissecting, analyzing, classifying. Some one had once remarked that he had a single-track mind. In one sense he had. The habit of it was to follow a train of thought to its logical conclusion. He did not hop from one thing to another inconsequently.

263

Just now his brain was working on his cousin James. He went back to the first day of his arrival in Denver and sifted the evidence for and against him. A stream of details, fugitive impressions, and mental reactions flooded through.

For one of so cold a temperament James had been distinctly friendly to him. He had gone out of his way to find bond for him when he had been arrested. He had tried to smooth over difficulties between him and Jack. But Kirby, against his desire, found practical reasons of policy to explain these overtures. James had known he would soon be released through the efforts of other cattlemen. He had stepped in to win the Wyoming cousin's confidence in order that he might prove an asset rather than a liability to his cause. The oil broker had readily agreed to protect Esther McLean from publicity, but the reason for his forbearance was quite plain now. He had been protecting himself, not her.

The man's relation to Esther proved him selfish and without principle. He had been willing to let his dead uncle bear the odium of his misdeed. Yet beneath the surface of his cold manner James was probably swept by heady passions. His love for Phyllis Harriman had carried him beyond prudence, beyond honor. He had duped the uncle whose good-will he had carefully fostered for many years, and at the hour of his uncle's death he had been due to reap the whirl-wind.

The problem sifted down to two factors. One was the time element. The other was the temperament of James. A man may be unprincipled and yet draw the line at murder. He may be a seducer and still lack the courage and the cowardice for a cold-blooded killing. Kirby had studied his cousin, but the man was more or less of a sphinx to him. Behind those cold, calculating eyes what was he thinking?

Only once had he seen him thrown off his poise. That was when Kirby and Rose had met him coming out of the Paradox white and shaken, his arm wrenched and strained. He had been nonplussed at sight of them. For a moment he had let his eyes mirror the dismay of his soul. The explanation he had given was quite inadequate as a cause.

Twenty-four hours later Kirby had discovered the dead body of the Japanese valet Horikawa. The man had been dead perhaps a day. More hours than one had been spent by Kirby pondering on the possible connection of his cousin's momentary breakdown and the servant's death. *Had James come fresh from the murder of Horikawa?*

It was possible that the Oriental might have held evidence against him and threatened to divulge it. James, with the fear of death in his heart, might have gone each day into the apartment where the man was lurking, taking to him food and newspapers. They might have quarreled. The strained tendons of Cunningham's arm could be accounted for a good deal more readily on the hypothesis of a bit of expert jiu-jitsu than on that of a fall downstairs. There were pieces in the puzzle Kirby could not fit into place. One of them was to find a sufficient cause for driving Horikawa to conceal himself when there was no evidence against him of the crime.

The time element was tremendously important in the solution of the mystery of Cunningham's death. Kirby had studied this a hundred times. On the back of an envelope he jotted down once more such memoranda as he knew or could safely guess at. Some of these he had to change slightly as to time to make them dovetail into each other.

8:45	Uncle J. leaves City Club.
8:55	Uncle J. reaches rooms.
8:55–9:10.	Gets slippers, etc. Smokes.
8:55–9:20.	Olson watching from W. fire escape.
9:10–9:30.	Hulls in Apt.
9:30–9:40.	*X.*
9:37–9:42.	Approximately time Olson heard shot.
9:20–9:42.	Olson busy on roof, with rope, etc. Then at window till 9:53.
9:40–9:53.	James in Apt.
9:44–9:50.	Jack and Phyllis in Apt.
9:55–10:05.	Wild Rose in rooms.

10:00.	I reach rooms.
10:20.	Meet Ellis.
10:25.	Call police.

That was the time schedule as well as he had been able to work it out. It was incomplete. For instance, he had not been able to account for Horikawa in it at all unless he represented X in that ten minutes of time unaccounted for. It was inaccurate. Olson was entirely vague as to time, but he could be checked up pretty well by the others. Hull was not quite sure of his clock, and Rose could only say that she had reached the Paradox 'quite a little after a quarter to ten.' Fortunately his own arrival checked up hers pretty closely, since she could not have been in the room much more than five minutes before him. Probably she had been even less than that. James could not have left the apartment more than a minute or so before Rose arrived. It was quite possible that her coming had frightened him out.

So far as the dovetailing of time went, there was only the ten minutes or less between the leaving of the Hulls and the appearance of James left unexplained. If some one other than those mentioned on his penciled memoranda had killed Cunningham, it must have been between half-past nine and twenty minutes to ten. The X he had written in there was the only possible unknown quantity. By the use of

267

hard work and common sense he had eliminated the rest of the time so far as outsiders were concerned.

Kirby put the envelope in his pocket and went out to get some luncheon.

'I'll call it a mornin',' he told himself with a smile.

CHAPTER THIRTY-NINE

KIRBY INVITES HIMSELF TO A RIDE

The Twin Buttes man had said he would call it a morning, but he carried with him to the restaurant the problem that had become the pivot of all his waking thoughts. He had an appointment to meet a man for lunch, and he found his guest waiting for him inside the door.

The restaurant was an inconspicuous one on a side street. Kirby had chosen it for that reason. The man who stepped into the booth with him and sat down on the opposite seat was Hudson, the clerk whom James had accused of losing the sheets of paper with the Japanese writing.

'I've got it at last,' he said as soon as he was alone. 'Thought he never would go out and leave the key to the private drawer inside the safe. But he left the key in the lock—for just five minutes—while Miss Harriman came to see him about something this morning. He walked out with her to the elevator. I ducked into his office. There was the key in the drawer, and in the drawer, right at the bottom under some papers, I found what I wanted.'

He handed to Kirby the sheets of paper found in the living-room of the apartment where Horikawa had been found dead.

The cattleman looked them over and put them in his pocket. 'Thought he wouldn't destroy them. He daren't. There might come a time when the translation of this writing would save his life. He couldn't tell what the Jap had written, but there might be a twist to it favorable to him. At the same time he daren't give it out and let any one translate it. So he'd keep it handy where nobody could get at it but himself.'

'I reckon that just about evens the score between me and Mr. James Cunningham' the clerk said vindictively. 'He bawled me out before a whole roomful of people when he knew all the time I hadn't lost the papers. I stood it, because right then I had to. But I've dug up a better job and start in on it Monday. He's been claiming he was so anxious to get these sheets back to you. Well, I hope he's satisfied now.'

'He had no right to keep 'em. They weren't his. I'll have 'em translated, then turn the sheets over to the police if they have any

269

bearing on the case. Of course they may be just a private letter or something of that sort.'

The clerk went on to defend himself for what he had done. Cunningham had treated him outrageously. Besides, they weren't his papers. He had no business to hold back evidence in a murder case because it did not suit him to have it made public. Didn't Mr. Lane think he had done right in taking the papers from the safe when he had a chance?

Mr. Lane rather dodged the ethics of the case of Hudson. He had, of course, instigated the theft of the papers. He was entitled to them. James had appropriated them by a trick. Besides, it was a matter of public and private justice that the whole Cunningham mystery be cleared up as soon as possible. But he was not prepared to pass on Hudson's right to be the instrument in the case. The man was, of course, a confidential employee of the oil broker. There was one thing to be said in his favor. Kirby had not offered him anything for what he had done nor did he want anything in payment. It was wholly a gratuitous service.

The cattleman had made inquiries. He knew of a Japanese interpreter used in the courts. Foster had recommended him as entirely reliable. To this man Kirby went. He explained what he wanted. While the Japanese clerk read in English the writing to him and afterward wrote out on a typewriter the translation of it, Kirby sat opposite him at the table to make sure that there was no juggling with the original document.

The affair was moving to its climax. Within a few hours now Kirby expected to see the murderer of his uncle put under arrest. It was time to take the Chief of Police into his confidence. He walked down Sixteenth toward the City Hall.

At Curtis Street the traffic officer was semaphoring with energetic gesture the east and west bound vehicles to be on their way. Kirby jaywalked across the street diagonally and passed in front of an electric headed south. He caught one glimpse of the driver and stood smiling at the door with his hat off.

'I want to see you just a minute, Miss Harriman. May I come in?'

Her long, dark eyes flashed at him. The first swift impulse was to refuse. But she knew he was dangerous. He knew much that it was vital to her social standing must not be published. She sparred for time.

'What do you want?'

He took this as an invitation and whipped open the door. 'Better get out of the traffic,' he told her. 'Where we can talk without being disturbed.'

She turned up Fifteenth. 'If you have anything to say,' she suggested, and swept her long-lashed eyes round at him with the manner of delicate disdain she held at command.

'I've been wonderin' about somethin',' he

271

said. 'When James telephoned my uncle, on the evenin' he was killed, that you an' he were on the way to his rooms, he said you were together; but James reached there alone, you an' Jack arrivin' a few minutes later. Did James propose that he go first?'

The young woman did not answer. But there was no longer disdain in her fear-filled eyes. She swung the car, as though by a sudden impulse, to the left and drove to the building where the older James Cunningham had had his offices.

'If you want to ask me questions you'd better ask them before Jack,' she said as she stepped out.

'Suits me exactly,' he agreed.

Her lithe, long body moved beside him gracefully, its every motion perfectly synchronized. In her close-fitting, stylish gown she was extremely handsome. There was a kind of proud defiance in the set of her oval jaw, as though even in the trouble that involved her she was a creature set apart from others.

'Mr. Lane has a question he wants to ask you, Jack,' she said when they were in the inner office.

Kirby smiled, and in his smile there were friendliness and admiration. 'First off, I have to apologize for some things I said two days ago. I'll eat humble pie. I accused you of somethin'. You're not the man, I've found out.'

'Yes?' Jack, standing behind his desk in the slim grace of well-dressed youth, watched him warily.

'We've found out at last who the man is.'

'Indeed!' Jack knew that Esther McLean had been found by her friends and taken away. No doubt she had told them her story. Did the cattleman mean to expose James before the woman he knew to be his wife? That wouldn't be quite what he would expect of Lane.

'Incidentally, I have some news for you. One of your uncle's stenographers, a Miss McLean, has just been married to a friend of mine, the champion rough rider. Perhaps you may have heard of him. His name is Cole Sanborn.'

Jack did not show the great relief he felt. 'Glad to hear it,' he said simply.

'Did we come here to discuss stenographers?' asked the young woman with a little curl of the lip. 'You mentioned a question, Mr. Lane. Hadn't we better get that out of the way!'

Kirby put to Jack the same query he had addressed to her.

'What's the drift of this? What do you want to prove?' Jack asked curtly.

The eyes in the brown face plunged deep into those of Jack Cunningham. 'Not a thing. I've finished my case, except for a detail or two. Within two hours the murderer of Uncle James will be arrested. I'm offerin' you a chance to come through with what you know

273

before it's too late. You can kick in if you want to. You can stay out if you don't. But don't say afterward I didn't give you a chance.'

'What kind of a chance are you giving me? Let's get clear on that. Are you proposing I turn state's evidence on James? Is that what you're driving at?'

'Did James kill Uncle James?'

'Of course he didn't, but you may have it in that warped mind of yours that he did.'

'What I think doesn't matter. All that will count is the truth. It's bound to come out. There are witnesses that saw you come to the Paradox, a witness that actually saw you in uncle's rooms. If you don't believe me, I'll tell you somethin'. When you an' Miss Harriman came into the room where my uncle had been killed, James was sittin' at the desk lookin' over papers. A gun was lyin' close by his hand. Miss Harriman nearly fainted an' you steadied her.'

Miss Harriman, or rather Mrs. James Cunningham, nearly fainted again. She caught at the back of a chair and stood rigid, looking at Kirby with dilated, horror-filled eyes.

'He knows everything—everything. I think he must be the devil,' she murmured from bloodless lips.

Jack, too, was shaken, badly. 'For God's sake, man, what do you know?' he asked hoarsely.

'I know so much that you can't safely keep

274

quiet any longer. The whole matter is goin' to the police. It's goin' to them this afternoon. What are you goin' to do? If you refuse to talk, then it will be taken to mean guilt.'

'Why should it go to the police? Be reasonable, man. James didn't do it, but he's in an awful hole. No jury on earth would refuse to convict him with the evidence you've piled up. Can't you see that?'

Kirby smiled. This time his smile was grim. 'I ought to know that better than you. I'll give you two hours to decide. Meet you at James's office then. There are some things we want to talk over alone, but I think Miss Harriman had better be there ready to join us when we send for her.'

'Going through with this, are you?'

'I'm goin' through in spite of hell and high water.'

Jack strode up and down the room in a stress of emotion. 'You're going to ruin three lives because you're so pigheaded or because you want your name in the papers as a great detective. Is there anything in the world we can do to head you off?'

'Nothin'. And if lives are ruined it's not my fault. I'll promise this: The man or woman I point to as the one who killed Uncle James will be the one that did it. If James is innocent, as you claim he is, he won't have it saddled on him. Shall I tell you the thing that's got you worried? Down in the bottom of your heart

275

you're not dead sure he didn't do it—either one of you.'

The young woman took a step toward Kirby, hands out-stretched in dumb pleading. She gave him her soft, appealing eyes, a light of proud humility in them.

'Don't do it!' she begged. 'He's your own cousin—and my husband. I love him. Perhaps there's some woman that loves you. If there is, remember her and be merciful.'

His eyes softened. It was the first time he had seen her taken out of her selfishness. She was one of those modern young women who take, but do not give. At least that had been his impression of her. She had specialized, he judged, in graceful and lovely self-indulgence. A part of her code had been to get the best possible bargain for her charm and beauty, and as a result of her philosophy of life time had already begun to enamel on her a slight hardness of finish. Yet she had married James instead of his uncle. She had risked the loss of a large fortune to follow her heart. Perhaps, if children came, she might still escape into the thoughts and actions that give life its true value.

A faint, sphinxlike smile touched his face. 'No use worryin'. That doesn't help any. I'll go as easy as I can. We'll meet in two hours at James's office.'

He turned and left the room.

CHAPTER FORTY

THE MILLS OF THE GODS

Kirby Lane, did not waste the two hours that lay before the appointment he had made for a meeting at the office of his cousin James. He had a talk with the Hulls and another with the Chief of Police. He saw Olson and Rose McLean. He even found the time to forge two initials at the foot of a typewritten note on the stationery of James Cunningham, and to send the note to its destination by a messenger.

Rose met him by appointment at the entrance to the Equitable Building and they rode up in the elevator together to the office of his cousin. Miss Harriman, as she still called herself in public, was there with Jack and her husband.

James was ice-cold. He bowed very slightly to Rose. Chairs were already placed.

For a moment Kirby was embarrassed. He drew James aside. Cunningham murmured an exchange of sentences with his wife, then escorted her to the door. Rose was left with the three cousins.

'I suppose Jack has told you of the marriage of Esther McLean,' Kirby said as soon as the door had been closed. James bowed, still very stiffly.

Kirby met him, eye to eye. He spoke very quietly and clearly. 'I want to open the meetin' by tellin' you on behalf of this young woman an' myself that we think you an unmitigated cur. We are debarred from sayin' so before your wife, but it's a pleasure to tell you so in private. Is that quite clear?'

The oil broker flushed darkly. He made no answer.

'You not only took advantage of a young woman's tender heart. You were willin' our dead uncle should bear the blame for it. Have you any other word than the one I have used to suggest as a more fittin' one?' the Wyoming man asked bitingly.

Jack answered for his brother. 'Suppose we pass that count of the indictment, unless you have a practical measure to suggest in connection with it. We plead guilty.'

There was a little gleam of mirth in Kirby's eyes. 'You an' I have discussed the matter already, Jack. I regret I expressed my opinion so vigorously then. We have nothin' practical to suggest, if you are referrin' to any form of compensation. Esther is happily married, thank God. All we want is to make it perfectly plain what we think of Mr. James Cunningham.'

James acknowledged this and answered. 'That is quite clear. I may say that I entirely concur in your estimate of my conduct. I might make explanations, but I can make none that justify me to myself.'

'In that case we may consider the subject closed, unless Miss McLean has something to say.'

Kirby turned to Rose. She looked at James Cunningham, and he might have been the dirt under her feet. 'I have nothing whatever to say, Kirby. You express my sentiments exactly.'

'Very well. Then we might open the door and invite in Miss Harriman. There are others who should be along soon that have a claim also to be present.'

'What others?' asked Jack Cunningham.'

'The other suspects in the case. I prefer to have them all here.'

'Any one else?'

'The Chief of Police.'

James looked at him hard. 'This is not a private conference, then?'

'That's a matter of definitions. I have invited only those who have a claim to be present,' Kirby answered.

'To my office, I think.'

'If you prefer the Chief's office we'll adjourn an' go there.'

The broker shrugged. 'Oh, very well.'

Kirby stepped to the door connecting with an outer office and threw it open. Mr. and Mrs. Hull, Olson, and the Chief of Police followed Phyllis Harriman into the room. More chairs were brought in.

The Chief sat nearest the door, one leg

279

thrown lazily across the other. He had a fat brown cigar in his hand. Sometimes he chewed on the end of it, but he was not smoking. He was an Irishman, and as it happened open-minded. He liked this brown-faced young fellow from Wyoming—never had believed him guilty from the first. Moreover, he was willing his detective bureau should get a jolt from an outsider. It might spur them up in future.

'Chief, is there anything you want to say?' Kirby asked.

'Not a wor-rd. I'm sittin' in a parquet seat. It's your show, son.'

Kirby's disarming smile won the Chief's heart. 'I want to say now that I've talked with the Chief several times. He's given me a lot of good tips an' I've worked under his direction.'

The head of the police force grinned. The tips he had given Lane had been of no value, but he was quite willing to take any public credit there might be. He sat back and listened now while Kirby told his story.

'Outside of the Chief every one here is connected closely with this case an' is involved in it. It happens that every man an' woman of us were in my uncle's apartment either at the time of his death or just before or after.' Kirby raised a hand to meet Olson's protest. 'Oh, I know. You weren't in the rooms, but you were on the fire escape outside. From the angle of the police you may have been in. All you had

280

to do was to pass through an open window.'

There was a moment's silence, while Kirby hesitated in what order to tell his facts. Hull mopped the back of his overflowing neck. Phyllis Cunningham moistened her dry lips. A chord in her throat ached tensely.

'Suspicion fell first on me an' on Hull,' Kirby went on. 'You've seen it all thrashed out in the papers. I had been unfriendly to my uncle for years, an' I was seen goin' to his rooms an' leavin' them that evening. My own suspicion was directed to Hull, especially when he an' Mrs. Hull at the coroner's inquest changed the time so as to get me into my uncle's apartment half an hour earlier than I had been there. I'd caught them in a panic of terror when I knocked on their door. They'd lied to get me into trouble. Hull had quarreled with Uncle James an' had threatened to go after him with a gun in *two days* after that time—and it was *just forty-eight hours later he was killed.* It looked a lot like Hull to me.

'I had one big advantage, Chief, a lot of inside facts not open to you,' the cattleman explained. 'I knew, for instance, that Miss McLean here had been in the rooms just before me. She was the young woman my uncle had the appointment to meet there before ten o'clock. You will remember Mr. Blanton's testimony. Miss McLean an' I compared notes, so we were able to shave down the time during which the murder must

281

have taken place. We worked together. She gave me other important data. Perhaps she had better tell in her own words about the clue she found that we followed.'

Rose turned to the Chief. Her young face flew a charming flag of color. Her hair, in crisp tendrils beneath the edge of the small hat she wore, was the ripe gold of wheat-tips in the shock. The tender blue of violets was in her eyes.

'I told you about how I found Mr. Cunningham tied to his chair, Chief. I forgot to say that in the living-room there was a faint odor of perfume. On my way upstairs I passed in the dark a man and a woman. I had got a whiff of the same perfume then. It was violet. So I knew they had been in the apartment just before me. Mr. Lane discovered later that Miss Harriman used that scent.'

'Which opened up a new field of speculation,' Kirby went on. 'We began to run down facts an' learned that my cousin James had secretly married Miss Harriman at Golden a month before. My uncle had just learned the news. He had a new will made by his lawyer, one that cut James off without a cent an' left his property to Jack Cunningham.'

'That will was never signed,' Jack broke in quickly.

Kirby looked at Jack and smiled cynically. 'No, it was never signed. Your brother discovered that when he looked the will over at Uncle's desk a few minutes after his death.'

James did not wink an eye in distress. The hand of the woman sitting beside him went out instantly to his in a warm, swift pressure. She was white to the lips, but her thought was for the man she loved and not for herself. Kirby scored another mark to her credit.

'Cumulative evidence pointed to James Cunningham,' continued Kirby. 'He tried to destroy the proof of his marriage to Miss Harriman. He later pretended to lose an important paper that might have cleared up the case. He tried to get me to drop the matter an' go back to Wyoming. The coil wound closer round him.

'About this time another factor attracted my attention. I had the good luck to unearth at Dry Valley the man who had written threatenin' letters to my uncle an' to discover that he was stayin' next door to the Paradox the very night of the murder. More, my friend Sanborn an' I guessed he had actually been on the fire escape of the Wyndham an' seen somethin' of importance through the window. Later I forced a statement from Olson. He told all he had seen that night.'

Kirby turned to the rancher from Dry Valley and had him tell his story. When he had finished, the cattleman made comment.

'On the face of it Olson's story leaves in doubt the question of who actually killed my uncle. If he was tellin' the whole truth, his

283

evidence points either to the Hulls or my cousin James. But it was quite possible he had seen my uncle tied up an' helpless, an' had himself stepped through the window an' shot him. Am I right, Chief?'

The Chief nodded grimly. 'Right, son.'

'You told me you didn't think I did it,' Olson burst out bitterly.

'An' I tell you so again,' Kirby answered, smiling. 'I was mentionin' possibilities. On your evidence it lies between my cousin James an' the Hulls. It was the Hulls that had tied him up after Cass Hull knocked him senseless. It was Hull who had given him two days more to live. And that's not all. Not an hour an' a half ago I had a talk with Mrs. Hull. She admitted, under pressure, *that she returned to my uncle's apartment again to release him from the chair.* She was alone with him, an' he was wholly in her power. She is a woman with a passionate sense of injury. What happened then nobody else saw.'

Mrs. Hull opened her yellow, wrinkled lips to speak, but Kirby checked her. 'Not yet, Mrs. Hull. I'll return to the subject. If you wish you can defend yourself then.'

He stopped a second time to find the logical way of proceeding with his story. The silence in the room was tense. The proverbial pin could have been heard. Only one person in the room except Kirby knew where the lightning was going to strike. That person sat by the door chewing the end of a cigar impassively. A woman gave a strangled little sob of pent emotion.

'I've been leaving Horikawa out of the story,' the cattle-man went on. 'I've got to bring him in now. He's the hinge on which it all swings. *The man or woman that killed my uncle killed Horikawa too.*'

James Cunningham, sitting opposite Kirby with his cold eyes steadily fixed on him, for the first time gave visible sign of his anxiety. It came in the form of a little gulping sound in his throat.

'Cole Sanborn and I found Horikawa in the room where he had been killed. The doctors thought he must have been dead about a day. Just a day before this time Miss McLean an' I met James Cunningham comin' out of the Paragon. He was white an' shaking. He was sufferin' from nausea, an' his arm was badly strained. He explained it by sayin' he had fallen downstairs. Later, I wondered about that fall. I'm still wonderin'. Had he just come out of the apartment where Horikawa was hidin'? Had the tendons of that arm been strained by a jiu-jitsu twist? *And had he left Horikawa behind him dead on the bed?*'

James, white to the lips, looked steadily at his cousin. 'A very ingenious theory. I've always complimented you on your imagination,' he said, a little hoarsely, as though from a parched throat.

'You do not desire to make any explanation?' Kirby asked.

'Thanks. no. I'm not on trial for my life here, am I?' answered the oil broker quietly, with obvious irony.

His wife was sobbing softly. The man's arm went round her and tightened in wordless comfort.

From his pocket Kirby drew the envelope upon which he had a few hours earlier penciled the time schedule relating to his uncle's death.

'One of the points that struck me earliest about this mystery was that the man who solved it would have to work out pretty closely the time element. Inside of an hour ten people beside Uncle James were in his rooms. They must 'a' trod on each other's heels right fast, I figured. So I checked up the time as carefully as I could. Here's the schedule I made out. Mebbe you'd like to see it.' He handed the envelope to James.

Jack rose and looked over his brother's shoulder. His quick eye ran down the list. 'I get the rest of it,' he said. 'But what does X mean?'

'X is the ten minutes of Uncle's time I can't account for. Some of us were with him practically every other minute. X is the whole unknown quantity. It is the time in which he was prob'ly actually killed. It is the man who *may*, by some thousandth chance, have stepped into the room an' killed him while none of us were present,' explained Kirby.

'If there is such an unknown man you can cut the time down to five minutes instead of ten, providing your schedule is correct,' James cut in. 'For according to it I was there part of the time and Mrs. Hull part of the rest of it.'

'Yes,' agreed his cousin.

'But you may have decided that Mrs. Hull is X or that I am,' jeered James. 'If so, of course that ends it. No need for a judge or jury.'

Kirby turned to the man by the door. 'Chief, one of the queer things about this mystery is that all the witnesses had somethin' to conceal. Go right through the list, an' it's true of every one of us. I'm talkin' about the important witnesses, of course. Well, Cole an' I found a paper in the living-room of the apartment where Horikawa was killed. It was in Japanese. I ought to have turned it over to you, but I didn't. I was kinda playin' a lone hand. At that time I didn't suspect my cousin James at all. We were workin' together on this thing. At least I thought so. I found out better later. I took the paper to him to get it translated, thinkin' maybe Horikawa might have written some kind of a confession. James lost that paper. Anyhow, he claimed he did. My theory is that Horikawa had some evidence against him. He was afraid of what that paper would tell.'

'Unfortunately for your theory it was a clerk

of mine who lost the paper. I had nothing to do with it,' James retorted coldly. 'No doubt the paper has been destroyed, but not by me. Quite by accident, I judge.'

His cousin let off a bomb beneath the broker's feet. 'You'll be glad to know that the paper wasn't destroyed,' he said. 'I have it, with a translation, in my pocket at the present moment.'

James clutched the arms of his chair. His knuckles grew white with the strain. 'Where—where did you find it?' he managed to say.

'In the most private drawer of your safe, where you hid it,' Kirby replied quietly.

Cunningham visibly fought for his composure. He did not speak until he had perfect self-control. Then it was with a sneer.

'And this paper which you allege you found in my safe—after a burglary which, no doubt, you know is very much against the law—does it convict me of the murder of my uncle?'

The tension in the room was nerve-shattering. Men and women suspended breathing while they waited for an answer.

'On the contrary, it acquits you of any guilt whatever in the matter.'

Phyllis Cunningham gave a broken little sob and collapsed into her husband's arms. Jack rose, his face working, and caught his brother by the shoulder. These two had suffered greatly, not only because of their fear for him, but because of the fear of his guilt that had poisoned their peace.

James, too, was moved, as much by their love for him as by the sudden relief that had lifted from his heart. But his pride held him outwardly cold.

'Since you've decided I didn't do it, Mr. Lane, perhaps you'll tell us then who did,' he suggested presently.

There came a knock at the door.

A whimsical smile twitched at the corners of Kirby's mouth. He did not often have a chance for dramatics like this.

'Why, yes, that seems fair enough,' he answered. 'He's knockin' at the door now. Enter X.'

CHAPTER FORTY-ONE

ENTER X

Shibo stood on the threshold and sent a swift glance around the room. He had expected to meet James alone. That first slant look of the long eyes forewarned him that Nemesis was at hand. But he faced without a flicker of the lids the destiny he had prepared for himself.

'You write me note come see you now,' he said to Cunningham.

James showed surprise. 'No, I think not.'

'You no want me?'

The Chief's hand fell on the shoulder of the janitor. 'I want you, Shibo.'

'You write me note come here now?'

'No, I reckon Mr. Lane wrote that.'

'I plenty busy. What you want me for?'

'For the murders of James Cunningham and Horikawa.'Before the words were out of his mouth the Chief had his prisoner handcuffed.

Shibo turned to Kirby. 'You tellum police I killum Mr. Cunningham and Horikawa?'

'Yes.'

'I plenty sorry I no kill you.'

'You did your best, Shibo. Took three shots at ten feet. Rotten shooting.'

'Do you mean that he actually tried to kill you?' James asked in surprise.

'In the Denmark Building, the other night. at eleven o'clock. And I'll say he made a bad mistake when he tried an' didn't get away with it. For I knew that the man who was aimin' to gun me was the same one that had killed Uncle James. He'd got to worryin' for fear I was followin' too hot a trail.'

'Did you recognize him?' Jack said.

'Not right then. I was too busy duckin' for cover. Safety first was my motto right then. No, when I first had time to figure on who could be the gentleman that was so eager to make me among those absent, I rather laid it to Cousin James, with Mr. Cass Hull second on my list of suspects. The fellow had a searchlight an' he flashed it on me. I could see above it a

290

bandanna handkerchief over the face. I'd seen a bandana like it in Hull's hands. But I had to eliminate Hull. The gunman on the stairs had small, neat feet, no larger than a woman's. Hull's feet are—well, sizable.'

They were. Huge was not too much to call them. As a dozen eyes focused on his boots the fat man drew them back of the rungs of his chair. This attention to personal details of his conformation was embarrassing.

'Those small feet stuck in my mind,' Kirby went on. 'Couldn't seem to get rid of the idea. They put James out of consideration, unless, of course, he had hired a killer, an' that didn't look reasonable to me. I'll tell the truth. I thought of Mrs. Hull dressed as a man—an' then I thought of Shibo.'

'Had you suspected him before?' This from Olson.

'Not of the murders. I had learned that he had seen the Hulls come from my uncle's rooms an' had kept quiet. Hull admitted that he had been forced to bribe him. I tackled Shibo with it an' threatened to tell the police. Evidently he became frightened an' tried to murder me. I got a note makin' an appointment at the Denmark Building at eleven in the night. The writer promised to tell me who killed my uncle. I took a chance an' went.' The cattleman turned to Mrs. Hull. 'Will you explain about the note, please?'

The gaunt, tight-lipped woman rose, as

though she had been called on at school to recite. 'I wrote the note,' she said. 'Shibo made me. I didn't know he meant to kill Mr. Lane. He said he'd tell everything if I didn't.'

She sat down. She had finished her little piece.

'So I began to focus on Shibo. He might be playin' a lone hand, or he might be a tool of my cousin James. A detective hired by me saw him leave James's office. That didn't absolutely settle the point. He might have seen somethin' an' be blackmailin' him too. That was the way of it, wasn't it?' He turned point-blank to Cunningham.

'Yes,' the broker said. 'He had us right—not only me, but Jack and Phyllis, too. I couldn't let him drag her into it. The day you saw me with the strained tendon I had been with him and Horikawa in the apartment next to the one Uncle James rented. We quarreled. I got furious and caught Shibo by the throat to shake the little scoundrel. He gave my arm some kind of a jiu-jitsu twist. He was at me every day. He never let up. He meant to bleed me heavily. We couldn't come to terms. I hated to yield to him.'

'And did you?'

'I promised him an answer soon.'

'No doubt he came today thinkin' he was goin' to get it.' Kirby went back to the previous question. 'Next time I saw Shibo I took a look at his feet. He was wearin' a pair o' shoes that looked to me mighty like those worn by the man that ambushed me. They didn't have any cap pieces across the toes. I'd noticed that even while he was shootin' at me. It struck me that it would be a good idea to look over his quarters in the basement. Shibo has one human weakness. He's a devotee of the moving pictures. Nearly every night he takes in a show on Curtis Street. The Chief lent me a man, an' last night we went through his room at the Paradox. We found there a flashlight, a bandana handkerchief with holes cut in it for the eyes, an' in the mattress two thousand dollars in big bills. We left them where we found them, for we didn't want to alarm Shibo.'

The janitor looked at him without emotion. 'You plenty devil men,' he said.

'We hadn't proved yet that Shibo was goin' it alone,' Kirby went on, paying no attention to the interruption. 'Some one might be usin' him as a tool. Horikawa's confession clears that up.'

Kirby handed to the Chief of Police the sheets of paper found in the apartment where the valet was killed. Attached to these by a clip was the translation. The Chief read this last aloud.

Horikawa, according to the confession, had been in Cunningham's rooms sponging and pressing a suit of clothes when the promoter came home on the afternoon of the day of his

293

death. Through a half-open door he had seen his master open his pocket-book and count a big roll of bills. The figures on the outside one showed that it was a treasury note for fifty dollars. The valet had told Shibo later and they had talked it over, but with no thought in Horikawa's mind of robbery.

He was helping Shibo fix a window screen at the end of the hall that evening when they saw the Hulls come out of Cunningham's apartment. Something furtive in their manner struck the valet's attention. It was in the line of his duties to drop in and ask whether the promoter's clothes needed any attention for the next day. He discovered after he was in the living-room that Shibo was at his heels. They found Cunningham trussed up to a chair in the smaller room. He was unconscious, evidently from a blow in the head.

The first impulse of Horikawa had been to free him and carry him to the bedroom. But Shibo interfered. He pushed his hand into the pocket of the smoking-jacket and drew out a pocket-book. It bulged with bills. In two sentences Shibo sketched a plan of operations. They would steal the money and lay the blame for it on the Hulls. Cunningham's own testimony would convict the fat man and his wife. The evidence of the two Japanese would corroborate his.

Cunningham's eyelids flickered. There was a bottle of chloroform on the desk. The

294

promoter had recently suffered pleurisy pains and had been advised by his doctor to hold a little of the drug against the place where they caught him most sharply. Shibo snatched up the bottle, drenched a handkerchief with some of its contents, and dropped the handkerchief over the wounded man's face.

A drawer was open within reach of Cunningham's hand. In it lay an automatic pistol.

The two men were about to hurry away. Shibo turned at the door. To his dismay he saw that the handkerchief had slipped from Cunningham's face and the man was looking at him. He had recovered consciousness.

Cunningham's eyes condemned him to death. In their steely depths there was a gleam of triumph. He was about to call for help. Shibo knew what that meant. He and Horikawa were in a strange land. They would be sent to prison, an example made of them because they were foreigners. Automatically. without an instant of delay, he acted to protect himself.

Two strides took him back to Cunningham. He reached across his body for the automatic and sent a bullet into the brain of the man bound to the chair.

Horikawa, to judge by his confession, was thunderstruck. He was an amiable little fellow who never had stepped outside the law. Now he was caught in the horrible meshes of a murder. He went to pieces and began to sob. Shibo stopped him sharply.

Then they heard some one coming. It was too late to get away by the door. They slipped through the window to the fire escape and from it to the window of the adjoining apartment. Horikawa, still sick with fear, stumbled against the rail as he clambered over it and cut his face badly.

Shibo volunteered to go downstairs and get him some sticking plaster. On the way down Shibo had met the younger James Cunningham as he came out of the elevator. Returning with first-aid supplies a few minutes later, he saw Jack and Phyllis.

It was easy to read between the lines that Shibo's will had dominated Horikawa. He had been afraid that his companion's wounded face would lead to his arrest. If so, he knew it would be followed by a confession. He forced Horikawa to hide in the vacant apartment till the wound should heal. Meanwhile he fed him and brought him newspapers.

There were battles of will between the two. Horikawa was terribly frightened when he read that his flight had brought suspicion on him. He wanted to give himself up at once to the police. They quarreled. Shibo always gained the temporary advantage, but he saw that under a grilling third degree his countryman would break down. He killed Horikawa because he knew he could not trust him.

This last fact was not, of course, in Horikawa's confession. But the dread of it was there. The valet had come to fear Shibo. He was convinced in his shrinking heart that the man meant to get rid of him. It was under some impulse of self-protection that he had written the statement.

Shibo heard the confession read without the twitching of a facial muscle. He shrugged his shoulders, accepting the inevitable with the fatalism of his race.

'He weak. He no good. He got yellow streak. I bossum,' was his comment.

'Did you kill him?' asked the Thief.

'I killum both—Cunnin'lam and Horikawa. You kill me now maybe yes.'

Officers led him away.

Phyllis Cunningham came up to Kirby and offered him her hand. 'You're hard on James. I don't know why you're so hard. But you've cleared us all. I say thanks awf'ly for that. I've been horribly frightened. That's the truth. It seemed as though there wasn't any way out for us. Come and see us and let's all make up, Cousin Kirby.'

Kirby did not say he would. But he gave her his strong grip and friendly smile. Just then his face did not look hard. He could not tell her why he had held his cousin on the grill so long, that it had been in punishment for what he had done to a defenseless friend of his in the name of love. What he did say suited her perhaps as well.

'I like you better right now than I ever did before, Cousin Phyllis. You're a good little sport an' you'll do to ride the river with.'

Jack could not quite let matters stand as they did. He called on Kirby that evening at his hotel.

'It's about James I want to see you,' he said, then stuck for lack of words with which to clothe his idea. He prodded at the rug with the point of his cane.

'Yes, about James,' Kirby presently reminded him, smiling.

'He's not so bad as you think he is.' Jack blurted out.

'He's as selfish as the devil, isn't he?'

'Well, he is, and he isn't. He's got a generous streak in him. You may not believe it, but he went on your bond because he liked you.'

'Come, Jack, you're tryin' to seduce my judgment by the personal appeal,' Kirby answered, laughing.

'I know I am. What I want to say is this. I believe he would have married Esther McLean if it hadn't been for one thing. He fell desperately in love with Phyllis afterward. The odd thing is that she loves him, too. They didn't dare to be aboveboard about it on account of Uncle James. They treated him shabbily, of course. I don't deny that.'

'You can hardly deny that,' Kirby agreed.

'But, damn it, one swallow doesn't make a summer. You've seen the worst side of him all the way through.'

'I dare say I have.' Kirby let his hand fall on the well-tailored shoulder of his cousin. But I haven't seen the worst side of his brother Jack. He's a good scout. Come up to Wyoming this fall an' we'll go huntin' up in the Jackson Hole country. What say?'

'Nothing I'd like better,' answered Jack promptly.

'We'll arrange a date later. Just now I've got to beat it. Goin' drivin' with a lady.'

Jack scored for once. *She's a good scout, too.'*

'If she isn't, I'll say there never was one,' his cousin assented.

CHAPTER FORTY-TWO

THE NEW WORLD

Kirby took his lady love driving in a rented flivver. It was a Colorado night, with a young moon looking down through the cool, rare atmosphere found only in the Rockies. He drove her through the city to Berkely and up the hill to Inspiration Point.

They talked only in intermittent snatches. Rose had the gift of comradeship. Her tongue never rattled. With Kirby she did not need to make talk. They had always understood each other without words.

But tonight their silences were filled with new and awkward significances. She guessed that an emotional crisis was at hand. With all her heart she welcomed and shrank from it. For she knew that after tonight life could never be the same to her. It might be fuller, deeper, happier, but it could not hold for her the freedom she had guarded and cherished.

At the summit he killed the engine. They looked across the valley to the hills dimmed by night's velvet dusk.

'We're through with all that back there,' he said, and she knew he meant the tangled trails of the past weeks into which their fate had led them. 'We don't have to keep our minds full of suspicions an' try to find out things in mean, secret ways. There, in front of us, is God's world, waitin' for you an' me, Rose.'

Though she had expected it, she could not escape a sense of suddenly stilled pulses followed by a clamor of beating blood. She quivered, vibrating, trembling. She was listening to the call of mate to mate sounding clear above all the voices of the world.

A flash of soft eyes darted at him. He was to be her man, and the maiden heurt thrilled at the thought. She loved all of him she knew— his fine. clean thoughts, his brave and virile life, the splendid body that was the expression of his personality. There was a line of golden down on his cheek just above where he had shaved. Her warm eyes dared to linger fondly there, for he was still gazing at the mountains.

His eyes came home to her, and as he looked he knew he longed for her in every fiber of his being.

He asked no formal question. She answered none. Under the steady regard of his eyes she made a small, nestling movement toward him. Her young and lissom body was in his arms, a warm and palpitating thing of life and joy. He held her close. Her eyelashes swept his cheek and sent a strange, delightful tingle through his blood.

Kirby held her head back and looked into her eyes again. Under the starlight their lips slowly met.

The road lay clear before them after many tangled trails.

Chivers Large Print Direct

If you have enjoyed this Large Print book and would like to build up your own collection of Large Print books and have them delivered direct to your door, please contact **Chivers Large Print Direct**.

Chivers Large Print Direct offers you a full service:

✧ **Created to support your local library**

✧ **Delivery direct to your door**

✧ **Easy-to-read type and attractively bound**

✧ **The very best authors**

✧ **Special low prices**

For further details either call Customer Services on 01225 443400 or write to us at

Chivers Large Print Direct
FREEPOST (BA 1686/1)
Bath
BA1 3QZ

COVENTRY LIBRARIES

Please return this book on or before
the last date stamped below.

PS130553 Disk 4

To renew this book take it to any of
the City Libraries before
the date due for return

Coventry City Council

BBC